**What is the true story
behind the Romulan-Klingon
alliance? How did Spock end up joining
Star Fleet? What roles do women
play in Star Trek?**

These are just a few of the questions answered
in this terrific new collection of articles about the
Star Trek phenomenon. You'll learn about the
stars, the shows, science, history, and everything
else that has brought this imaginary universe so
vividly alive for so many dedicated fans the world
around.

# THE BEST OF TREK® #2

# SIGNET Books of Special Interest

# THE BEST OF TREK #2

## FROM THE MAGAZINE FOR STAR TREK FANS

EDITED BY WALTER IRWIN AND G. B. LOVE

A SIGNET BOOK

NEW AMERICAN LIBRARY

TIMES MIRROR

SIGNET, SIGNET CLASSICS, MENTOR, PLUME, MERIDIAN AND NAL BOOKS
are published by The New American Library, Inc.,
1633 Broadway, New York, New York 10019

First Printing, March, 1980

1  2  3  4  5  6  7  8  9

PRINTED IN THE UNITED STATES OF AMERICA

# ACKNOWLEDGMENTS

Thanks go to many people who helped with the realization of this collection and the continued existence of *Trek:*

Elaine Hauptman, for slaving for hours over a hot typewriter; Sheila Gilbert of NAL, for being charitable with the blue pencil; Jim Houston, resident Barrel of Laughs, and constant gadfly; Leslie Thompson, Lady of Mystery; and, of course, our readers, subscribers, contributors, and advertisers . . . We couldn't do it without y'all!

# CONTENTS

# INTRODUCTION

If you purchased *The Best of Trek #1*, you most likely read our rather lengthy introduction in which we gave our views on the future of Star Trek, its eventual effect on our society, and a few of the reasons why we publish *Trek*.

None of our feelings have changed. In fact, having had the opportunity to meet and correspond with thousands of fans over the past eighteen months, we are even more sure that Star Trek will have a lasting and beneficial effect on the way we live.

As you read this, the long-awaited Star Trek movie will be showing in theaters. This multimillion-dollar production is a wonderful thing, as its very existence supports our contention that Star Trek will never die. And as long as Star Trek is alive, the ideals and hope which it represents will live also.

We'll keep the introduction short this time, but we would like to mention a few more things. If you like the articles in this collection, we invite you to turn to our ad at the back of this book, where you can find information on ordering and subscribing to *Trek*. And if you feel you would like to write an article yourself, please write one and send it to us. We are always looking for new writers with fresh ideas. And finally, we would like to hear from you in any case. Reader response and communication are the heart of our magazine—after all, why do you think we call it "The Magazine For Star Trek Fans"?

Enjoy this collection. We hope these articles entertain you, excite you, and educate you. Live long and prosper.

WALTER IRWIN
G. B. LOVE

# 1.
# KLINGON UPDATE

## by Leslie Thompson

*Over a year after we published the first issue of* Trek *in which Leslie's Klingon article appeared, we decided to reprint the article in the first issue of* Trek Special, *as the negatives for* Trek #1 *had been destroyed, and fans were clamoring for a reprint of some sort. When Leslie heard we were planning the reprint, she asked if she could rewrite the Klingon article to answer questions and add new information which she had received over the past year. As part of the purpose of Special #1 was to preserve what had been lost from* Trek #1, *we had to refuse, but asked if she would like to do a separate article updating the original for the same issue. Lesie agreed that this was the best solution, and her addendum has been just as popular and thought-provoking as the original. And now she and the fans both are starting to clamor for an update of the update. . . .*

Since the publication of *Trek* #1, almost three years ago, I have received many letters about my Klingon article. They run from praising my "inside knowledge" of the show to complaints about everything from my spelling to the conclusions drawn in the article. But the most frequently asked question has been: "Just how do *you* know so much about the Klingons?"

To be truthful, I don't know any more than any other Star Trek fan. All of the hard factual evidence I have is what was given in the episodes; and, as everyone knows, that is very little.

When I wrote the Klingon article, I used a form of writing which I call "speculative faction." In simple terms, I take what is known and let my imagination (tempered by scientific laws and a knowledge of human nature) take it from there.

Human nature? When writing about aliens? Yes, because we have no other frame of reference by which to judge. Think of it in terms of translating a language. A literal translation may sometimes take an entirely different meaning than the spirit of what is intended. So it is with this type of writing. Something alien—be it action or speech—cannot be understood until it is put into our frame of reference. Therefore, human nature is the guide by which we must go.

Now to reader's comments. By far the most often asked questions and complaints have been about the character of Kling.

Kling is not intended to be real or factually based (although we must always remember that all of this could happen, just as Kirk and Spock and the *Enterprise* could happen). His character is just a handy tool with which to outline a logical process by which the Klingon race could have evolved a space-going empire.

Look at our own history. Every major advance in government forms has been through the direct influence of one person or group of persons—Genghis Khan, William the Conqueror, Adolf Hitler, the Continental Congress, and many others.

Because I have received so many letters, I will try in this article to answer some of the recurrent questions, and to clarify some of the points which were left hazy (even to me) in the original article.

I took the name Kazh mainly because Star Trek had established the practice of alliterating the names of Klingons with the first letter K. Kazh sounds fairly alien, has a strong single syllable, and could conceivably be a curse of some sort. If the Klingon home planet is the inhospitable place I describe, then its inhabitants would be unlikely to have any strong affection for it. Therefore, "Kazh," spat out gutturally, would make an excellent curse. (The next time some Trekkie bothers you, tell him to go to Kazh.)

The Klingons are dark-skinned. Therefore one would assume that they were exposed to a very strong sunlight and radiation level. So we can assume their planet is close to their sun, most likely the second planet in the system. Since they are stronger than humans, while possessing a similar mass and size, a heavier gravity would account for superior musculature.

A major and fairly valid complaint has been that a planet with sparse vegetation and salty, shallow seas could not produce the necessary amounts of oxygen to support humanoid life forms. Ah, but it could, if the seas were almost entirely filled with great plankton chains, and the ground vegetation was of a highly respirative type. And a "greenhouse effect" would be avoided because the strong radiation from the nearby sun would burn away cloud cover and prevent condensation in the upper atmosphere.

The result? A hot, dry, sandy, and highly oxygenated atmosphere, which, because of the high oxygen level, would cause the humanoids living on the surface to be excitable, restless, and somewhat "high" all the time.

The closer to a sun a planet is, the less the angle of incidence with which the light from the sun strikes it. Therefore, a planet which has little tilt to its axis would receive just about the same amount of light, radiation, and heat over all its surface. Effect? Same climate. No heat changes? Very little wind. No mountains? No heat layers or inversions and therefore little change in scenery or topography.

Now to the governmental systems. Questions keep cropping up about my comparison of the Klingon system to communism. After some thought, I agree. Klingon government would be much more analogous to a completely militaristic government, such as that of the Nazis during World War II.

This analogy also affords a clearer view of how a Klingon may achieve high status in a system where he is literally "owned" by the state.

Such a rise may be achieved through gathering political or military power (in many instances the same thing) and then using it to advantage when the opportunity presents itself. As I stated, assassination, deceit, etc. are all part of this process.

Too, it is not the average Klingon who rises to the top. It takes a person of superior intelligence and drive to wend his way through such treacherous surroundings; and the dull, lackadaisical, or cowardly never become involved in situations which could lead to a rise to the top.

Consider this: If your entire life is spent under the tutelage and guidance of the state, then you have to show some smarts pretty darn early to keep from being quickly and permanently designated as kitchen guard, fourth class. When a Klingon youth fails to pass on to the next level of education, he is trained to serve in a less necessary and less responsible position.

Now to the question of Klingon "women's lib." I have constantly had the character of Mara from "Day of the Dove" thrown at me. Yes, I know that Mara was science officer of the Klingon ship. Yes, I know that it is the second most responsible position on a starship. And, yes, I know that Kang did not treat her like "chattel," that he treated her with affection, admiration, and respect.

There is a difference between the beliefs and practices of people and what is often given as official policy. In general, male Klingons consider women an inferior species and the laws of the Klingon Empire give women no legal rights or status. However, Klingons are always very quick to make use of any tool which will help them achieve their aims, and if one of those tools happens to be a female whose intelligence and training make her valuable to the state or an individual, only lip service is paid to chauvinism. In this respect, at least, the Klingons are much like us.

In the case of Kang, this was very likely the situation. He, through the power of his position, was able to make use of the best science officer he could find, and the fact that she was a woman was only secondary to the efficient running of his ship. To strengthen his position, however, he married her, and only later did he begin to depend on her as wife and confidante rather than as a competent crew member. Whatever love there was in their marriage grew from this relationship.

Some readers have wondered how a civilization can function when its members are constantly striving to displace one another in the hierarchy of power and status. Again, I point out that level of service is determined by level of intelligence. The average Klingon is interested only in his immediate sphere—in elevating his own life-style and comforts. He does not aspire to become senator in chief, only head of the department. And on these lower levels, the struggle is more psychological than physical. The average Klingon will try to outfox or outmaneuver his superiors, not outfight or out-terrorize them.

Add to this the fact that if the performance levels of any one organization or department fall below acceptable competence because of infighting, the higher-ups will cause heads to roll, and everyone will lose. So your average Klingon worker will make sure his work is done long before he has his fun and tries to get rid of a superior.

Now to Kazhian history and the rise of Kling.

The analogy to the Arab was an obvious one, since he wanders across the vast expanses of the Sahara, Gobi, and Sinai deserts, seeking food and sustenance when and where he can, just as I had my early Kazhians do. The Arab, while not among the most inventive of humans, certainly ranks among the most resourceful. The Kazhian too would be resourceful; having so little to start with that he would make the most of what he had.

Scientists tell us that it is theoretically possible for a nomadic tribe to cover an amazing amount of territory in a given length of time. And if that time is virtually limitless, so too could be the distance covered. And with the planet's landmass virtually unbroken by oceans or mountain chains, there is no place where a nomadic tribe could not go. So my statement that some of the Kazhian tribes could have encircled their world is not so ludicrous as it may first sound.

In a world of limited food and water, there would certainly be war. The fact is unavoidable. Those who have pointed out that Arab tribes of Earth often go out of their way to avoid contact with each other are not considering that the Arab is an essentially peace-loving and reticent person. Not so with the Kazhians, who were in a constant state of agitation from their oxygen-rich atmosphere; and who were not forced into such conditions or chose to live in them but had always lived in them.

As the tribes increased, the nomadic wanderings would cease because of the need to remain near and protect any fairly bountiful supplies of water and food. This would facilitate the growth of cities and trade.

Astute viewers of the series have noticed that there are two types of Klingons, one a bit lighter-skinned than the other. However, this does not invalidate my thesis that racial differences had been eliminated by interbreeding in Kazhian prehistory. The coloration difference is so slight that it hardly matters, and is obviously a case of genetic "sport" cropping up in some members of the race.

The development of Klingon society and weaponry was intentionally glossed over in the original article. The scenario is familiar—just look at the dual development of government and warfare on our own world. I did not intend to suggest that the Klingons went from barbarism to atomic warfare overnight. I was just making a long (and sadly familiar) story short. The same goes for the development of space flight.

All of the information about the actors and the Klingons they played is factual. As to who was the best, and why, that is purely my own opinion.

The weaponry is listed in episodes and textual materials. Uniforms have been designed from what was shown on television and by extrapolation of stated material. The Empire's inner workings is an educated guess; the aims, obvious.

If I had any specific intention in writing the article in the way that I did, it would have to be stated as an effort to stretch my imagination and the imaginations of my fellow fans. And to have some fun with my favorite villains.

To all of you who have written, I thank you. Your comments, suggestions, refutations, and opinions have made me very happy that so many of you will take the time and trouble to let me know what you think of my work and of the magazine in which I publish.

# 2.
# "JUST" A SIMPLE COUNTRY DOCTOR?

by Joyce Tullock

*Leonard McCoy always finishes a solid third in every fan poll, but for some reason, very few fans seem to want to write about the good doctor. This is easy enough to understand, as we feel that McCoy is the most complex and intricate character in Star Trek. It is difficult to examine his character with any degree of objectivity—but why should this be so? In her article, Joyce Tullock gives what could be an explanation, and at the same time, a key as to why "Bones" McCoy is such an essential part of Star Trek.*

I have a confession to make! Mr. Spock is not my favorite Star Trek character. Neither is Captain Kirk. Nope! I see in Leonard McCoy a valuable, gentle hint to the world of today. He represents the positiveness to be found in the "average" man. Everyone knows that part of Mr. Spock's appeal to Star Trek fans is his cool reserve. It is continually pointed out that his ability to remain calm in an emergency is a highly admired, even envied, trait. That's true. His emotionlessness is often compared to McCoy's rash, excitable nature.

But there is also something to be said in favor of that erratic, emotional Dr. McCoy. He offers to many viewers a very positive example of the other side of the coin. He is more, much more, than a balance for the Star Trek threesome. In taking a close look at the McCoy personality, we find him to be a valuable element, not only for the Kirk/Spock relationship, but for the very success of Star Trek. He is the voice of today, the face of the twentieth century; a kind of Everyman. McCoy is today's connection with tomorrow. For some viewers (myself, at least) he makes the

7

future world of Star Trek more than just believable. He makes it natural.

McCoy, in spite of his highly sophisticated twenty-third-century training, is a twentieth-century man. When he speaks, his words so very often might have been spoken by anyone of our century cast into the world of the *Enterprise*. His thoughts, worries, and insights reach from our world to his. He is concerned about the existence of man in the machine age. While McCoy uses the tools of technology in his work, he is not dependent upon it. He would be a doctor regardless of the age in which he was born. The technology of medicine is important to him, but he does not try to hide his instinctual distrust of machines. In fact, he openly quarrels with them whenever he gets the chance. We all know about his standing quarrel with the transporter, but this is more than the chronic complaining of a bickering eccentric. It is a highly spirited attempt to keep machine and man in their proper places.

The doctor's biting comments about his world reveal a touching concern for the spirit of man. He probably takes machines for granted; he must, for they're a part of his world. But his focus is on humanity.

We find him time and again making statements which Mr. Spock finds ridiculous and illogical. But are they really, from the human point of view? His "emotional" decisions and insights are sometimes the correct ones. Had McCoy not offered himself to the Vians in "The Empath," Spock would have never been able to use his logic to save the day. And in "Return to Tomorrow," McCoy warns Kirk that the incredibly superior beings could "squash" them "like an insect." Now, for once, let's give the doctor credit! He was right! For all Kirk's noble speech about the chances for knowledge and advancement, his decision was at least partially in error. He did not even attempt any kind of compromise plan, but went along wholeheartedly (and somewhat recklessly) with the aliens' wishes. Really, what would have been so wrong with the exercise of just a little caution?

But Captain Kirk often shows us that he values McCoy's judgment and insight. He tells Spock to seek out McCoy's advice in "The Tholian Web," and in "A Private Little War," Kirk insists that the doctor's insight may aid him in solving the problem of Tyree's people. When Kirk and McCoy have a violent disagreement about the means of providing a balance of power, we see one of McCoy's most important functions outside the realm of medicine: He provides the Captain with an intelligent, honest, and uninhibited sounding board for ideas. He is no "yes man." He is refreshingly outspoken.

McCoy reminds us, then, that emotion can be a positive force. And for humans, it is essential. Let's not forget that the ancient Vulcans' inability to control their emotions with moderation has forced them to suppress that part of their nature totally. Well, that may work for Vulcans, but Dr. McCoy knows that it is not a thing to be desired in humans.

In "Plato's Stepchildren" we learn the equally beautiful aspects of the two natures. Spock advises his friends to express their emotions just as he must "master" his. Healthy or unhealthy, the expression of emotion is vital to human well-being. And as mankind has learned countless times, the suppression of emotion in the human animal can ultimately lead to disastrous effects. We are not Vulcans. We are built to display emotions, we operate through them. We depend on them to guide our heart and conscience. It is emotion which causes one human to make sacrifices for another. That's just the way we are. It's how we exist. And McCoy knows that the humans of Star Trek are not inferior to the Vulcan race because they are emotional.

Indeed, man has done the Vulcans one better, as Kirk points out in "Spectre of the Gun" and "Arena," for instead of denying his emotional nature, he is learning to overcome its negative aspects. Today, he simply will not give in to his desire to kill! The man of the twenty-third century is learning to harness his emotions in order to put them to good use; a fine display of human logic! And this is the kind of emotion represented in McCoy. Emotion is not to be repressed, but channeled. And as a doctor and humanitarian, McCoy has developed the use of emotion to an art.

So Dr. McCoy also knows how to lighten the tension of his world. And as a doctor he obviously sees more suffering than any of his friends aboard the *Enterprise*. Also, as a doctor, he shares the confidence of many aboard the *Enterprise*—and so bears the burdens that must accompany such a responsibility.

But to McCoy, this is what life is all about: people (yes, and Vulcans, too). He values them. And we get the feeling that he sees a special treasure in Mr. Spock. He goads Spock. Teases him. Tricks him into not taking himself quite so seriously. He won't let Spock forget that he is half human, because McCoy knows, as Spock's mother knows, that being human is good too. So because McCoy feels that it is important, he reminds Spock of his own humanity. And McCoy no doubt believes that the human part of Spock has a need for recognition; for that is basic to human nature. This is why he asks Spock's mother about his childhood. Because he worries about Spock's human half hiding inside. He serves as a gad-fly, constantly challenging Spock to face the reality of his complex nature.

In fact, it is through this interaction with McCoy that Mr. Spock reveals much of his human side. Spock clearly enjoys correcting the doctor's illogic, and often goes out of his way to get a rise from McCoy. McCoy falls to the bait, not be-cause he is stupid, but because he is keenly aware of the Vul-can's need to make some kind of contact. No one, not even a Vulcan, can live in total isolation. While Kirk offers binding friendship, McCoy offers Spock something else which is es-sential. In forcing Spock to react to his illogic, his emotional outbursts, and his passionate caring, McCoy provides a kind of therapeutic human experience. The Spock/McCoy feud is simply a sign of friendship. How else could they be expected to communicate?

The doctor often seems almost out of place and uncom-fortable in that technological world. He reacts to his world more like a common man from our own time. This, however, is only one way in which he represents twentieth-century man. His responses to problems and dangerous situations are perhaps the most realistic.

In "Return to Tomorrow" he worries quite naturally about beaming down into solid rock. He is less likely to forge too quickly into a dangerous situation. Kirk, in this very episode, states that McCoy is too cautious. But it is this very tendency toward caution which makes McCoy such an attractive char-acter. He is, at times, the reluctant hero.

Let's face it: Kirk and Spock, compared to McCoy, are "macho" men. Their courage and determination in the face of the gravest dangers is legend. They are military men. They've trained themselves to have nerves of steel. McCoy, however, is not one to "rush in where angels fear to tread." While all three think things over carefully before taking ac-tion, McCoy tends to consider the negative side most cau-tiously. More than once he argues with Kirk's decision to enter a risky situation. And his advice often proves to be very sound indeed.

Because McCoy is not "macho," because he is more likely to display his heroic reluctance, he becomes a very honest, true-to-life character. And when he takes a chance or makes a sacrifice, we can appreciate it all the more. You can almost feel the butterflies in his stomach! Spock once accused him of having a martyr complex ("The Immunity Syndrome"). But Leonard McCoy is no martyr. He doesn't like danger. When he takes a share of the danger, it is more out of love than devotion to duty. His decision to protect Spock and Gem from the Vians is a very complicated one. Knowing McCoy, it is hard to believe that he made that decision solely because it was logical. As a matter of fact, he probably would have done it whether it had been logical or not. He cared about Spock and Gem; and the doctor is notorious for allowing his emotions to guide him.

"The Empath" is often discussed in connection with both Spock and Dr. McCoy. And it is perhaps one of the most intensely emotional episodes of the series. It was certainly one of Nimoy's most clever performances, for he managed to display very deep concern for his friend with such subtlety that he avoided stepping out of character. Somehow, Kirk's outward display of emotion diminishes before the quiet worry in Spock's eyes.

Of course, this may all only be in the eyes of the beholder. With Spock, it is hard to tell how much we see and how much we superimpose through our own emotions.

But one thing is clear: Kirk and Spock's concern for the doctor runs through Star Trek as a general motif. It would be interesting to count the number of times he is pushed aside, left behind, held back, knocked out or hushed (his big mouth is often his gravest danger) simply for his own protection. In short, McCoy's friends show a tendency to shelter him from danger whenever possible.

This adds another charming aspect to McCoy's nature. He is not a bumbler, but he is an innocent in the military world. First and last he is a doctor. And he is constantly pointing this out to Kirk and Spock. Because he thinks like a doctor, he thinks like a civilian—and that takes us back to his essential value to Star Trek.

Kirk, in "The Alternative Factor," is a busy man trying to find answers to the "winking out" problem. He becomes annoyed with McCoy's natural (and once again realistic) way of describing the unusual recovery of his patient, Lazarus. To Kirk, a man trained in the military sense, McCoy is beating around the bush. McCoy, on the other hand, claims to be "just a simple country doctor." He is puzzled, embarrassed, bewildered, and a little bit amused by his own problem. Here we can clearly see that Kirk's tremendous responsibilities force him to be more serious. The very nature of Dr. McCoy's work, however, has taught him to arm himself with a sense of humor—which is sometimes his only defense (and in some episodes, Star Trek's only salvation).

McCoy's insistence that he is "just a simple country doctor" provides more reinforcement for that "Everyman" quality of his character. He is uncomfortable in social surroundings. He hates the dress uniform and makes an embarrassed, half-hearted attempt to give Sarek the Vulcan salute in "Journey to Babel." His "country" attitude offers a colorful contrast to the world of the twenty-third century.

It's those little touches (which may have seemed insignificant at the time they were written and performed) which fill out his character and make it so real. Most viewers, to some extent at least, can identify with his distaste for formality, regulations, and computers. McCoy is much the ordinary guy, like one of H. G. Wells' contemporary characters cast into a world with which he is a little out of touch. And we can somehow admire his determination not to adjust too well. He is always a little at odds, and he likes it.

McCoy is not a character just to be admired. Kirk and Spock fulfill that basic hero need. He is a character to be "recognized." And what we may see of ourselves in him (both the good and the bad) allows us to step easily into Star Trek's world. He is the conduit, the connection. His awe and disbelief reflect our own. When he speaks, we may not always agree with him, but we "understand" the way he thinks. And when he beats around the bush or has difficulty understanding Spock's scientific jargon, that's when we like him most of all. That's when we feel at home on the *Enterprise*.

McCoy's informal attitude should not be taken too seriously, either. After all, he is a man who knows his business. Even Mr. Spock admires his abilities (although he seldom admits it). He compliments the doctor's expertise in "Spectre of the Gun," has confidence in his ability to operate on Sarek, and is in puzzled awe of his scientific method in "Miri."

Incidentally, it would have been nice to just once hear someone say thanks after being brought back from near death by McCoy. All right, so you can't expect it from Vulcans. But still . . . McCoy's medical talents might have been brought out a little more clearly in the series. He does get to isolate countless viruses and create antidotes once in a while, but for the most part he fulfills his medical task by announcing that fatal message: "He's dead, Jim!" (If anyone has ever bothered to count them, I don't want to hear about it!)

Still, for the most part, Dr. McCoy's dialogue provides some of the most entertaining and memorable moments of Star Trek. When McCoy comes on the screen, the viewer knows he's in line for some humor, tension, or real drama. His comments and facial expressions can animate an otherwise dry or trite script. He was not always utilized to the fullest in Star Trek, and when he is missing the show is usually the poorer for it. In "Let That Be Your Last Battlefield" he makes what I like to call his "special guest appearance" early in the program and is never heard from again. I felt cheated! But then, that was one of those shows that . . . well, what can I say? McCoy's presence invariably provided a snappiness and tension which helped to keep the show running smoothly in spite of it all.

The doctor's relationship with Mr. Spock, of course, is essential. It tells us more about the Vulcan than we could ever know directly. The Spock/McCoy contrast (note—not "conflict") is beautiful, for it most clearly emphasizes the IDIC concept. Here are two completely different natures, each serving by contrast to emphasize and display the beauty of the other.

Just as many viewers value Spock's cool control, McCoy's humanity must be appreciated, too. His ability to display uninhibited emotion is a thing to be admired in our own too often tight-lipped society. McCoy is a man of old Earth warmth, charm, even elegance, and these positive qualities are derived from his emotional essence. His outward gruffness only emphasizes the grace of his true character as we learn to know him. As we become more aware of McCoy the humanitarian, McCoy the cynic becomes justified.

Like the real people of today's world, Leonard McCoy has been hurt in love. He does not have Kirk's knack of being a lady-killer or Spock's built-in shield of emotionlessness. He feels very deeply, and we get the impression that he is very cautious about those feelings. Once again, he is very much the average man. But McCoy handles his life quite well. The fact that his personal problems are recognizable as being common today just adds more to his character. While they no doubt color his personality, they do not weigh him down. After all, as McCoy would say, "A little suffering is good for the soul." So we may assume that the doctor is able to channel those bad emotional experiences and use them for good. His depth of understanding and concerned empathy with others is clear.

Leonard McCoy's presence aboard the USS *Enterprise* provides a sometimes subtle—but always essential—flavor to Star Trek. Without diminishing the value of Kirk and Spock, it must be said that McCoy gives Star Trek an element of credibility in his own right.

He is texture. He is the click of recognition which helps make Star Trek work. Barely noticeable at times, his is the life spark which tricks us into believing that it's all real. He makes us feel at home. For the most part, he says what we would say and does what we would do if cast into such a world. Or at least he says what we might "like" to say or do.

He moves on his own in a highly controlled world and refuses to be a cog in the machine. McCoy is not afraid of eccentricity. He does not take himself or his elaborate education too seriously. He charms us with his illogical, erratic, and emotionally volatile nature. He touches us with his human warmth. In a way, he represents the mankind of today at its best. Perhaps he is the antithesis of Mr. Spock in many ways. Perhaps he touches us for the very opposite reasons that Mr. Spock does. All the more to the benefit of Star Trek and the philosophy of IDIC.

# 3.
# SUBSPACE RADIO AND SPACE WARPS

## by Mark Andrew Golding

*The technology of the time of Star Trek is beyond our ability to duplicate, of course (too bad . . . transporters would certainly solve the gas shortage!), but we do have the means to work with current knowledge and provide ourselves with possible explanations for some of the mechanics of the future. Mark Golding has been doing just that for some time, and his efforts have won him a reputation as one of the leading "experts" on Federation physics, hardware, and theory. In the following article, Mark turns his attention to one of the most fascinating and exasperating facets of that technology: the subspace radio.*

In a previous article I have postulated that a system of space warps leading from solar system to solar system is necessary to explain many puzzling aspects of the Star Trek universe. I call those space warps Gateways, at least until the Great Bird of the Galaxy gives them an official name.

The subspace radio is among the aspects of the Star Trek universe which enables us to make deductions about the arrangement of the system of Gateways.

In several episodes Kirk seemed to carry on direct conversations with Starfleet admirals instead of merely receiving answers to his messages hours after they had been sent. They include "Amok Time" (near Vulcan?), perhaps "The Trouble with Tribbles" (near Sherman's Planet), "For the World Is Hollow and I have Touched the Sky" (near Daran V), "Mark of Gideon" (at Gideon), and perhaps "Alternative Factor" (a distant planetary system).

Since even the three-second round trip of radio from the

Earth to the Moon and back causes a noticeable time lag in conversations, it can be assumed that in those cases the round-trip time of the subspace radio was less than three seconds.

Thus if we assume a certain distance between Starfleet Headquarters and the position of the *Enterprise* during those episodes, we can deduce a minimum speed for subspace radio communication.

If we assume that the five solar systems involved are the five closest to Starfleet HQ (which would in turn necessitate the assumption that Starfleet HQ is not in our solar system, for it seems unlikely that the systems of Vulcan, Sherman's Planet, Daran V, Gideon, and Lazarus' Planet are those of Alpha Centauri, Bernard's Star, Wolf 359, Lalande 21185, and Sirius), then it is likely that their distances range from four to nine light-years from Starfleet HQ. Since even at a distance of nine light-years subspace rays take less than three seconds for a round trip, the speed of subspace rays must be greater than 189,345,600 times the speed of light.

Even if Starfleet HQ is in the densely crowded core of the galaxy, or in a globular star cluster, it still would require a distance of a light-year or two to include the five nearest stars. Even in that case the minimum speed of subspace rays would be about 20,000,000 times the speed of light.

Those are the minimum speeds; there's no reason why the actual speed of subspace rays couldn't be tens or millions of times greater. Since there are hundreds of billions of stars in the galaxy, and the *Enterprise* has visited only a hundred or so of them in the various episodes, and since about 5 percent of that insignificant fraction of the total number of stars in the galaxy are within conversational range of Starfleet HQ, it seems likely that those five stars aren't the five stars closest to Starfleet HQ. They could be hundreds of light-years away, which would make the minimum speeds of subspace radio that much faster.

At speeds of 189,000,000 C (the speed of light), it would take 4.6 hours to travel the 100,000 light-years from one end of the galaxy to another, the greatest possible distance within the galaxy. Even at speeds of only 20,000,000 C it would take only 1.826 days to cross the greatest possible distance within the galaxy.

But in "Balance of Terror" it took hours to get an answer from Starfleet to messages sent from the Romulan Neutral Zone, while in "The *Enterprise* Incident" it was said that it would take *three weeks* to send a message to Starfleet, to say nothing of receiving an answer. Thus it would seem that the maximum speed of subspace radio in "The Enterprise Incident" would have to be 1,733,333.3 times C, even if that part of the Romulan Neutral Zone was 100,000 light-years from Starfleet HQ!

In "Whom Gods Destroy" there was reference to a Romulan ship destroyed near Tau Ceti, probably the one destroyed in "Balance of Terror"; and since a comet was shown with its streaming tail, it must have been within a few hundred million miles of whatever star was involved.

If the part of the Romulan Neutral Zone in "Balance of Terror" is the same one that is near Gamma Hydra, about 150 light-years from Earth in "The Deadly Years," then the necessary speeds of subspace radio would range from 9,163,-000 C if the round trip is 3.5 hours to 121,800 C if the round-trip time is 24 hours.

Thus we see that if conversations with no noticeable time lag are to be possible over the distances between even the nearest stars, speeds of at least 20,000,000 times the speed of light, more likely at least 200,000,000 times the speed of light, will be necessary. If there is to be anyplace in the galaxy that it would take three weeks to reach by a subspace message, then subspace radio must be slower than 1,700,000 times the speed of light, while there is a possibility that the speed of subspace radio may be within the range of 9,000 to 60,000 times the speed of light!

According to the inverse square law, the particle density of a burst of radiation will be inversely proportional to the square of the distance; at twice the distance it will be ¼ as great, at three times the distance it will be ⅑ as great, etc. Thus at a certain distance from a starship the density of radiation from its subspace radio will be too low to be detected.

If each individual particle is made more energetic, it will be possible to detect the message even when the particle density is lower, so perhaps the amount of energy given to each particle of subspace radio radiation will vary with the distance the message will have to be sent.

If the amount of energy carried by a subspace radiation particle is inversely proportional to its speed (i.e., the faster it goes the less likely it will be to be detected, as would be the case with the hypothetical Tachyon particles), then messages sent over long distances would travel slower than messages sent over short distances.

If you made assumptions about the distances of Vulcan, Daran V, Gideon, Sherman's Planet, Lazarus' Planet, and the sections of the Romulan Neutral Zone mentioned in "Balance of Terror" and *"Enterprise* Incident" you could calculate the ratio of distance/speed for subspace radio messages.

That theory would explain the contradictions between the speed of subspace radio in various episodes. But I prefer another theory which is even more useful.

If the Gateways, the space warps which allow instantaneous travel between solar systems, are used for transportation, why wouldn't they be used for communications also? Just as even the faster-than-light speeds of starships are not enough to travel the great distances of the galactic civilization of Star Trek in reasonable times, so too the faster-than-light speeds of subspace radio are not fast enough to permit conversations over interstellar distances without being relayed through the system of Gateways.

If there are two Gateways in each solar system, at equal distances from the star, then they are likely to orbit opposite one another, and thus a message being relayed through that system would travel twice the distance from a Gateway to the star.

If there are three Gateways arranged in an equal triangle, or four arranged in an equal tetrahedron, then the distance traveled by a message traveling through the solar system will be equal to 1.7333 times the distance between a Gateway and the star

It seems logical to assume that manned or unmanned space stations are kept at each end of the Gateways leading between civilized solar systems, to beam messages through the Gateways and relay those which are received to the other Gateways leading out of the solar system or one of the planets in the system if that planet is the destination of the message.

Naturally, when a starship travels far beyond the borders of explored space, passing through Gateways no Earth ship has passed through before, there will be no space stations to relay its subspace messages back through the Gateways it has passed through. The starship will have to beam the message across space instead of sending it through the shortcuts of the Gateways.

It is rather surprising that that appears to be the procedure when sending messages to Starfleet HQ from the Romulan Neutral Zone. We would expect a system of space stations in the Gateways to relay such messages as fast as possible. Perhaps Starfleet fears that such a system would make it too easy for the Romulans to track down the location of Earth and other Federation planets if they crossed the Neutral Zone to invade the Federation.

If we assume various speeds for subspace radiation and various numbers of Gateways and solar systems the messages are transmitted through, and allow for the distance the messages travel through in each solar system to be either 2 times or 1.7333 times the average distance from a Gateway to the star it orbits, we can chart the various figures for that average distance D.

Assume that the distance a subspace message travels through in a solar system is twice the distance D between a Gateway and its star, that a round trip takes 1 second, and that the total distance traveled equals the number of solar systems passed through times 4 D.

In "Operation Annihilate!" Kirk described the planet Deneva as having been settled a century earlier as a stop on the route between the asteroid mines and the outer planets. Since there is no planet Deneva in our solar system, we can assume that it is in another solar system and that the outer planets are in still more distant solar systems. The asteroid mines mentioned are probably, though not necessarily, those in our own solar system.

Thus, the route through the Gateways from the asteroid mines through Deneva to the outer planets would also be the (or a) route from Earth and the rest of the solar system to Deneva and the outer solar systems. It would have been referred to as the route from Earth, unless the entry point of the Gateway in question is situated closer to the asteroid belt than to Earth. Let us say the endpoint of the Gateway in question must be between $2.0 \times 10^8$ kilometers from the sun and $8.0 \times 10^8$ kilometers from the sun, as compared to Earth's distance of $1.495 \times 10^8$ kilometers.

That limits the possibilities considerably. If you assume there are two Gateways connected to each solar system, then a starship which has entered it through one of them will have only one Gateway through which to pass to reach another solar system. If it started from one solar system it would have to travel through hundreds of billions of solar systems and Gateways in order to have a 100 percent certainty of reaching any other particular solar system.

On the other hand, if there are three gateways leading out

of each solar system, then a starship which enters a solar system through one Gateway will have two different Gateways to choose from which will lead to different solar systems. If it starts its voyage from within a solar system it will have three Gateways to choose from the first time and two to choose from in each succeeding solar system.

The number of solar systems which are accessible through a specific number of Gateways, or through a lesser number, will be almost twice the number accessible through exactly that number of Gateways. Since there are several hundred billion stars in our galaxy, we can assume that a few percent of them might be accessible through 30 Gateways. Of the stars visited by the *Enterprise*, a few percent are close enough to Starfleet HQ for conversations via subspace radio to be possible without any noticeable time lag, by sending the messages through the system of Gateways.

This suggests that the average distance between the mouth of a Gateway and the star it orbits is about $2 \times 10^8$ kilometers to $8 \times 10^8$ kilometers, and the speed of subspace radio waves will be between 68.965.51 times the sped of light and 277,777.7 times the speed of light.

This indicates that since it took at least three hours to get a reply from Starfleet in "Balance of Terror" then the section of the Romulan Neutral Zone that was the setting of that episode must not have been near Tau Ceti. Spock's reference to the Romulan ship "we" destroyed there must have been to some other, unfilmed, adventure of the *Enterprise* or to an incident involving another starship.

If the speed of subspace radio is 70,000 times the speed of light, "Balance of Terror" could have taken place about 16 light-years from Earth if the answer took 4 hours getting to the *Enterprise* and about 96 light-years from Earth if the round trip of the message took 24 hours. If the speed of subspace radio is 275,000 times the speed of light, "Balance of Terror" could have taken place 63 light-years from Earth if the message took 4 hours for the round trip and 375 light-years from Earth if the message took 24 hours for the round trip.

In *"Enterprise* Incident," it was said that a message from the section of the Romulan Neutral Zone in which that episode took place would take three weeks to reach Starfleet HQ.

The fact that a Romulan ship was once destroyed near Tau Ceti, only 11 light-years from Earth; the fact that part of the

Romulan Neutral Zone is near Gamma Hydra, 150 light-years from Earth in the opposite direction; the fact that still another part of the Romulan Neutral Zone is 4,000 to 16,000 light-years from Earth; and the fact that the parts of the Romulan Neutral Zone in "'Deadly Years" and *"Enterprise* Incident" seem to be shaped like spheres only a dozen or so light-years wide all seem to prove that the Romulan Empire consists of many spherical volumes of space which are connected only through the Gateways, and are scattered across the galaxy, mixed in with segments of the Federation, the Klingon Empire, the Tholian Assembly, etc.

A speed of 70,000 times the speed of light is equal to about warp 41.5, 100,000 C to warp 46.5, 150,000 C to warp 53.5, 200,000 C to warp 58.5, 250,000 C to warp 63, and 275,000 C to warp 65.

You will notice that traveling through 37 or 38 Gateways would be sufficient to reach any star in the galaxy from any other star. How long would that take?

Assuming that the distance a starship would have to travel between Gateways in a solar system is equal to 1.733 times the distance between a Gateway and its star, and that the distance between a Gateway and its star is in the range of 200,000,000 kilometers to 800,000,000 kilometers, the following can be deduced.

Since it should only be necessary to pass through 38 Gateways to reach any solar system in the galaxy from any other, it should take only 8.74 seconds to 4.878 hours to reach any solar system in the galaxy from any other.

In "Obsession," Sulu told Kirk it would take 1.7 days to reach Tycho IV from Argus X, 1,000 light-years away, and return. If the *Enterprise* traveled through space all the way it would take 10 years at warp 6 for the round trip, but the best route through the Gateways would take only 20.14 to 81.32 seconds at warp 6.

It would seem that the Federation has mapped only a tiny fraction of the Gateways, and the best-known route through them from Argus X to Tycho IV must be many times as long as the best possible route would be—about 7,292.9 to 1,-806.19 times as long.

In "That Which Survives," Spock calculated that it would take at least 11.33 hours at warp 8.4 to travel 990.7 light-years. Traveling through space all the way would take 14,-652.4 hours, while at warp 8.4 it would take only 7.4062 seconds to 29.63 seconds to travel through 38 Gateways, the maximum needed to reach any planet in the galaxy. Thus, it would seem that the best-known route back to the Kalandan outpost planet was 1,376.6 to 5,507.28 times as long as the shortest possible route.

Of course, it is possible that the Kalandan computer in "That Which Survives" threw the *Enterprise* into a region of space which was far from the nearest entrance to a Gateway. In 11.33 hours at warp 8.4 the *Enterprise* could travel 6,-715.291 light-hours—0.76061 light-years. If it was that distance from the nearest Gateway it would have to travel for almost all the 11.33 hours to get to that Gateway and then swifly make its way through the system of Gateways to the Kalandan Outpost planet in a matter of a minute or so.

Then too it may be that starships can't travel at their maximum speed in the narrow confines of a solar system between Gateways. But in "Elaan of Troyius," it was considered unusual for the *Enterprise* to crawl at slower-than-light speeds between two planets in the Tellun star system.

Perhaps an added maneuvering time reduces the number of Gateways a starship can pass through in an hour. Perhaps.

In the examples cited, the *Enterprise* traveled through 1,-000 to 7,000 times as many Gateways as the 38 that would be the maximum necessary to reach any star in the galaxy if every Gateway had been charted by the Federation. Since hundreds of billions of Gateways would have to be traversed to get from one star to another if one didn't know anything about the proper route to take, it would seem that the Federation has explored 2,500,000 to 1,000,000 times as much of the galaxy as a group that knew nothing of the Gateways and their arrangement would have.

Thus it would seem that about 0.001 percent or so of the galaxy has been mapped by the Federation, presumably starting less than 200 years before the time of Star Trek with the invention of the warp drive by Zefrem Cochrane.

In "Obsession" and "That Which Survives," the *Enterprise* makes journeys through 38,000 to 250,000 Gateways, indicating that the Federation's sphere of exploration extends through that many Gateways in at least one direction of travel. But if it had explored every solar system which could be reached through a mere 38 Gateways from Earth, it would have explored the entire Galaxy.

If the Federation has explored 0.001 percent of the Galaxy, it has explored the equivalent of every solar system within 26 or 27 Gateways of Earth. Since it has explored thousands of times as far through the system of Gateways in some directions, it must have explored far less than 25 Gateways away in other directions.

It seems rather illogical to explore thousands of times as far in one direction as another. Of course, Earth had two separate phases of interstellar exploration, according to my historical reconstruction.

First Zefrem Cochrane of Alpha Centauri led a fleet from Earth which traveled through hundreds or thousands of Gateways, and then destroyed their records so that the route back to Earth would never be discovered by their enemies. Then they founded a new Earth and formed the realm which overthrew the evil power which had monopolized interstellar travel. They then began the long, slow search by trial and error for the route back to Earth.

Later the slower-than-light ships of Earth discovered the Gateways and explored through them, colonizing many planets and fighting the Romulan War and the War with Axanar. The reunion of the two groups was only a few years in the past at the time of the first visit of the *Enterprise* to Talos IV, and the resulting area of explored space extended hundreds of Gateways long in the connecting axis between the two former spheres of exploration.

Also, many of the Gateways may be inactive for some reason or their ends leading into various solar systems may be blocked by defensive force shields, or there may be mighty space empires which forbid the ships of the Federation to travel through the Gateways in their regions of space.

As you'll remember, in "This Side of Paradise," it was said that the colonists on Omicron (Mira) Ceti III had traveled a year from Earth. Omicron Ceti is a little more than the 216 light-years a ship traveling at warp 6 could travel in a year away from Earth, but it is more likely that the colony ship traveled at warp 2 or warp 3, going through the system of Gateways except at one point when it traveled 10 or 20 light-years across space from one solar system and its Gateways to another solar system and the routes through the Gateways that led from it. There may be no known route through the Gateways from Earth to the New Earth without some flight over several light-years between neighboring stars and their Gateway systems.

There are 175 or so star systems mentioned in various Star Trek episodes. I have determined with greater or lesser accuracy the distances of about 57 of them. Eight, possibly 16, are in the 10,000 to 80,000 light-year range from Earth; about 3 to 12 are in the 1,000 to 10,000 light-year range; 11, or perhaps 19, are in the 100 to 1,000 light-year range; and 18 to 21 are in the range of up to 100 light-years.

It is true that some of the stars closest to Earth may be reached not through the Gateways but by direct flight across 10 or 20 light-years of space, but as I argued in an earlier article, Pollux, only 40 light-years from Earth, must be beyond the range of such exploration and reachable only through the Gateways. All stars farther than 40 light-years from Earth must be reached through the system of Gateways.

We find that there are 29 to 40 worlds within 1,000 light-years from Earth, and a volume of only 0.0004 percent of the volume of the Galaxy. Yet the stars mentioned in that tiny area are from 0.1657 to 2.22857 percent of the total number of stars mentioned in all the Star Trek episodes. The volume of space within 1,000 light-years of Earth seems to have been explored 276.2 to 380.95 times as much as the rest of the galaxy—even allowing for the stars closer to Earth than Pollux is, the stars which might not have been reached through the Gateways.

Thus it can be seen that Gateways are more likely to lead to nearby solar systems than to far-distant ones. However, many of them do lead to far-distant solar systems. Some of the star systems visited by the *Enterprise* must be close to the far side of the galaxy, despite the fact that only a small fraction of the stars in the galaxy have ever been visited.

The arrangement of the Gateways is not orderly. If it was, you could pass from one solar system to its neighbor in the direction you wanted to go and then the next star system in line, and so on in a straight line. Instead, you may zigzag across the galaxy many times while making a journey between stars only a couple of dozen light-years apart. One Gateway may lead between stars 10 light-years apart and the next one between stars 10,000 light-years apart.

It is possible that when the system of Gateways was created it was orderly, with each solar system linked to its three closest neighbors, and each of the neighbors linked to the three closest stars, etc. Since each star has a slightly different orbit around the center of the galaxy, over millions of years the relative positions of the stars would change—the system would become as it is in the time of Star Trek.

That is assuming that the Gateways are attached somehow to the stars they connect, that the ends of each Gateway must remain at the same distance from those stars no matter how much those stars move from their original positions.

· If that was not the case, if the mouths of the Gateways did not move with the stars and yet averaged only a few hundred million kilometers distant from each star, they would have to be scattered in space a few hundred million kilometers apart.

If that was the case, a planet that traveled with its star would run into a Gateway every 40,000,000,000,000,000 kil-- ometers or so at the least, or every 10,000,000 years (Earth is about 5,000,000,000 years old). That would not be healthy —to lose a chunk of matter or to be transported entirely to a spot light-years from any sun. Every planet in the galaxy would be a frozen orb wandering between stars by now!

It seems logical to assume that the system of Gateways does not lead to other galaxies. Otherwise a Gateway leading to another galaxy would probably have been discovered by now.

It is true the Kelvans would need enough Gateways to reduce the 2,000,000-light-year distance to Andromeda to 400,000 light-years if they were to make the trip at warp 11 in a mere 300 years as seen in "By Any Other Name." But perhaps they intended to increase their speed from warp 11 to warp 18.821, or 6,666.96 times the speed of light, which would be the right speed to make the trip in 300 years.

I can't imagine why Spock would have been surprised by any figure the Kelvans quoted from the trip to Andromeda unless he knew that the system of Gateways didn't extend beyond the edge of our galaxy, and that any voyage to Andromeda would have to be through all the 2,000,000 light-years between the two galaxies.

It seems likely that the system of Gateways was created by a now extinct civilization long ago for its own use. Or a benevolent super-civilization may have created it for the use of lesser civilizations such as the Federation, the Tholians, the Gorns, the Klingons, etc. It is impossible to say whether it was created long ago in an orderly condition and developed into its present confusion as the positions of the stars in the galaxy slowly changed, or if it was recently created in its present condition.

Since only about 0.001 percent of all the stars in the galaxy have been explored through Gateways by Earthmen, and yet Sirius, Canopus, Alpha Centauri, Arcturus, Vega, Capella, Rigel, Altair, Spica, Antares, Pollux, and Deneb— 12 of the 20 stars which are best known to Earthmen of our time—are accessible and explored in the time of Star Trek, it is safe to assume that whoever created the system of Gateways planned to have the most famous stars known to Earthmen among those which would first be discovered through the Gateways.

Probably the Preservers, who scatter primitive human cultures from Earth on dozens and hundreds of planets across the galaxy, and yet have not done so with nonhuman races, are responsible for creating the system of Gateways with its arrangement so clearly planned with Earth in mind.

# 4.

# THE ROMULAN/ KLINGON ALLIANCE

## by Patrick R. Wilson

*The "truce" between the Klingons and the Romulans was originally designed as an easy and economical way to use the same starship models for both races, but to Star Trek fans, that simply wasn't proper and fittin'. The fans see the Star Trek "universe" as real, and therefore require a realistic and detailed explanation for whatever happens within that universe. However, no such explanation was forthcoming, and it was not until last year that Patrick Wilson decided it was high time for one. We think he did an excellent job, and it becomes even more entertaining and informative in the "official report" format he suggested for it.*

Official Use Only
O Mark O R5PC

Starfleet Command
Starfleet Headquarters
United Federation of Planets
THE STARFLEET ACADEMY

Patrick R. Wilson
Chief of Planetary Relations

Stardate: 7806.10

TO: Commodore D. H. Garth
    Chief, School of Military Arts
    Starfleet Academy

RE: The Romulan/Klingon Alliance

Sir:

In compliance with your request of Stardate 7806.1, herein is a résumé of the current evaluation of the Romulan/Klingon Alliance to facilitate your lectures to the incoming cadets now beginning the summer semester at the Academy.

Not since the first years of the Outreach following the Eugenics Wars and the subsequent first encounters with the Klingon and Romulan Star Empires has Starfleet been faced with a more serious challenge than is represented by this alliance.

The specific reasons and circumstances of the alliance can only be matters of speculation, as the negotiations were necessarily secret. Indeed, the very existence of the alliance was unknown until random intelligence and chance encounters suggested it. Confirmation was not forthcoming until the much exaggerated *"Enterprise* Incident" of 5031.3, in which the USS *Enterprise* (Capt. James T. Kirk, SC937-0176CEC, commanding) strayed across the Romulan Neutral Zone through an error in navigation (the officially logged explanation) and first reported both visual and sensor confirmation of the Romulans' use of Klingon battle cruisers.

In any event, it is currently believed that the primary reasons for the alliance were rooted in concerns for greater collective security, exchange of technological data, and possibly offensive designs against the United Federation of Planets or other powers.

That collective security as a goal is obvious, but it is unclear how the allies will be able to exercise it. The distance between the two empires at their closest point is something over 5,000 parsecs and this route skirts the energy barrier at the galaxy's edge. Compounding the problems of direct communication are the Outpost Colonies monitoring the Romulan Neutral Zone, which should be able to prevent any unobserved contacts. Ironically, it may have been these very disadvantages which prompted the quest for the alliance. After all, the Romulans and Klingons both perceive themselves threatened by the burgeoning economic and military power of the Federation, and view their relative isolation as an invitation to eventual attack.

Recently acquired intelligence supports the theory that both sides were seeking diplomatic contact with each other at the time of the last major breach of the Romulan-Federation Peace Treaty.

This incident occurred on Stardate 1709.1, when a Romulan ship, equipped with their new cloaking device and a plasma beam, attacked the Outpost Line on the Neutral Zone, destroying several of the stations before it was itself destroyed. The holes thus torn in the monitoring system could only partially be filled by small patrol craft during the solar year required to reestablish the entire line.

It was during this period that a Klingon battle cruiser (tentatively identified as the *Thanatos*) apparently made the passage through the Neutral Zone and delivered the first proposals. Representing the Klingon Empire in these negotiations was a certain Kainord, believed to be Senior Advisor for Alien Affairs to the Klingon Supreme Council, a position he still holds, according to latest available reports. His opposite number in the negotiations was Thalone, personal representative of Praetor Raznak, who has since been given a squadron of his own and the rank of Commander.

Details of the negotiations are wanting, but a mutual understanding was reached in a remarkably short time, and an instrument of alliance was signed on or about Stardate 2856.25. Again, full specifics of the agreement are unknown, but some points have come to light.

Both empires are committed to the defense of the other in the event of attack on either party by the Federation; and there is reason to believe that there is a movement toward the completion of an offensive treaty as well, which would commit both parties to an eventual attack on the Federation. While of obvious concern, there is no reason to expect imminent hostilities arising from the influence of these agreements.

However, one of the proofs of the sense of collective security deriving from the treaty is the evidence of hostilities between the Romulans and their immediate neighbors, the Gorn. With the promise of Klingon support and the acquisition of new weapons, the Romulans have set about securing their borders against this small but technologically sophisticated reptiloid race. The progress of this conflict is of great concern to the Federation, as success for the Romulans may herald the beginning of whatever offensive operations they and their new Allies may have in mind.

It is to be expected that before the Romulans begin any such operations, they will have dealt with the fleet of the First Federation which operates within the space of the Federation Exploration Territory and in the area just beyond the territory of the Gorn. The monitoring of these areas and potential or ongoing conflicts are of primary concern at this time to the Chief of Planetary Relations.

Of immediate concern to all current and future Starfleet personnel is the exchange of military and technological hardware and data. Prior to the Romulan/Klingon Alliance, the Romulan space force had been in a long-term state of disorganization and technological stagnation resulting from the stalemate and staggering losses during the Romulan War. This period of relative inactivity came to an abrupt halt with the confirmation of Raznak as Praetor.

He instituted a major reoranization of the fleet, eliminating many of the old class distinctions between officers (usually from the Equestrian order) and enlisted men (Plebeians). Further, he authorized the design of weapons that would counter what was seen as the Federation's greatest military asset, the warp drive, something then beyond Romulan capabilities. This culminated in the development of the Romulan's invisibility screen and the plasma beam. Both were then ruthlessly perfected under combat circumstances during a ten-year campaign to reestablish the Praetor's supremacy within the fragmented sections of the empire.

With the conclusion of the alliance, one of the first benefits to accrue to the Romulans was delivery of seven of the Klingon's D-6 Class battle cruisers, which were immediately formed into two squadrons, with one ship in reserve. In a *quid pro quo* arrangement, the Romulans have given over to the Klingons the specifications of their invisibility screen and the plasma beam. The D-6 battle cruisers, with their seven phaser banks and twin disruptors, were even then becoming obsolete, and were being phased out in favor of the more heavily armed and versatile D-7 Class.

It would seem that the Klingons had gotten the better deal, but the Romulans appear to be satisfied with the gain of the warp drive, which had eluded them for so long. However valuable the invisibility screen (or cloaking device, as it is termed when installed in Klingon-style ships) may have been to the Klingons at this time, it is now generally conceded that the "chance" acquisition of one of these units by the Federation has restored the technological balance between the superpowers.

The plasma beam appears to be the only concrete benefit the Klingons have received from the alliance, and this is of military significance. It is not known if the treaty requires the continued trading of newly developed hardware or was limited to the specific needs of the signees at the time; but with the advent of the Klingon stasis field generator, there is a possibility that it will eventually be fitted in Romulan vessels as well.

One of the most puzzling aspects of the Romulan/Klingon Alliance is why the Klingons were apparently so eager to give up the secret of their warp drive to a power they are likely to betray someday. In a full-scale war, the side with a warp-drive system must be victorious over any culture that does not possess it. Thus the apparent contradiction of the Klingons' giving a future enemy (and one must remember that the Klingons are the avowed enemies of *all* cultures in the galaxy) the means of resisting effectively.

Of course, this may only be a matter of expedience for the Klingons. They may be willing to give up this advantage in order to improve their overall strategic position vis-à-vis the Federation. But there is also evidence to support the belief that the Klingons have driven a particularly hard bargain with the Romulans in this regard.

Some intelligence sources and miscellaneous random leaks suggest that the battle cruisers now in Romulan hands may have Klingons supervising or completely manning the engineering sections of the ships. The commanders and sub-commanders of these ships have full operational control over their vessels, but are only nominally in command of their Klingon "technical advisers."

This theory is supported by the obvious problem (at least in the early stages of the alliance) that the Romulans had no qualified engineers in warp drive technology, and the Klingons would have been obliged to supply the necessary expertise. However, even with the intervening years, there is no sign that the Klingons have relinquished their authority over their engineering domain.

The significance of this cannot have been lost on the Romulans, and should not be by Federation Starfleet personnel either. The inevitable distrust and communications problems such a system must engender is a potentially serious limitation on the deployment of the vessels so affected. Evidence of the degree of real harmony between the allies is small, but at least an indication can be gleaned by the fact that Klingon engineers have (according to recently confirmed intelligence) override control of their engines, and are required to scuttle and/or permanently damage their ships either on direct orders or if in danger of being forcibly removed from their posts.

As intimated earlier, there is currently no evidence of imminent hostilities resulting from this alliance, but the reasons for this fact are of great significance to those who would serve in Starfleet.

The Organian Crisis of Stardate 3198 may have been largely precipitated by the conclusion of the alliance between the Klingons and the Romulans. Hostilities had already begun at this time, and a general fleet action between Starfleet Task Force 33 and Klingon Battle Group Kor was imminent. But, as everyone somewhat shamefacedly remembers, the "helpless" Organians imposed their terms of peace on both parties.

At the time of the crisis, there were no reported incidents along the Romulan Neutral Zone, so it is impossible to tell if "the war that never was" was intended to be a general galactic one. What *is* known is that with the establishment of the new Neutral Zone between the Klingon Empire and the Federation Treaty Exploration Territory, the Klingons had become even more isolated than before the alliance had been signed.

Since hostilities within the Neutral Zone are forbidden by the Organians, neither side lets vessels of the other out of the zone into their territory, thus limiting the Klingon's access to Romulan space.

This problem may have been partially—and literally—circumvented by reported Klingon successes in piercing the energy barrier at the edge of the galaxy and navigating outside of the galaxy to reenter into Romulan space. It is not known how often this very hazardous undertaking has been tried, but Starfleet's own experience suggests that failures would have been many and spectacular. For this reason, it is believed that this method of communication is used solely for the most important dispatches carried by the fastest and best vessels in the Klingon fleet.

Since the Romulans do not appear, as yet, to have any such dispatch vessels themselves, it is clear that communications between the allies are somewhat one-sided as only the Klingons can initiate the dialogue, and have to return with the answer before anything can be firmly decided by the allies. For this reason alone, close coordination for military purposes seems impractical for the allies. But it is an axiom of our age that yesterday's impossible is tomorrow's mundane, and advancing technology may yet solve their problem.

There are other inherent limiting factors to the Romulan/Klingon Alliance worthy of note, not the least of which being the natures of the "allies" themselves.

The Klingon attitude toward treaties, pacts, agreements,

understandings, and even personal relationships is universally known and has set the standard for betrayal and treason throughout the galaxy. This is so obvious, in fact, that one wonders why the Romulans have decided to "ride the tiger's back." But, from reasons previously discussed above, it may be that the Romulans are the ones with the most to gain from this alliance.

It may very well be that they have no intention of honoring every clause or requirement of the alliance, and are simply using it as a level to improve their standing with—and against—the Federation itself. Indeed, the Romulans have become a major power again after nearly a century of quiet decline.

The distance between the Allies removes a great deal of the "pressure potential" which the Klingons would otherwise be able to exert on the Romulans to act in their behalf. And as the Romulans are only peripherally affected by the Organian Peace Treaty, they are the only ones with any real opportunity to increase the pressure on the Federation. Thus, they can demand even further concessions from their ally before consenting to use their newly won power in the Klingon's interests.

Finally, the Romulans must know that they are next on the Klingons' now delayed timetable after the Federation. Therefore, it is unlikely that they will encourage a war against the Federation that would remove it as a counterweight against Klingon ambitions. These factors, coupled with the personal mistrust and doubts held by both sides, conspire to limit the full potential of the alliance.

In spite of these severe problems, the Federation Council has taken the threat presented by the Romulan/Klingan Alliance seriously. Between Stardates 3220 and 5930, over 100 new *Constitution* Class heavy cruisers, 26 *Saladin* Class destroyers, 25 *Hermes* Class destroyers and dispatch vessels, and over 120 *Ptolemy* Class transport/tugs have been authorized, and construction is well on the way to completion.

But perhaps the most significant reaction to the alliance was the final authorization for the construction of the *Federation* Class dreadnoughts in the appropriation of Stardate 6066. The twenty vessels projected for this class represent the first major addition to Starfleet since the original twelve *Constitution* Class starships were authorized in the Federation's first military appropriation.

The firepower and sophisticated combat systems these ships

will carry are more than a match for any presently known Romulan or Klingon vessels, on hand or in the design stage. Probably only the economic might of the Federation could support these ships, and it seems unlikely that the alliance (or any other currently known powers) will be able to match or exceed the capabilities of these ships in the foreseeable future.

Thus, it may be said that the failure of the Romulan/Klingon Alliance to significantly alter the balance of power early in its existence has permitted the Federation to prepare adequately enough to maintain a probably decisive edge. Indeed, it may prove that the greatest result of the Romulan/Klingan Alliance was to energize the opposition into a greater position of strength and security (vis-à-vis the alliance) than ever achieved before. Though perhaps a bitter irony to the allies, this may eventually hasten the end of the period of confrontation and usher in an era of cooperation which will someday allow the entire galaxy to be opened.

Such is one possibility arising from the alliance, but there is another that must be considered and prepared for: war.

Exactly how much our adversaries know about Federation plans and capabilities is uncertain. But they cannot have missed the building that continues apace in Starfleet, the expansion of the Academy to train the thousands of new crews and officers to man the new ships, or the increasing economic might that supports it all.

Recognizing their limitations, their growing numerical inferiority, and the simple fact that time is against them, they may choose to strike before the situation is irretrievably lost—before the new construction is completed and can take position, before the new crews are graduated and experienced, and (perhaps above all), before the dreadnoughts are ready.

A detailed report on the military strengths and capabilities of the allies is beyond the scope of this résumé, but conservative estimates still credit them with sufficient power to have a chance of victory in a full-scale war.

And each of the allies has something that is not to be underestimated: will, and a *joie de combattre* second to none in the universe. Who can forget Kor, Military Governor of Organia, who remarked upon hearing of the Organians' intervention that prevented the battle between the Klingon fleet and that of the Federation: "A pity. It would have been *glorious!*" Or the last recorded transmission from the Romulan commander of the ship that attacked the Outpost Colonies, who said, just prior to ordering his ship to self-destruct, "Just one more duty to perform."

We, members of the Federation, who share what we believe to be more "civilized" attitudes, must not forget the bitter lessons of our collective history: that unshared idealism is dangerous, and that the Romulans and Klingons have their own perception of the universe and their—and our—place in it.

Thus, until the time comes when war and conquest once again prove themselves the grand illusion they always were—to *all* powers—we of Starfleet must remain on call. We must be prepared to resist the threat of the Romulan/Klingon Alliance, and the key to successful resistance is proper preparation. Thus this brief résumé of the current thought on this subject.

I have the honor to be, sir, your colleague,

Patrick R. Wilson
Chief of Planetary Relations

# 5.

# THE FALL OF
# THE FEDERATION

## by Philip Carpenter

*We never really learned much about the internal workings of
the United Federation of Planets from Star Trek episodes on
television. So to complete a vital part of the background of
the Star Trek "universe," fans created an entire system of
laws, organization, and background for the UFP. Philip Car-
penter took this creation one step farther: He looks at what
could happen to the Federation when all of the carefully
crafted pillars of interstellar cooperation begin to fall apart.
It is also a commentary on how our civilization could end—
not with a bang . . .*

It is said that nothing created by man can be truly immortal, and this applies especially to his systems of government.
One thinks about the ancient Roman Empire, the various
Chinese dynasties, and the kingdoms of the Middle Ages and
realizes that a powerful society, at one time prosperous and
thriving, will inevitably decay and crumble. Such is the
nature of man: always rejecting, always seeking for something new and better.

Numerous political, economic, sociological, and technological pressures are constantly applied to societies, and eventual
destruction is to be expected.

Such will be the fate of Star Trek's United Federation of
Planets: While healthy in Kirk's and Spock's era, the time
will come someday when relentless pressures force the disso-
lution of this growing society.

But when will this happen? The Galactic Empire, as established in "Mirror, Mirror," has only about 240 years after
Star Trek's time period until the revolt of the slave classes
leads to its demolition. It is probable that the empire, with its

36

extreme internal pressures, is a more unstable system than the Federation. Yet the Federation also has internal pressures, and paradoxically, the more civilizations are admitted to the Federation, the more chances there are for voices of discord to be heard.

Thus, the breaking point will come, not in 240 years, but in 8,000. That will be the critical point, when the responsible forces come together and exceed the limits of tolerance.

What, specifically, are the events leading to this end? Undoubtedly there are distinct events which historians will point at and declare, "Here marks the beginning of the end." Yet in order for those events to happen there have to be certain conditions conducive for their occurrence. Thus it is necessary to outline the state of the Federation several centuries before the fall; several centuries because only lengthy, momentum-gathering events could possibly affect such a huge, interlocking system.

One must consider the economic background of the Federation. In Star Trek's time, about 10 percent of the galaxy had been explored; but several centuries before the fall about 95 percent had been explored and charted. The remaining 5 percent belonged mostly to other races which, out of hostility or other reasons, refused the Federation admittance to their domains. Thus, for all practical purposes, the Federation found its growth coming to a halt.

True, there were unlimited worlds beyond the Milky Way Galaxy, and there were numerous expeditions sent to places from the halo group of stars surrounding our galaxy (just outside the energy barrier)—to places such as the 2 Magellanic Clouds, the Draco cluster, the Sculptor system, the 2 Leo systems, and the Andromeda Galaxy.

However, even the best advances in propulsion technology could not bridge the vast distances in any reasonable length of time. To travel to Andromeda, for example, required nearly 50 years (as contrasted to Star Trek's Kelvans, who could adapt engines for travel within 300 years). Obviously, one cannot build an alliance of worlds where it would take decades to communicate with all the members. Thus, while establishing outposts outside the Milky Way, the Federation was confined to this galaxy.

And this limit to growth had a severe effect on the expansionist economy used by the Federation, an economy somewhat similar to the economic policies of nineteenth-century Earth. To see just why a catastrophe is imminent under such conditions, let us take the oversimplified example of a single mining company.

This company has ships, work crews, and monetary capital. After discovering a new planet rich in minerals, the company mines out the ore and sells it, making a profit. This income is then used to buy more ships, and these new ships are used to explore more planets for more ore . . . and so on.

As long as we don't run out of planets, this procedure is profitable. However, the instant that there are no more planets to be mined, this system collapses. No more ships are bought, capital is unused, crews are laid off, and companies are left begging for ore.

This situation was realized by the Federation some time before the end of galactic exploration, and the proposed solution was to convert the economy over from an expansionist one to the cyclic policy.

To understand what would happen under a cyclic economy, let's look again at the example of our mining company.

Our company is in the business of supplying ore, which it can now do only by buying old, obsolete ships and tearing them apart into their constituent substances, which are then sold to make new ships. Thus, old materials are recycled into new products, and the number of usable products remains constant.

Obviously, our mining company can no longer actually be a "mining" company, but instead changes to a reconversion company. To do so means selling the mining equipment (to a company which already has reconversion equipment to break down the mining equipment) and using the income to purchase machinery for reconversion. However, there has to be a market for obsolete mining equipment; if there isn't, then the company will find it difficult to raise the necessary capital. But if the changeover to reconversion comes gradually enough, then enough markets can be found in which to raise that capital.

Unfortunately, procrastination set in. Until almost the end of the exploration period, the economy was expansionist, and very few businesses set themselves up for the inevitable change. As a result, the changeover was rushed and panicky when it finally happened, and the result was a prompt depression.

Huge numbers of people found themselves no longer needed in the system; especially farmers and miners. Reconversion machinery had been perfected to the point where sand or water could be put in, and anything from caviar to computer tapes extracted. This technological milestone was predicted, yet had the citizens paid attention earlier, farmers, miners, and others could have trained for more useful occupations.

Thus, just before the fall, the Federation was struggling with an economic depression. But there were also unusual political forces at work.

The Federation had, for the most part, adopted a policy of tolerance for other life forms and their thoughts, no matter how bizarre. Indeed, many members of the Federation consider it a privilege to be considered as such.

However, at about the same time that depression was settling, a new movement was slowly growing to power within high government circles. It was called the Disciplinarian Movement, and its advocates preached a harsh treatment of any life forms or cultures which held any belief other than the Federation's total tolerance policy.

Put simply, they believed, "We believe in total tolerance for all life forms, but if you don't think so, then we don't like you." This rather improbable attitude, it must be remembered, was more or less the result of a long historical record of fiascoes for the Federation, apparently stemming from the open-arms, tolerance policy. (Such fiascoes had occurred rarely, of course, but there was such a record.)

Thus, Disciplinarianism seeped among the ruling bodies, and, due to several crises within a couple of centuries prior to the fall, grew to overwhelming proportions. There are a good number of these crises, and two of the more important ones will be related here for illustration.

1. The Husseans are a relatively primitive people, yet their planet contains enormous quantities of valaschite, trichromium, and other rare minerals. Mining agreements were greatly desired, but the Husseans were less than fully cooperative. They regarded any and all Federation representatives with suspicion and hostility; in fact, their religion establishes one god, who is Hussean, and innumerable demons, which are outworlders.

Their unfriendliness was noted, yet so great was the demand for the minerals that an agreement was pushed through anyway after years of tedious negotiations with them. However, after a treaty was established, only disaster followed.

Ore mined by the natives and shipped out inevitably

proved to be useless dirt and rock. Payments sent to them were burned in religious rituals. And any Federation official who remained on the planet for any length of time was eventually killed. So after only a couple of months the agreement was ended and the Federation thoroughly humiliated.

2. Contact with the Ha'alah race inevitably turned into interstellar battle. They seemed to be something of a threat, yet the Federation never ceased to propose peace. Finally, hostilities were suspended and a careful cultural exchange took place. The Ha'alah seemed almost too friendly and too open. In fact, they were just that: They learned as much of Federation technology as they could, then retreated, built a fleet of warships, and attacked in one of the bloodiest wars in Federation history. They were finally defeated and taken under Federation probationary rule, but the bitter memory remained.

Thus, with these and other significant events, the policy of total tolerance was doubted, and the Disciplinarian Movement came to power. After some time, many of the highest officials were either advocates of the movement or else were influenced to concur with it (by numerous political and partisan forces).

As a matter of note, Earth and Vulcan never entirely gave themselves to the movement; in fact, they filed several protests to the high command, Earth claiming that the advocates were too unforgiving, Vulcan stating that their position was irrational.

Internal pressures began to build. Many Federation member worlds had societies which were less than fully democratic, and under the movement they found themselves the brunt of increasing pressures, political, economic, and sociological, to conform their cultures to more acceptable standards.

This, then, was the state of the Federation just prior to its collapse. The economy was depressed and struggling, internal pressures had built between worlds, and public optimism and spirit were sinking. But what specific events marked the fall? In this writer's opinion, the first significant occurrence was the secession of the Antilles Colonies.

The planet Antilles, a member of the Federation for 1,000 years prior to this point, had colonized over a dozen nearby planets in its vicinity when it was discovered that the parent sun would nova and destroy Antilles. The population was relocated before the catastrophe, and the newly formed colonies joined together as one unit—the Antilles Colonies. But why did the colonies want to secede? There are three reasons which seem to be important.

1. Sociological: After two or three generations had been born on the new planets, the people began to feel that these were their homes and as such deserved their allegiance instead of their ancestors' home planet, which stood as a symbol of the Federation. They had had to terraform the new planets, plant crops, battle predatory animals, build villages and cities, and preserve their arts. Thus they felt far more involved with the lands that their own hands had brought to submission than with some far-off Federation government.

2. Political: Following the system used on the original planet Antilles, the colonies formed a government based on extremely differentiated castes.

At the top was a small group of ruling families with every luxury and many rights; in the middle the artisan, scientific, and business classes; and at the bottom the majority of the population—the working classes, which had virtually no rights and no luxuries.

Indeed, it was a common custom to work these lower classes so hard that thousands died from exhaustion in any given month. The workers had no voice in any affairs; their religions were suppressed, their possessions often seized, their personal preferences ignored.

And it was exactly this form of society that soon brought rebuffs from the Disciplinarians.

At first, the Antilles ambassadors were merely snubbed by others, but soon considerable pressure was brought to bear in the hope that the colonies would change their system. Taxes were laid on imports, markets were reduced for exports, art trade was restricted, and fewer political members supported their policies. Needless to say, these actions alienated the Antillians.

3. Economic: As stated before, the Federation was in the grip of a depression, and with the additional restrictions levied on the colonies, the Antillians suffered considerably. The belief began to spread that if the colonies separated themselves from the Federation, their near-totalitarian system could force their economy into a more healthy state.

Workers, many of whom were currently idle, would be forced to work at virtually any task, producing great quantities of goods, while their wages were kept to a minimum to reroute the monetary flow into the hands of the leaders who could extend credit and increase capital.

Thus, with all these factors, the Antilles colonies eventually applied for secession. Rather surprisingly, their request was granted; perhaps it was felt by the prominent Federation members that Antilles was a thorn in their side.

Whatever the reason, Antilles gathered together a few sympathetic worlds and formed the Antilles Federation. At last they were free of "unfair" pressures, and their economy, while lacking the might of the Federation's resources, did improve.

But this secession proved to be a dangerous precedent. The planet Markolith also maintained a culture of nontolerance in that its citizens were segregated according to religious status, such status being derived by virtue of a person's birth. They too had borne the brunt of many attacks by Federation rulers, and so they applied for secession not long after the Antilles move. It was granted, and along with several sympathetic worlds they retreated to form the Markolith Federation.

By now it was hoped that this would be the end. However, it was only the beginning.

The Disciplinarian Movement was beginning to lose followers, and its advocates put forth great efforts to remain influential. At this point the highest general ruling body of the Federation—now named Federation Prime—was the Grand Council, to which every member world sent one representative. Within the Grand Council, a little over half a dozen of the more rigid Disciplinarians exerted as much partisan and political influence as they could, and eventually rose to dominance within the Council.

This group was formally called the Coalition of Eight, although the exact number of the group is uncertain. While theoretically the Grand Council was as democratic as possible, in practice nearly all policy was dictated by the Coalition. Many other Council members were controlled by the Coalition, and those who weren't were outnumbered. Those latter members found their voices either ignored or squashed.

Obviously, this gave rise to greater disagreement than ever. Alienation was rampant, and finally dozens of offended members demanded secession. Some of them may have felt that they could have later rejoined Federation Prime, but in fact that probably never could have happened.

So one secession after another cut down the numbers of

Federation Prime. Eventually, though, it was correctly realized that any further reductions would leave Federation Prime dangerously weak. Thus secession was forbidden, and stiff penalties were levied on anyone who suggested such.

Yet that did not stop many angry worlds. Tensions blazed, and while other members (such as Earth and Vulcan) tried to soothe over hostilities, nothing could prevent the outbreak of civil wars.

These wars were on a grander scale than had ever before been seen. Some proposed secessions were defeated but others succeeded. Out of these battles came such organizations as the Perseid Federation, the Spica Federation, the Eridani Federation, and the Al Nasl Federation.

The most definitive victory by a secessionist group was the Sualocin Federation; their enormous population (over 200 worlds were grouped together!) and extensive military strength gave them a distinct advantage.

Possibly the bloodiest conflict involved the group which had intended to call itself the Lacertaen Federation. The casualties were so heavy on both sides that had the group won, there would not have been enough people to form the federation.

Finally the struggles declined, as all those with any grievance had peeled off into their own groups. However, another danger was brewing. About this time various races which were not friendly to the original Federation learned of the situation and decided to take advantage of it.

It must be remembered that in Star Trek's time period only three empires of incompatible predatory races were discovered (the Klingons, the Kzinti, the Romulans).

However, by the time of the Great Secessions, well over two dozen hostile races had been encountered. These predators learned of the weakened state of Federation Prime and its spinoffs and hastily sent in attack fleets to destroy and conquer. At last their dreams of galactic rule seemed at hand.

However, Federation Prime and the others put up a valiant fight, despite their weakened condition. It was inevitable that they would be overthrown, yet they prolonged the battles to the point where both defenders and invaders were severely damaged. It seemed that the predators made the mistake of being too hasty (understandable in the circumstances), and thus were not too knowledgeable on the distribution of the federations' strength.

An interesting point: The Organian Peace Treaty established millennia earlier forbade the Klingon race from attacking the Federation, but that applied only to Federation Prime. As the new federations were technically and practically not members, they were released from the treaty. Thus, at no time did the Klingons actually attack Federation Prime, but instead invaded the "spinoff" federations.

There were some efforts by some of the federations to join forces and become more effective in repelling the predators (the best example of this was the Battle of Ras Alegthi, where ships from the Ruchbach, Monoceros, Denebola, and Tarazed federations combined forces to demolish a fleet of Syntatic invaders), yet for the most part each federation had its hands full just trying to cope with its enemies.

As a matter of fact, had the invading races decided to join forces, the wars would have been much swifter and more decisive. However, there was a simple matter of distrust; none of the predators trusted any others to keep their word.

This was a practical policy; at first the Zeonistics formed an alliance with the Klingons, but this proved a mistake, as the Klingons had a habit of allowing Zeonistic ships to "strafe and sack" a planet, then beaming the treasures aboard their ships and destroying the other ships from the rear.

Needless to say, this alliance was quickly broken.

In fact, it was this distrust that proved at times more dangerous than any federation forces. As a case in point, the Battle of Aquila 2127 was almost more comic than tragic as Romulan, Kzinti, and Mal'kanstan ships simultaneously converged upon and claimed this planet. Ships from the Aquilan federation waited for the invaders to attack, but instead the disputes grew so hot that the predators began fighting among themselves, and the battle was so devastating that when it was over, there were no ships left to attack the federation ships—which had not fired a shot themselves.

Despite such antics, the Great Invasions lasted for somewhat over 600 years; the exact figure is not available as many records are lost from that period.

But finally all the forces had destroyed each other and virtually no warships remained; whole populations had been decimated, cities and planets burned to dust, vast numbers of people relocated, cultures forgotten or lost.

There had been many raids by federation forces into the predators' territories, and thus they suffered the same fate. No one seemed untouched by the devastation (except for the worlds of vastly superior beings, who had held themselves above the hostilities).

Priceless information was lost. Many worlds had lost all of their inhabitants, and on those which had not, the citizens reverted to very primitive societies.

Probably the only ones escaping the wreckage were the Federation extragalactic outposts; but they soon learned that their Federation no longer existed, and so they were forced to develop their own independent societies.

Since so many records were lost, the number and location of these outposts will remain a mystery forever, as they themselves will learn if they try to locate the others. Indeed, they themselves may forget their own origins after several generations, or they may develop exotic legends about the Federation or their neighbors.

Because of this, these outposts have been called the Missing Settlements.

And so ends the life of the United Federation of Planets. There is an ancient Earth saying that we should learn from history, or else we will be condemned to repeat it.

What lessons are to be drawn from this mighty collapse remains to be seen, as the historians will undoubtedly bicker among themselves for some time to come.

It will be a great testament, to be sure, to the many planets such as Earth and Vulcan which fought by the side of the original Federation to the very end.

It will be a testament, also, to the philosophies of peace and cooperation that allowed the Federation to survive for as long as it did.

But there are many questions. What civilizations will rise out of the ashes of the galaxy? What will the few remaining humans, Vulcans, Klingons, Romulans, and others scattered across the Milky Way make of themselves? Will they ever return to their former glory, or is the stage set for different creatures to star in a new experiment of life?

The answers, as always, will be revealed in due time.

# 6.
# WOMEN IN
# THE FEDERATION

## by Pamela Rose

*Try an experiment for yourself: Go to any convention, find a group of fans, and casually ask them, "How do you feel about the position of women in the United Federation of Planets?" And then prepare to spend at least several hours listening to dozens of different opinions, complaints, and good old-fashioned arguing. Fans refer to such slugfests as the Pro-miniskirts versus the Anti-miniskirts, but it goes much deeper than that. In this article, Pamela Rose neatly sidesteps these extremes and probes a more important problem: "Is there equality in Star Trek?" And the answer may surprise you.*

It has been stated in several episodes of Star Trek that the philosophy of the Federation is equality. When examined a little closer, however, there may be a few cracks in this noble view. Superficially everyone is treated equally, but there have been numerous incidents when individuals have been less than tolerant.

In "The Omega Glory," Captain Tracy is openly prejudiced against Spock, and more than a few other crewmen voice distaste and doubts about Vulcans. As far as that goes, Spock makes no secret of the fact that he considers humans to be somewhat inferior, or at least inefficient, due to their lack of logic. And even Spock's father, Sarek, speaks of Tellarites in a less than complimentary manner.

This could all be taken as natural pride in one's own race, but it definitely does not lead to trust or perfect harmony in the galaxy. (It also keeps Star Trek from being boring.)

I am not talking about Federation laws. I think we can take for granted that there are some definite laws establishing equality or the Federation would fall apart rather rapidly. But laws can be circumvented occasionally—and usually are. It looks as if it might take longer than a couple of hundred years for all our basic prejudices to be resolved—especially sexual prejudices.

In "Turnabout Intruder," Kirk says that Janice Lester's bitterness and resultant insanity were caused by her belief that she was treated unfairly because she was female. She felt that if she were not a woman she would have been placed in charge of a starship. We can agree with Kirk that she is totally unsuited to that type of position—and probably always was.

But I have wondered if there is not some basis to her feelings of male chauvinism in Starfleet and the Federation in general. Ridiculous, of course! This is the future. Remember equality?

If you examine the role of women in Starfleet, you get a disturbing feeling that they are there in token positions only. With the exception of Uhura and one or two others, they seem to spend most of their time passing coffee and carrying fuel reports for the Captain to sign—when he gets time after saving the galaxy. Now, I realize these fuel reports and such are important to the running of a starship, but why is it never a *male* yeoman?

Of course, there are exceptions, but in many cases when a woman is in a position of importance, she is a cold bitch ("Metamorphosis"; "Where No Man Has Gone Before"), or she is emotionally unstable ("Is There in Truth No Beauty"). Nine out of ten times there is something wrong with her. There were quite a few unstable and idiotic men as well, like Nils Baris and Daystrom, but the men still have a much better average than the women in responsibility and intelligence.

Janet Wallace in "The Deadly Years" is competent in her field, but she seems to have a father fixation and prefers her men to be at death's door, which doesn't appear too normal to me.

I am not forgetting Number 1 in "The Menagerie," who is definitely in a position of importance as first officer. (She is nixed pretty quick, though, which is just as well or we wouldn't have Spock as he is.) But I can't like the fact that she was supposed to be so cold and unemotional. Just because a woman has risen to a position of responsibility, why does she have to squelch her emotions? Kirk and Pike certainly don't. In fact, they are both highly emotional men. We see this several times in the series. When a woman is in a position of importance, more often than not, she has toned down her femininity and acts hard as nails. It is usually a facade, but it is interesting that they feel they must have this mask at all.

I get the distinct impression from some of the episodes that three-fourths of the women in Starfleet are there to find a husband. Or are present for the convenience of the male crew members. "Have to keep the men happy in the voids of deep space."

Why else the short uniforms? Surely not for the women's convenience. Those mini-skirts appear a bit impractical—except when Janice Rand wants Kirk to look at her legs. Hmmmmmm.

In the original episodes ("The Menagerie" and "Where No Man Has Gone Before"), the women, quite sensibly, wore pants. Some lecherous old man back at Starfleet Command must have suggested the change. (Or more likely, back at NBC.)

I have no quarrel with the uniforms, however. They are very attractive. But I can't help feeling sorry for some brilliant female technician with bow legs and knobby knees. But, of course, there are no ugly women in Starfleet—unless they stuff them up the Jeffries Tubes.

To be fair, there aren't too many ugly men either. (Such are the requirements of television.) Maybe they've bred it out of the race.

There are a few sparse examples of intelligent, efficient women, however. Dr. Ann Mulhall in "Return to Tomorrow" is quite sensible. And Areel Shaw in "Court-Martial" certainly doesn't put her emotions above her duty in prosecuting Kirk. That was refreshing, as generally when a woman is emotional she goes overboard. Remember Lieutenant Marla McGivers? She not only disregards her duty, she mutinies—all for the sake of a pretty face and an incredible set of muscles. Carolyn Palamas comes close to doing the same in "Who Mourns for Adonais?" but Kirk gives her a macho speech and she pulls herself together at the last moment. Ah, frail womanhood!

Dr. Helen Noel in "Dagger of the Mind" is intelligent and responsible, but even though *she* is the trained psychologist, it takes Kirk's unfeminine intuition to figure out something is fishy. It also seems a little unprofessional of her to choose a "love" suggestion for their experiment on the neural neutralizer.

Edith Keeler is the only real example of a totally committed, intelligent, and compassionate woman. She is not weak, but her strength does not detract from her femininity. She is a woman with a goal and a meaning to her life. And they had to find her in the 1930s!

Where are these women in the twenty-third century? Are they really so rare (quite possible), or are they just too hard to fit into an action/adventure plot (also possible)?

As for some other contemporary women who cross the *Enterprise*'s path:

Mira Romaine in "The Lights of Zetar" does prove to be less pliant and to have a stronger self-will than first indicated. But it still takes the decompression chamber to get rid of the critters.

Mudd's women are frankly after husbands to take care of.

Irina Galliulin in "The Way to Eden" is easily led and gullible.

Leila Kalomi seems to prefer the dreamy world of the spores of Omicron Ceti III to reality.

Lenore Karidian ("Conscience of the King") and Marta ("Whom Gods Destroy") are both homicidal maniacs.

Droxine, whom Spock finds so intellectually stimulating ("The Cloud Minders"), is really quite heartless and unfeeling until Spock points out her failing.

Why, among all the starship captains, commodores, ambassadors, scientists, and heads of state contacted during the *Enterprise's* swing around the galaxy, are the few women such unflattering examples?

Alien women, in or out of the Federation, fare hardly better. True, the Romulans have a female commander, but she is amazingly easy to deceive. I must admit that Mr. Spock might be able to turn my head also, but it doesn't say much for her intelligence or efficiency as a flagship commander that she is taken in so completely.

Elaan, the Dohlman of Elas, is far from weak or helpless, but she is undoubtedly a spoiled brat.

As for Vulcan women, we see only two of them and it is difficult to know for certain just what place a woman has in Vulcan society. T'Pau is said to be influential and powerful, and she is the only person ever to turn down a seat on the Federation Council. (Maybe she knows something we don't?)

The less said about T'Pring the better. I, for one, will never see the logic in choosing shifty-eyed Stonn over Spock.

It is stated in "Amok Time" that the bride becomes the property of the victor, and from Amanda's quick obedience to Sarek in "Journey to Babel," it might be inferred that this is not only the case when Challenge is given, but the traditional place of women on Vulcan.

And how does that equate with T'Pau's power? It is possible that at the death of the mate, the wife assumes his power and station in life if she is at all qualified. But that is pure conjecture.

Spock's mother, Amanda, is one of the few truly sensible and three-dimensional women found in the Star Trek universe. Unfortunately, she has a tendency to submerge her personality in Sarek's. Having chosen her life on Vulcan, she takes the logical course of following Vulcan tradition. She also seems a little ashamed of her humanity. Or possibly it was her dressmaker who felt that way.

We only get to meet one female Klingon. Mara, in "Day of the Dove," is certainly an improvement on the male Klingon. (She would have had to be, or the race would have died out long ago.) There are definite indications that Klingon men don't understand their women any better than human males do. When Kang sees Mara's torn tunic, he automatically decides she has been raped—and that she liked it! He thinks that is the reason she tries to get him to listen to Kirk. Well, no one ever accused a Klingon of being logical.

There are supposedly about 150 women on the *Enterprise.* I have often wondered just what all these women do.

I have never seen a female in security, or at least I don't remember it. I see no reason why there shouldn't be some in the age of space karate and phasers. But then, I can't recall seeing a crewwoman fire a phaser at all. (Perhaps Starfleet feels they would be unable to hit the side of a barn.)

Angela Martine ("Ballance of Terror") is a phaser specialist, but I got the impression she is more of a repairman than a sharpshooter. I could be right, for she is later transferred to life sciences ("Shore Leave")—and she does run smack into a tree in that episode!

I have noticed very few women in the engineering section either. One notable exception is Lieutenant Masters ("Alternative Factor"), who is in charge of the energizing section of engineering.

On the average, however, women are generally yeomen,

historians, secretaries, or assistants of one type or another. You certainly see a lot of them in the corridors and rec rooms. They look very graceful when they fall after a phaser blast or an alien attack on the ship. (I love to watch Christine Chapel fall in "The Way to Eden" during the ultrasonic blast by the space hippies. No grace there. She falls like a ton of bricks.)

Looking at the main characters' attitudes toward women might reveal something about women's place in the Federation.

Kirk's charm is, in the main, a cover for his inability to communicate with women. He is uncomfortable with them and has trouble relating in any other than a sexual or a protective sense. After all, why waste your time trying to be logical when you can seduce them and get what you want? (Examples include "Is There In Truth No Beauty," "Conscience of the King," and "The Gamesters of Triskelion.") It doesn't always work, but he has a good batting average.

Scotty approaches women as if they were china dolls, or at least extremely delicate objects. Whenever he is in love, he goes a little batty. The rest of the time he's too wrapped up in his engines to notice.

Spock usually treats women the same as he does men—logically. But he is somewhat protective of Uhura, and is definitely uncomfortable around Christine.

McCoy is ordinarily the most realistic in his relationships with women—perhaps because he knows from experience they are not all sugar and spice, but have gallstones, hangnails, and gas just like the he-men. However, that does not keep him from turning on the southern charm occasionally—thank goodness.

As for the two most notable crewwomen, Christine Chapel is a career woman and definitely dedicated to her work. But she joined Starfleet to find her lost love Roger Corby. When that didn't work out, she stayed—almost as if to say, "Since I didn't find a husband, I don't have anything better to do." She promptly falls in love with Mr. Spock, and has another reason for living.

It has been suggested that Christine is really a full-fledged doctor. If that is the case, I wonder why she is always addressed as "Nurse"? I think I would resent that a great deal after studying for years to achieve a degree. Especially when it is usually a situation of "Hand me the thermocumbobulator and stand aside."

Uhura is a different matter entirely. She is an expert in her field, and has even been known to fix equipment that Spock could not. And she still remains a complete, total woman.

There are a few times when she flashes her lashes at the Captain and admits in a trembling voice that she is afraid (something I can hardly imagine Scott or Sulu doing), but generally she is quite able to hold her own.

This article is not intended as a radical woman's-lib tirade. Nor did I mean to take nitpicking to a fine art. I think Star Trek did an admirable job of portraying women for that time in television. It even broke some new ground.

But Janice Lester may have a valid point to make somewhere in the root of her insanity. It is doubtful if a woman could have become a starship captain in the Federation of Star Trek.

However, I hear things are looking up. Janice Rand is to be the new transporter chief in the upcoming movie. Maybe Lieutenant Kyle decided to get married and keep house.

We've come a long way, baby.

# 7.

# ON SHIP-TO-SURFACE TRANSPORTATION

## by Richard G. Van Treuren

*Rich Van Treuren's articles on the Star Trek miniatures in
The Best of Trek #1 proved to be among the most popular in
that collection. So armed with dozens of laudatory letters, we
prevailed upon Rich to once more turn his writing attentions
to Star Trek. His first few submissions to us were a series of
excellent photo-oriented articles, which, sadly, we are not
able to include in this collection. However, just before our
deadline for this book, Rich wrote and informed us he had "a
little something on the transporter" that was mostly text, and
might be suitable for inclusion. The "little something" turned
out to be the most detailed and entertaining article on the
transporter we have ever seen! We believe you will think so
too.*

It was September 1964. The new, unique television show
was taking shape. Its science-fictional spaceship, created by
artists/aviators, had been whittled out in model form. The pilot film story had been chosen. Even though the first-script
draft was carefully prepared by an experienced entertainer
with wide aviation experience, the opinion of an aerospace
professional was solicited. The physicist took exception to
only one major point—something called the "transporter."
"What kind of fun is that?" he wrote. "Where is the suspense?"

The scientist, of course, was H. P. Lynn; he was offering
criticism to creator Gene Roddenberry. The story was made
public in *The Making of Star Trek*.

Here we had the most perfectly credible science-fiction
space project ever attempted for television. (Admittedly, that
is not saying very much.) Every facet had been either created
or supervised by knowledgeable types. The pilot script was a

mass of logical predictions, honest guesswork, and excellent entertainment. Yet here, amid this perfection, sticking out like a sore thumb, was a machine that disassembled living beings, moved their disassociated bodies across space, and reassembled them hundreds of miles away—without any sort of reception device. Was the physicist complaining about the imagined machine from a scientific viewpoint? Incredibly, he actually was not, at least not at this point. He was pointing out that the machine would offer *dramatic* problems.

Just what's wrong with the transporter, anyway? Two hundred years from now, almost anything is possible. Who can say what will or will not be? And what difference does that make when it comes to dramatic television right now?

First off, we have to accept that the transporter device, taken out of the Star Trek context, is entirely possible. With as much time as 200 years to carry out research toward its creation, it might even be probable.

What is *not* possible is its placement in a civilization at the technological level predicted in Star Trek. A practical living-being transmitter/reassembly device on board the United Space Ship *Enterprise* is like finding a nuclear-powered scanning X-ray machine amid the oarsmen on Cleopatra's barge. The transporter is so inconsistent as to be highly improbable, which means Star Trek, as a dramatic television program, had to be less than it could have been.

Inconsistency has always been a problem with future-oriented science fiction, particularly that brought to television. At the first Trek Convention in New York City in 1972, s-f great Isaac Asimov illustrated the point. He offered a line that could have come from television: "We must be getting close to Earth; we just passed Octans and Uranus. That's like saying," he pointed out, "we must be getting close [to New York City] because we just passed India and Jersey City."

Before we go any further in discussing the transporter either scientifically or dramatically, let's see how this mess got started. Was the machine a part of the series from the beginning?

Contrary to popular belief, it was not. The first series outline—dated March 1964—contained no mention of anything so fantastic. The problem of transit between the large ship and any surface was handled by the only obvious answer, a "small shuttle rocket." There were no story springboards involving a machine which would destroy the characters' concept of distance and transportation times.

It is not entirely clear why the transporter appeared. Perhaps it was an attempt to jazz up the concept, to throw in something a little outlandish, and make the series more salable. After all, CBS had turned it down.

At any rate, its inclusion in August 1964 really presented no problems. Nothing had been nailed down, and there were any number of ways such a machine could work within the framework of the rest of the created technology. The spaceship was to have force shields of some sort, as well as practical artificial gravity. The transporter might function with a combination of these two technologies. But whatever, if the machine proved too difficult to either create or get across to the audience, it could be cured with a pencil slash.

The next month saw the construction of the show's spaceship miniatures. The major model, some eleven feet long, included an area for a hangar bay, but this was not completed. The cost of these models was staggering, and could not have helped the young series at this point, before a script was ready.

It was around this time that the fateful decision was made. Hundreds of thousands of dollars were being poured into the two major sets, those of the planet exterior and the cruiser control center. Would there be money for the shuttle rocket, or would there be some cheaper method of getting the characters down to the planet's surface?

Before you think it was an easy decision, consider the cost of a shuttlecraft. First, since the starship models had been built rather modestly (compared to thirty-five-foot and even fifty-six-foot miniatures at Fox and MGM), a separate hangar bay airlock set would have to be constructed. More money would have to be allotted to complete the hangar bay doors on the cruiser models. A full-size section of hangar bay would have been desirable.

Next, a new miniature of the shuttle rocket would have to be created. It could be on the same scale as the hangar bay, but since it had to be small enough to handle on the film effects stages, it could not be used in scenes with actors.

So, a full-size exterior mockup would have to be built. It would have to be portable so as to be moved from set to set easily, and should even be suitable for trucking to locations.

This exterior mockup could not be used for interior shots, so a separate shuttlecraft interior set would be necessary. It would have to have breakaway overhead, side, and floor panels.

As if all that weren't enough, the optical effects necessary for shuttle realism would be extremely difficult—and therefore expensive. Space shots are no problem, but making an imaginary vehicle lift off or touch down on a surface is damn near impossible. Even expensive new projects like *Star Wars* avoided the question when they could.

Even in 1964 dollars, all this stuff—what the whole shuttle rocket was made of—would have cost more than $100,000. All that for a three-minute part of an hour-long film that might not make it to series anyway? If you remember the desperate, hungry situation Desilu was in at the time, you can see that there was simply no way.

It was a *financial* necessity that the transporter be the sole method of ship-to-surface transit. The transporter set was brought in for less than one-tenth that estimated cost. It was simply a door, three walls, and the platform. Even the control panel was brought in from the cruiser control center set. If this sounds like a cheap trick, remember that there probably would have been no series today had anyone insisted on the shuttle rocket.

Even at this point it was not too late for the machine to have made sense. Had Roddenberry been consulting a science-fiction expert as he had been aerospace experts, it just might have been done. Unhappily, there was no one to tell him that s-f was loaded with "world without distance" concepts, from the comic book *Magus: Robot Fighter* to Robert Heinlein's *Tunnel in the Sky*. Any number of ideas could have been used to explain the machine's functioning, in keeping with the rest of the imaginative technology.

Evidently, the only method which came to mind was that of dematerialization for distant reassembly. This probably came about because the only such concept that had reached film at that time was said to have worked this way. In the late-1950s s-f/horror picture *The Fly*, David Hedison played an inventor who had created a machine capable of sending living things along wires in the manner of a telephone. It's tragic that a similar idea was used to explain Star Trek's transporter, because it was not only hopelessly inconsistent, but would create more dramatic problems than could ever be solved.

First let's examine the transporter problem from a purely scientific point of view. Modern technology did not just happen overnight. It was created by a stepladder of separate discoveries, and one step would not have been possible without the one before it. Primitive man did not move from ox carts to Volkswagens; certain discoveries had to be made to permit the construction of any modern device.

The internal-combustion engine could not have been built until a quick-burning liquid fuel was refined. De Forest would never have come up with the triode vacuum tube had not Edison first invented the incandescent light bulb. Neil Armstrong would not have walked on our moon had not the Wright brothers proved that mathematically impossible heavier-than-air flight *was* possible.

So, on the stepladder to Star Trek's transporter device, certain discoveries will have to be made. We will have to once and for all prove the present atomic theory. Then, assuming it is correct (and that's assuming a lot, by the number of its unexplained mysteries), we would have to come up with a way to take atoms apart without setting off a chain reaction.

No doubt we would start with the simplest element, hydrogen. We would have to peel away the one electron orbiting each of the hydrogen nuclei. That's no small task, even forgetting what happens in a hydrogen bomb. Remember, scientists disagree as to whether electrons are actually particles or just energy. Either way, electrons move right along, and they'd be hard to catch.

Now, assuming we discover a way of doing that peacefully, we would be able to weave the subatomic particles through just about anything, if the theory about spaces between atoms is correct. But how do we pick the particles up and get them anywhere? Telephones, radios, and televisions are poor analogies because they simply couldn't do the job.

Modern communications equipment doesn't actually send any matter anywhere; it is nothing more than vastly improved sun mirrors and smoke signals. When the cavalry wanted to speak to the infantry across the plain, the signalman would wiggle his mirror to reflect the sun in a manner predetermined to have meaning. Later, similar impulses were carried along wires, and eventually Alexander Bell came up with a way to make voices produce electrical impulses. Eventually, it was possible to modulate radio waves with these representations of intelligence. Now, we do the same with pictures. But remember, even though a two-dimensional image of Captain Kirk was seen on 20,000,000 screens at a time, the original film of William Shatner was undisturbed. In that vein, we are no closer to perfecting a matter transmitter than were the ancient Egyptians.

So, we must have a way of picking up those same particles and moving them where we want. It would have to be some sort of force, and would work like a length of adhesive tape capturing a string of ball bearings. This same force beam would also be capable of moving whole objects, but they would not fit through solid matter—like the bulkhead of a spaceship.

After taking our hydrogen atoms apart and sending the particles somewhere, we would have to undo the process to reassemble the atoms and place them back in their previous vibratory patterns. We would probably have some sort of reception and reassembly device for this delicate task. We would more or less have to assume that our present atomic theory is correct—that is, the basic atomic building blocks are all the same. Thus it would not matter if we lost count and got electrons from nuclei 689,059,546 and 689,059,547 mixed up. They would happily circle either nucleus once returned to orbit.

Once we completed that fantastic feat, we would move onto the next challenge on the element chart—helium. We would now be peeling two electrons away, for later reinstatement. However, if all atomic building blocks are identical, we would be tempted to try an experiment. If we disassembled samples of hydrogen and helium at the same time, mixed up the particles, and rebuilt the same original quantities of gases, some of the electrons that had been part of hydrogen atoms would now be part of helium atoms, and vice versa. It wouldn't make any difference to the gas, but what a discovery we would have made. We could have the machine memorize how to reassemble helium, then feed in hydrogen for disassembly. Obviously, there would be a slight drop in quantity, but the machine could take the hydrogen's particles and rebuild them as helium. This would have been particularly useful to the German airship industry in 1937.

There would be no stopping us as we moved right on down the chart. We would have more lead than gold, so we would make the old alchemist's dream come true. Any element could be rebuilt out of the pieces of any other element. And it would be the same as we got into compounds: gasoline could be made out of seawater, or out of thin air. It would cease to be necessary to go anywhere to get anything. All things could be made on the spot. In Star Trek's time, dilithium crystals could be made out of dirt, or even cow manure.

So, long before beginning to experiment with living things,

we would have changed the nature of our civilization. But even if we could ignore that incredible achievement and press on toward the teleportation of living beings, we would have a way to go.

It is a physical law that two particles of matter cannot occupy the same space at the same time. There was repeated reference in the series to the frightening possibility of materializing inside solid rock. Yet there is very real matter around us all the time; we are at the bottom of an enormous ocean of air. Breathable atmosphere occupies space, and we could no more reassemble matter inside it than inside granite. So, we would have to create some sort of force shield exactly the size of the object we wished to rebuild, then pump out every iota of air to make a more perfect vacuum than interstellar space. (This idea, incidentally, was one of many experimental optical effects given tests during the post-production of the first pilot. The red outline, however, would not have actually made sense since the force field would have been an envelope.)

It would also be necessary to have a shield during the disassembly process to prevent foreign particles from mixing in accidentally. *The Fly* demonstrated one idea of what might happen if a human and insect were confused in the transport process, but there are of course millions of less spectacular but more deadly dangers. If a bubble of air got mixed in the bloodstream, for instance, it would be curtains for the hapless transportee.

There is the further problem of isolating the essence of life. Some scientists now believe even bacteria have a simple intelligence and can communicate; plants are also blessed with something that separates them from the soil they grow in. Whatever *life* is would have to be discovered, and made suitable to send along with the matter.

Unless most every human religion is wrong, people have an immortal, supernatural side; their emotions, personality— their soul, if you will. One more supernatural enigma that would have to be solved. (The late James Blish toyed with this question in his novel *Spock Must Die!*)

Now, given all that, we would have a very complex machine indeed. It would have to be delicate enough to take the total person—muscle, bone, blood, air in lungs, electrical nerve impulses, brain waves, and soul—down to subatomic particles. How could it *not* be able to recognize foreign material in the body—like viruses, or even bullets? This obvious development was also forgotten.

The last step, reassembly without a receiver, was unique to Star Trek. There could be no receiver for the same reason there could be no shuttlecraft in the first place. The idea is possible, of course, and might not take as many basic discoveries as we have mentioned so far. Distant receiverless assembly of matter would have to come *after* the same was first possible with two-dimensional light images, however. In other words, if a person could be sent anywhere, it would be child's play to send a two-dimensional light image for distant reassembly. Hence, the civilization would be devoid of television screens and even walkie-talkie radios.

Jumping ahead a bit, we see how this bit of inconsistency made one episode look more ridiculous. In "Return of the Archons," Kirk should not have been at all impressed with the projected image of Landru. "But beautiful, Mr. Spock," he said, "with no apparatus at this end." If Kirk's civilization could do the same with living beings, this trick should have been no surprise. He would have been doing the same thing, instead of toting a little radio about or watching a viewscreen on his ship.

The preceding pages would not mean anything had Star Trek been just another product for the lobotomy box. But it was supposed to be credible and consistent. The Writer's Guide states that technology must be consistent, informing the writer that the enemy should not be given starflight capability and then attack with grappling hooks and swords.

All right, all right. So the transporter *was* inconsistent. So what? It wasn't *that* important a part of the series. It was to be a *people* show, with such controversies being avoided. So it *was* created from hunger. Didn't it solve a lot of problems? Didn't it "speed up" the action?

It's a shame someone pressed Roddenberry for an answer about the transporter without giving him time to think. What he is quoted as saying just doesn't jive, and must have been made up in the heat of the moment.

"Land a ship fourteen stories tall on a planet surface every week?" he supposedly said. But even from the very first day, the ship was not to land regularly, if ever. The shuttle rocket would have done the transporting. He then supposedly complained that landing the ship would take so much time the story would be slowed down. That's not only forgetting the shuttle rocket, that's forgetting the age-old film device of the lap dissolve. The old boy was undoubtedly rushed when he said that.

Would a shuttlecraft landing be slow or boring? Some fans complained that the eventual shuttle design resembled a butter dish. But whatever its shortcomings, it could not have taken too much time, even if one forgets the dissolve. The miniature would not be (and was not ever) shown for more than a few seconds at a time, since it was not detailed and would interfere with character development. So, five seconds to show it leaving the hangar, a few more to enter the atmosphere, and five more to touch down. That's less time than the original transport process took.

Besides, such an obvious procedure—hardly more bizarre than sailors going on liberty via boat—could be omitted regularly. It could have even been included as part of the opening credits, educating the audience while it livened up the repetitious starship flybys. No, the shuttle would not have slowed any story, it just would have killed the fledgling series.

Okay, granted the transporter was inconsistent, and the excuses given for its existence were feeble ones. But it just *wasn't* that important a series element. It would not occupy a full minute of any of the nearly hour-long shows! It *could* be tolerated, couldn't it?

Perhaps it could have been, if there had been some sort of operating parameters adhered to. That proved to be impossible. The machine proved to be irresistible to writers either in a bad spot or devoid of a story altogether.

For instance, teleportation was to be a difficult, power-consuming process, possible along only short, line-of-sight distances. (This tied in with VHF and higher-frequency radio waves, with which many are familiar.) That's good for drama, since anytime someone needed to be stranded, the writer needed only to move him out of clear view of the ship.

This was adhered to in several episodes, like "Dagger of the Mind." Kirk and Noel beamed down to an open surface, walked into a building, and took an elevator down to the colony. Even as late as "This Side of Paradise," Spock says, "I'll meet you at the beam-down point," which proved to be a big open field. These examples ignored the fact that air is matter, perhaps, but offered some semblance of believability.

However, there was no way to resist the magic machine, even from the beginning. Roddenberry was faced with the problem of getting the starship women down into the Tholosian community without another time-consuming illusion, capture, elevator stuffing, and so on. It was too easy to throw out the idea of a starship in synchronous orbit beaming things down along a clear line of sight. So there they went, beaming through solid rock.

The major reason given for rejection of the first pilot was that it went over the heads of many in the audience. The transporter helped make the situation intolerable. Mind control, illusions, and the like would have been more understandable had there been a better definition of who was doing the visual magic. Remember, the starshipmen disappeared, traveled hundreds of miles, and then reappeared while the "advanced" Tholosians took elevators or simply walked. This inconsistency might seem ridiculous to the show fan, but it was very real to the casual viewer.

This is a frustrating damned-if-you-do-or-don't situation with ordinary people and science fiction. If the space s-f is cheap and simple, they say it's kid stuff. If it's made good, accurate, and entertaining, they say they don't understand it. Somewhere in there, a fine line of acceptability divides the two. And that's the line you have to stay on to be a success in the mass media.

Needless to say, after the first pilot was finally passed by a test audience—and NBC agreed to a second film—there was a long hard look at the idea of bringing quality s-f to television. Small wonder the second pilot featured Kirk shooting a big ray gun. Was transporter elimination discussed? Possibly it was, but the budget pressure hadn't let up. "Where No Man Has Gone Before" was completed with the construction of only one (very simple) new ship set.

As they had to, the transporter-based story problems got worse in regular production. There were several basic oversights that people began to ask questions about as time went on.

It was obvious that the hand-held communicator would be built to control the transporter. Remote controls date way back, and even in 1976 they were sophisticated enough to allow Earthbound engineers to control machines on Mars. Would such simple technology be forgotten? No, but for dramatic reasons, it had to be.

Even more obvious was the fact that any such spaceship would have several transporter machines, including ones for cargo and others for backup. Believability was shattered when time and again "the" transporter was broken. Later on, someone in the publicity department was not applying the proper brand of television no-think. He or she released material which said the ship had several of the machines; some were larger and used for cargo. Somehow, the word was not passed to the script supervisor, nor was the Writer's Guide ever changed to say so.

The first two shows made in regular production presented no transporter problems. However, the third, "The Enemy Within," blew the fragile lid off.

In case you've tried to forget this one, the transporter "malfunctioned" and caused a duplicate Kirk to be made. Since there could be only one personality of Kirk, it was split between the two bodies. This writer heard one fan remark (not realizing when this episode was filmed) that "they had begun to run out of ideas when they made that one." So it would seem, in spite of William Shatner's excellent performance and the skillful direction of Leo Penn.

You can bet your most prized possession that no one would have given a damn about Kirk getting passionate with his yeoman. Everyone would have been down in the transporter room trying to figure out how the machine managed to duplicate a man and a dog with no raw matter whatever. We have seen that such a machine could easily "duplicate" inanimate objects by reassembly of basic atomic particles. But doing it with no raw matter at all is more like what gods are supposed to be able to do. It would make the accidental discovery of penicillin—when some lab samples got moldy—very pale by comparison.

As if that weren't bad enough, of course, the machine was used to reassemble the duplicated bodies, which was predictable from the moment the duplicate stepped off the transporter chamber without his shirt symbol. No one asked how the whole incident might have happened, nor how they might harness the discovery. This ridiculous episode had no place in an otherwise plausible series, and it opened the door for later writers (and script editors) to further abuse the privilege.

While this was going on, the show still needed some sort of shuttlecraft. Just after the pilots, the major *Enterprise* miniature had been considerably modified, including the addition of hangar bay doors. There was still no money, however, to make the shuttlecraft. As more shows were completed, the point of no return was approaching. If something was not done soon, the stopgap would become a show fixture.

Unhappily, shuttle money was not freed up for several months—not until the second batch of shows was ordered by

NBC. It was well into October, and more than a dozen shows had been shot.

Even though there was no hope of forgetting about the magic machine, little effort was spared on the shuttlecraft. A very impressive twenty-two-foot exterior mockup was constructed in Arizona, at the same shop that built the car and other vehicles in *The Man from Uncle*. It was trucked to Hollywood and set up on Stage Ten at the Desilu Gower Studio for filming of the first of the second-batch shows, "The Galileo Seven." Meantime, studio personnel constructed an interior set.

Had the exterior mockup been available earlier, someone might have thought the interior set too big. It turned out to be about one-third larger than the acual unfinished interior of the portable mockup. This allowed even the taller actors to stand erect wihout hitting the removable overhead panels. The interior set was constructed for ease of filming, as its sides and even bottom were removable. The complicated three-part door of the mockup was not duplicated.

One could argue that the shuttlecraft was less than perfect, of course. The designer knew the views from the ship would have to be limited to either optical mattes or what could easily be moved by stagehands, so only three small ports were installed. It also suffered in execution, since complete instructions were not passed to everyone. For instance, director Robert Gist had two actors exit through the rear of the shuttle interior set, and a door sound effect was added. Yet the same show revealed the aft end of the craft, and there was no door. In later shows, stock footage of the same shuttle views were used over and over again. On the whole, however, one could see that quite an effort was made, and it is a terrible shame the money could not have been spared in 1964.

It was far too late to go back and erase the transporter, with so many in the can and several already broadcast. The men stranded by transporter failure in "The Enemy Within" could not be rescued by shuttle, since millions had already seen the episode. And, unhappily, it was not possible to continue without the silly machine.

Incredibly, the story device of stranding people via transporter failure was *still used*. Some of the scripts had been written back before the shuttle was available, true. But what excuse could be offered for the later ones?

As time went on, there was more abuse. Dorothy Fontana had the machine reassemble future people inside their past bodies, which we won't honor by discussing. In later shows, it was used to spread atoms across space, provide transit between dimensions, and so on, without mentioning the insane inconsistencies of the cartoon series. The transporter's expanding powers could not be maintained.

The machine is so well rooted in the Star Trek universe by this time that we will never be rid of it. It's as indispensable as the series lead, the Captain.

Science-fiction writers and producers can learn from this unfortunate error, however, and remember that consistency is at least as important as anything else in their project. The lesson won't strike home, however, unless the audience appreciates what is going on and demands consistency.

# 8.
# I LOVE SPOCK
## (with apologies to Mrs. Nimoy)

### by Beverley Wood

*When rock stars and actors have it, it's called sex appeal.*
*When politicians and other public figures have it, it's called*
*charisma. But when you apply it—and most assuredly, "it" is*
*love, pure and simple—to a character in a science-fiction TV*
*show, well . . . Reams have been written about fans' feelings*
*for Spock, but Beverley Wood expresses it best—in what can*
*only be called a love letter.*

Say you're crazy about Kirk—nobody questions your san-
ity. Say you adore McCoy—that's fine. Say you love Spock
and suddenly you're a target for the prying questions, nasty
snickers, and outhouse philosophies of hordes of amateur psy-
chiatrists. In discussions of the Star Trek phenomena (and
there are a lot), few writers are able to resist dissecting the
psychology of Spock's female fans. Cheerfully they agree that
"Kirk's women" are normal, lusty wenches while Spock's fans
are repressed, erotic, and crazy to boot. I object. Strenuously.
In fact, I would like to reply with a two-syllable rebuttal that
is itself a little outhousy; but, being a lady . . .

Yes, I love Spock. I go on record here and now as stating
quite calmly that there is nothing wrong with loving a Vulcan. Too often have I and a lot of other intelligent women
been labeled "neurotic," "dirty old broads," or worse. I'm
sick and tired of being the butt of such outright prejudice;
the abuse we have to take is truly appalling, and for what
reason? Because we happen to love a Vulcan! Amanda is a
strong-willed woman, but if she'd had to put up with such
harassment, even she might have given up; then she wouldn't
have had a son and we wouldn't have our problem. Thank
goodness, she knew what she wanted, got it, and means to

66

keep it; and since Spock's father is very attractive, I don't blame her a bit. (If I'd seen Sarek first—well, never mind.)

Why shouldn't we love Spock? For that matter, why do we? Why do I, why does Christine, why did Leila, Zarabeth, the Romulan woman commander, Droxine, and all his other fans love that most famous alien? I can speak only for myself, but I'll bet I'm not alone in saying that I love Spock for the same reasons any woman loves any man. For me to love a man he must be (in order, not of importance, but of simple sequence): (1) attractive, (2) strong (physically and mentally), (3) gentle, (4) perceptive, and (5) real.

In the natural order of events when we meet a person our senses rush into operation, making contact with forgotten memories and impressions, computing and cross-referencing. Almost at once the personal verdict lights up on the screen: "ATTRACTIVE" (or not, as the case may be). Further acquaintance can change that original verdict—it's only a snap judgment, after all—but it's the first step, and a logical one, in loving a person.

Many women admire the brawny frame and classic good looks of Kirk/Shatner. Even I admit to a certain tingle when he unleashes that famous smile. Others, including my sister, insist that McCoy/Kelley is the ideal man, and although I don't entirely agree with them, I respect their choice. McCoy and Kirk have their charms. Undoubtedly, all of the Star Trek regulars are very attractive men and women, but I happen to adore tall, lean, handsome men. (I married one thirty years ago, and at once we set out enthusiastically to produce four more tall, lean, handsome young men; also one tall, slender, lovely young woman.) A nice, flat midriff with a hint of ribs and hipbones showing turns me on far more than bulky shoulders and well-padded biceps. As for the ears— stunning! (I've been considering some minor plastic surgery for my husband.)

Amanda and I aren't the only admirers of Vulcan good looks. First there's Christine—beautiful, misunderstood, trying-to-make-the-best-of-a-bad-situation Christine. She can't help loving Commander Spock, tries not to bother him, and isn't given enough credit for her strength of character.

In "The Cloud Minders," Droxine tried to make us think she admired Spock's intelligence only, but you can't tell me his mind was all she was after. That terrific Romulan commander had excellent taste in men, but the poor woman came out second best in a conflict of loyalties ("The *Enterprise* Incident").

Leila Kalomi ("This Side of Paradise") carried the torch for our alien for six years before she got the spores on her side. Lucky girl, when she went on to that new colony, she at least took an interesting memory with her. Oh, you didn't catch that? Next time you watch that episode, look at the grass! Overcome by unnatural emotion, Spock embraced Leila, dropping his communicator in the fresh, untrodden grass. Later, as Kirk tried to contact his errant first officer, the communicator was shown still lying where it fell, the once-crisp stalks now thoroughly crushed and bent. Hmmmmm!

Then there was lovely, lonely Zarabeth ("All Our Yesterdays"). Did she really end up as lonely as when we first saw her? When McCoy burst in on the cozy pair, their blissful glassy-eyed expressions were surely indicative of a bit more than a kiss or two. Maybe Zarabeth had a very small someone to keep her busy and share her exile before a year was out; I like to think so, anyway.

Ah ha, you say, I've got you now; any fool knows about Vulcans and the seven-year cycle! All right, but listen: Remember in "Amok Time" Spock says, "I had thought I might be spared this." Now tell me, what made him think that? Why would he hope to be spared the ordeal of the *pon farr* unless he had good reason to believe he was more human than Vulcan in that respect? And just try to convince me that Amanda—a very human, emotional, and enthusiastic woman—could manage for seven years without something more from her Vulcan husband than the clasp of two fingers? The real story is this—and I have it direct from the latest files in McCoy's lab, thanks to Christine, always a good friend:

"It is quite true that every seventh year Vulcan males suffer the impact of such an uncontrollable and violent compulsion to mate that the only alternative is death. This *pon farr* time, or time of fertility, is a natural evolutionary development; its occurrence is, of course, not simultaneous with all males, being a function of the onset of the individual's physical maturity. The seven-year cycle of male fertility works effectively to keep the population within the limits necessitated by a somewhat hostile environment, while at the same time the irresistible power of the *pon farr* drive guarantees the continuance of the species. As a further safeguard, it is believed (although undocumented at the present time) that Vulcan females are fertile at all times, thus ensuring conception during *pon farr*."

See? And just because Vulcan males aren't fertile between times doesn't mean that they can't or don't . . . well, you figure it out. Of course, being Vulcan, they don't volunteer the information, and the misconception (no pun intended) does tend to keep them out of embarrassing situations.

Moving right along, the next item on my list is strength. I'm incurably old-fashioned and I do like "a proper man"—one who is physically and mentally strong. There's no doubting Spock's great physical powers. Even half-dead with *pon farr*, he could have killed Kirk easily in "Amok Time," and the poor gladiators in "Bread and Circuses" never had a chance. For a nonviolent man he sees a good deal of action and handles it competently.

No question about mental strength either. Spock can read the delicate sensors directly, and interprets the computer's complex responses without waiting for correlation. The answers are all there, all neatly arranged in the Vulcan's logical mind, almost before the questions are asked. But notice that unless the questions *are* asked, the answers aren't forthcoming. Never, unless it is a life-or-death matter, will Spock overstep his authority; never will he volunteer information if he sees that Kirk is (albeit more slowly) coming to the same conclusion. He may make discreet suggestions, but he supports and sustains his commanding officer by allowing Kirk to think matters through and make his own decisions. Spock has chosen to accept Kirk's leadership, and his loyalty is complete and believable. What an asset to a starship captain—not just to have such a man as second in command, but to have him by the Vulcan's own choice! Spock is of command rank, thoroughly capable and qualified to command a ship, but the fact is, he has no ambition for command ("The Galileo Seven"). He is far more interested in the fields of science and research. Not so strange—there are plenty of brilliant minds that do not care to be in a management position.

Gentleness is an important part of Spock's nature. It's not the opposite of strength, you know; tenderness doesn't conflict with strength. To be gentle is not to be weak. I, for one, love both in a man. We've all seen the gentleness in Spock's behavior—touching the Horta's eggs ("The Devil in the Dark"), stroking the tribble ("The Trouble with Tribbles"), comforting the little horned dog doomed to die in the transporter ("The Enemy Within"). It's harder for him to show that side of his nature with humans, but not impossible—it's there in his regret for Christine's unhappiness ("The Naked Time"), his concern for the dying McCoy ("The Empath"), his poignant whisper "Forget" to the anguished captain ("Requiem for Methuselah"), his care not only for Kirk, but for Kirk's opinion of himself ("The Enemy Within").

The Vulcan mind meld in its various forms is always initiated with a gentleness approaching emotional love. Surely not less intimate than physical love, the mind meld may very likely be an important part of Vulcan sex life. Indeed, the Vulcan males' abhorrence of the *pon farr* may be due in part to the fact that in the primitive passions that drive them at that time there is no place for the tender subtlety of the mind meld.

Perception is one of the many fine things about Star Trek as a whole, especially when particular characters or events are shown by the actions or reactions of others—for instance, Kirk's compelling personality as shown by Spock's loyalty, Spock's emotions by McCoy's declarations that he has none. The love between two men couldn't be more beautifully demonstrated than by the silent smile Kirk flashes his first officer ("The Ultimate Computer") in gratitude for the alien's almost-whispered words of loyalty.

Spock's perception goes beyond the physical. He is, as all Vulcans are, marginally telepathic. He knows things humans can't know and is ever aware of feelings and emotions that must be abrasive to his too-sensitive nature. It is for that very reason that a Vulcan/human relationship such as Spock/Kirk is seldom found; it is simply too painful for the overreceptive Vulcan mind. In Spock's case, he had excellent training for the ordeal, having lived his youth in the presence of an exceedingly human mother. Thus, he is able to relate to humans more easily than are other Vulcans. (I can't help wondering about Sarek's mental state, for that poor man had no such early indoctrination. However, it was his own choice, and life with the vivacious Amanda no doubt has its benefits, even for a staid Vulcan.)

Spock's perception has made him well aware of the reason behind McCoy's constant badgering. (Knowing that the worst thing that could happen to Spock is for him to become too human, McCoy reminds him continually and acidly about his

half-Vulcanity.) The doctor is an artist with the intentionally
barbed remark, and Spock ably adds his part to the deception
of mutual dislike. It has developed into a game the two
play—at times almost unconsciously, yet each knowing and
knowing the other knows. Fooled for a while, and considerably worried about the bickering of his officers, Kirk has finally understood that the feud isn't real. He has found, too,
that it has beneficial side effects. The accustomed arguments
not only amuse the crew, they tend to relieve the tension at
critical moments (for if Spock and McCoy are "at it again,"
things can't be too bad, right?).

The final question, even if he fits my requirements so far,
is: Is the Vulcan real? Oh, absolutely. At first, he was robot-
stiff with officers and crew (less real), but then we began to
see his realness and it affords us no small amount of amuse-
ment when we catch glimpses of it. He is sometimes stub-
born, annoyingly meticulous, often too correct. He worries
miserably about Kirk and the others. He indulges in occasional humor and has become less averse to revealing himself.
But still Spock is a hard man to know. It took the captain
some time to break down the barriers of his own dislike to
find the Vulcan knowable on his own terms.

I didn't know Spock myself until just a couple of years
ago. In the "real" Star Trek years (i.e., the late '60s), I never
had time to sit down and get acquainted with him; I saw the
show only through a haze of supper and dishes and ironing
and mending. It was only when I quite accidentally saw a
rerun of "The Devil in the Dark" two years ago that I suddenly locked on, cried "Wow" or words to that effect, and became an instant Trekkie. For there was the sum total of
Spock's complex personality—divining the significance of the
rock/eggs, rebelling against killing and then ready to kill
without question to save his captain, and finally accepting the
ultimate involvement of mind meld with the Horta.

One of the most "real" things about Spock is his nagging
self-doubt. He doesn't quite trust himself, and persists with
what almost amounts to paranoia in being Vulcan beyond the
demands of ordinary healthy Vulcanity. Because of his mixed
ancestry, Spock has *expected* to be "different," to be deluged
with human reactions and emotions. He sees his own churn-
ing feelings as purely human, whereas they are actually Vulcan. A good chat with Sarek years ago might have dispelled
these fears, for, of course, Vulcans do have emotions—such
terribly strong ones that they will overwhelm them if given

half a chance. In their control lies the strength and serenity of the Vulcan mind. Sarek, with no reason to doubt his innate Vulcanity, allows himself to smile at his wife, enjoys a tender touch, and shows definite signs of a very real and deep love. He shows signs of other emotions, too, such as aggravation at his son's rejection of his fatherly choice of a career for Spock ("Journey to Babel").

Spock holds himself in check too sternly, guards too closely against the flood of human illogic he imagines to be latent within himself. I have mixed feelings about this—I want Spock to be at ease with himself, I want him to accept himself, because I, too, have things within me that frighten and repel me and because I want very much to be acceptable to myself. However, if he could trust himself, if he could forget his human heritage, if he could be a typical Vulcan, he wouldn't be Spock. So I don't really want him to achieve the ease and security that would change him; Spock, as he is, is too important an individual.

In some of the less-than-beloved third-year episodes the individualities of Kirk/Spock/McCoy began to overlap and blend. (I can't abide the spineless way Spock behaved in "Turnabout Intruder"; he must have been seriously ill with some undiagnosed Vulcan disease.) This interchangeability of character was dangerous and could have been disastrous to the discipline of the *Enterprise* and the fulfillment of her mission, for any organization, in order to function successfully, must be headed by strongly defined key people. Three men, each a composite of Kirk/Spock/McCoy, would have little value as senior officers of a starship.

Yet the problem of personality change was understandable. In real life, in situations of long association, a mixing and sharing of traits often occurs in just that way. At first Kirk would probably have been pleased to find things running so smoothly on the surface (as would have happened had the three begun to think more alike), but it wouldn't have taken him long to understand the threat to his ship. By that time, McCoy would have caustically diagnosed the trouble and he and Spock would have been well on their way to stiffening up and getting back into character.

Thus, the last requirement: The man I love must not only be attractive, strong, gentle, perceptive, and real, but he must possess an integrity of person and personality that resists blurring, that can be itself even though loved and loving, even though I or others might want to and try to change him.

As the Companion ("Metamorphosis") said, with a slightly different meaning, "He must continue."

It's said that love is a many-splendored thing, and this is true in part; but it's not just one thing, it's a whole lot of things. Love is stretchable, elastic, expandable enough to include many people at the same time, even unreal ones. Relatives and those whose lives we actually touch make up a large part of our loves, but there are others—maybe a little less durable, less tangible, somewhat vicarious, but not any the less true. For example, happily married women (pregnant ones) normally fall briefly in love with their obstetricians; and grown men, sane in most ways, have been known to adore a poster or a TV commercial. Actors and actresses receive a good deal of this kind of love just because they are so widely in view; and what an ego trip it must be to know that there are thousands of men or women in love with the "person" they portray. (Scary, too, I suppose, and maybe a downright nuisance at times, but surely pleasant nevertheless.)

Vicarious loves are predestined to nonfulfillment, for they are clearly not compatible with the real world. The love I had for my obstetrician, for instance, was certainly true in its own way; yet now I can't even remember what he looked like (although God knows I lived in his office for seven years). My feeling for Spock exists, but as for meeting the real Spock/Nimoy (if such an unlikely event were to occur)—naturally, my rosy fantasy shows me brilliant, witty, and charming, but honesty forces me to admit the likelihood of a somewhat less comfortable picture. In real life, if I weren't struck mercifully dumb, my sparkling wit would probably be voiced in my most fluent "dingbatese" (a dither of the first degree), and I would wish I were thoroughly dead.

In spite of the incompatibility of these "other loves" with the real world, they are true; they exist and have meaning. It would degrade my human integrity to suggest that my love for such people is only imaginary. It's not, nor is it psychotic. True love enriches the lives it touches, and the love of Spock has enriched mine. I love him as he is (not some erotic, meaningless fantasy of him), and I wouldn't think of demeaning him or myself by any kind of distasteful demonstration. He doesn't have to guard his Vulcanity against me, for I respect and cherish it. I can join Christine in declaring honestly and with simple dignity, "I love Spock."

And if you will allow me one final succinct observation—*T'Pring was nuts!*

# 9.
# CHARACTERIZATION RAPE

by Kendra Hunter

*It will come as no surprise to anyone who purchased this book that hundreds of original Star Trek stories are published each year in fanzines. This flood of new ST is the most outstanding feature of the fan subculture, and will eventually be responsible for an entire new crop of authors, poets, screenwriters, and reviewers—many of whom would never have dared to try their hand at writing if Star Trek had not come along to stimulate their imaginations.*

*But this plethora of "fanfic" has caused some dissension in fandom. Kendra Hunter discusses what this dissension is and why it occurs, and at the same time exposes some of the flaws that should be avoided in writing your original Star Trek story.*

Somewhere in the vastness of interstellar space, the Starship *Enterprise* sails smoothly at warp factor 2. Commander Spock, standing at his station on the bridge, can be overheard explaining to Dr. Leonard McCoy that "fascinating" is a word he would use in the description of the unexpected. The phenomenon that is Star Trek must certainly qualify as "fascinating."

On March 11, 1964 (Star Trek, first draft), a man by the name of Gene Roddenberry sat at his typewriter and began to shape a dream into reality. Because he believed in the intelligence of television viewers and loved science fiction, Mr. Roddenberry created Star Trek. This created-for-television series had such a wide format that many current social problems could be aired in the episodes. "Let This Be Your Last Battleground" exposed prejudice for the ridiculous idea that it is, and in "The Trouble with Tribbles" an environmental problem was illustrated while we were being entertained. The show allowed the expression of the IDIC, the evaluation of freedom, and the individual rights of beings. In the turbulent decade of the '60s, with the Vietnam War, the assassination of John Kennedy, the college campus riots, and the space program, which took us from Alan Shepard's historic fifteen minutes to Neil Armstrong's "giant leap for mankind," Star Trek was a platform for writers to express the dreams of peace and freedom.

The writers, under the guidance of the Great Bird of the Galaxy, and director Gene L. Coon, produced quality scripts wherein the personalities of the characters began to develop. The actors projected much of themselves into the stories. Captain Robert M. April became James T. Kirk, commanding one of Starfleet's finest vessels. According to the outline, April was a colorfully complex personality, capable of action and decision, while continually battling with self-doubt and the loneliness of command. These same features manifest themselves in Kirk. William Shatner, with the help of Mr. Roddenberry and Mr. Coon, took Kirk and made him a living being. The same is true of Mr. Spock, a character whom the powers-that-be at NBC viewed with skepticism. No one had ever done this before, and they were afraid. Maybe television producers should be frightened more often.

Writing in the constant pressure of a television-production atmosphere must be debilitating at best, and the probability of committing what has been labeled "characterization rape" is great. This is done by professional writers in all aspects of fiction writing, so it was not surprising to find this offense in the volumes of fan fiction which began while Star Trek was still being aired in prime time.

In order to avoid committing characterization rape, a writer, either professional or amateur, must realize that she (those gentlemen readers must forgive my use of the feminine pronouns, but as the vast majority of fan writers are women, it seems only proper) is not omnipotent. She cannot force her characters to simply do as she pleases. Fictional characters are like newborn babies—from the moment of birth each is an individual with unique personality traits. When an author forces a character to walk out of sync, the result is an episode like "The *Galileo* Seven." Such a story leaves the reader or viewer frustrated, unsatisfied, and cheated.

The writer must have respect for her characters or those created by others that she is using, and have a full working knowledge of each before committing her thoughts to paper.

If the characters do not move in sync as living people do, the result is bad writing and the reader/viewer is left not caring. It is the caring for and loving of the Star Trek characters that necessitated fan fiction.

"The *Galileo* Seven," written by Oliver Crawford and S. Bar-David, is a prime example of characterization rape involving all the characters. The writers began with a preconceived notion of what a Vulcan was and were going to make Spock that Vulcan without taking the time to become acquainted with him. The beginning of the story states that although this half-Vulcan is first officer aboard the *Enterprise*, he has never commanded a mission. Oh, come now! What's he been doing for the last twelve years? A person does not achieve a place of responsibility in Starfleet without having earned it. Then the crew of the *Galileo* is forced out of sync as the writers continually demand insubordination from them. Regardless of how the crew feel about Mr. Spock or his ability to command, these people are militarily trained and as such would not vocalize mutinous opinions.

However, as with all the aired Trek, there is good with the bad. The only action taken by Spock that is totally within his character is the moment when he jettisons the fuel and ignites it—a command decision which was made when it had to be made, where it had to be made, in light of all available information. It was not an emotional outbreak, just a logical decision, a gamble to be sure, but a logical gamble with everything to gain and nothing to lose.

While "The *Galileo* Seven" is an example of characterization rape, there are examples of the lasting impression made when a character behaves true to form. "The City on the Edge of Forever" demonstrates the value of forcing the viewer/reader to care about a fictional character. When Kirk watches Edith die—and he must let her die—all of Trekdom cries. We all feel the pain and want to help. This is Kirk, the real Kirk, the man who touches our hearts.

Characterization is by far the most important aspect of fiction writing. The creating of men, women, children, and extraterrestrials must make them into entities, they must live and breathe as they move across the pages or the screen. If they do not, the reader/viewer has been cheated and the writer has failed. Whatever point the writer wished made will not be made because the reader does not care.

To make the reader/viewer care (without committing characterization rape) was a problem faced by the writers from the time the first Star Trek script was drafted and continues today in the hundreds of fanzines. The characters had been outlined by Roddenberry, but each writer has to further the development of each of them. And therein lies the trick—to maintain the characters in sync while expanding and exploring the interrelationships of the various characters. And there are a variety of relationships: Kirk/Spock, Kirk/McCoy, Spock/McCoy, Spock/Chapel, Kirk/Chekov, Kirk/Uhura, etc., each having value and depth. The majority of these relationships were only hinted at vaguely in the aired episodes, but they exist nonetheless and have been fully developed in the realms of fan fiction. The most apparent relationship of this group is the Kirk/Spock relationship. It was begun on the aired episodes and has grown and increased in fan fiction.

This relationship came into being because the fan writers loved the characters and cared about the ideas that are Star Trek and they refused to let it fade away into oblivion. It is these fans who are responsible for the volumes of fanzines which contain stories, novels, articles, poetry, songs, cartoons, and many other artistic expressions. If there was no fandom, the aired episodes would stand as they are, and yet they would be just old reruns of some old series with no more meaning than old reruns of "I Love Lucy." Because Star Trek is what it is; because the fans took to heart every word that was uttered, every expression that was filmed, every eyebrow that was raised and made it even more; because the fans took Kirk/Spock and developed it far beyond even what Roddenberry had imagined, the relationship has become as deep and rich and meaningful as the entire concept of Star Trek itself.

As an example, Commander Spock is briefly outlined in "The Star Trek Guide," Third Revision, April 17, 1967, as being biologically, emotionally, and intellectually a "half-breed" who has more advanced mental powers, as well as more fully developed physical strength, than the humans he serves with on board the *Enterprise*. In fan fiction Spock has been evolved from the time before his birth until his death. The history of Vulcan has been written and discussed. The Vulcan language has been analyzed and a dictionary written. Spock's parents have been written about from all angles, until they, too, have become living, breathing fictional characters.

It was this desire for a deeper understanding of the characters, who had become friends, companions, and even heroes, to the fans and the unwillingness to let them be forgotten that spawned the torrent of fan fiction.

There is no way to discuss fan fiction or characterization rape in fan fiction without discussing the worst offender: the Lieutenant Mary Sue story. Mary Sue stories are typical groupie fantasies in which, usually, a writer transfers herself from the 1970 era into the future by means of the Guardian of Forever, a time warp, or other device of time travel, and finds herself in the Star Trek universe. In general, Mary Sue is a single, thirty-year-old female, who is incredibly beautiful, super-loving, super-intelligent, super-everything. In the standard format, Kirk, Spock, and McCoy fall in love with her immediately and sometimes even Scott, Sulu, and Chekov are included in the emotional tangle. Mary Sue will choose one of the men to begin a relationship and complete her fantasy. In so doing, Mary Sue usually must save the *Enterprise* from some unimaginable horror while the command crew, whom Starfleet command has spent a great deal of taxpayer money to train, sit on their hands. Once the Big *E* is saved to fight another day, Mary Sue and whichever of the men (in my case, it's always Captain Kirk) she chooses ride off into the sunset to live happily ever after.

The criminal offense committed here is the obvious forcing of the characters to step out of their roles and become something that they are not. Kirk is not about to go off into the sunset with anyone because he is owned body and soul by the *Enterprise,* as men for centuries have been owned by their ships. The call of space is no different from the call of the sea. Kirk is not about to allow an untrained amateur on the bridge of his ship.

These stories are an exotic form of torture for the reader, but nonetheless, the Mary Sue story is a necessary part of fan fiction. It provides a place for the writer to begin to develop her writing talent, to let her thoughts flow from mind to paper.

When a writer sits down at her typewriter and creates a character, all aspects of that character are in her head, either consciously or unconsciously, and all she has to do is draw from that knowledge. In Star Trek writing, however, these new characters must function in a world inhabited by fictional characters already known quite well by the reader. The writer must then make sure her character has evolved according to her own individual personality, while at the same

**Captain of the *Enterprise***
*(Monica Miller)*

"Seeker Among the Stars"  ©MILLER '7

## Seeker Among the Stars
*(Monica Miller)*

**Right: Lee** *(Monica Miller)*
**Below: Kor** *(Monica Miller)*

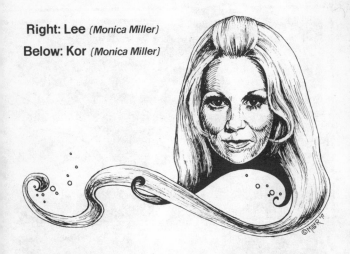

**Kirk's Fair Damsel**
*(Monica Miller)*

**Target Practice**
*(Steven Fabian)*

# Needlepoint Design

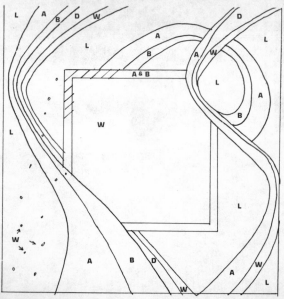

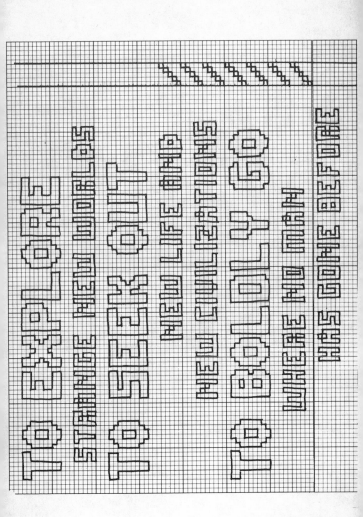

**Kzinti** *(P. Stout)*

time the previously created people are moving according to their personalities.

The officers and crew of the USS *Enterprise* are not real, a fact that is sometimes overlooked by the fans. Many writers have a difficult time relating from their point of view in the real world to the imaginary world of our beloved Kirk and company. Mary Sue and her many compatriots serve as a bridge to span this void between the real and the unreal. It is a step used by the writer to overcome a barrier which exists in the mind and allows her to relate on a one-to-one basis with the fictional characters.

However, when this method is used to force the other characters to act out of sync, then it produces bad writing. Unless a writer is prepared to write directly to her reader, she should never attempt to be published. If the writer wants to share her Mary Sue or other fiction work with the readers (there are thousands of eager readers in the realms of Trekdom), then she should endeavor to make that fiction as plausible as possible. Make Kirk, Spock, and company real and vivid, reacting as all the readers know they will react. Mary Sue must fit into the world of the *Enterprise* and not the other way around; and if she does not fit, transfer her off the ship and start all over again. The market is there—it doesn't pay much, but the market does exist and the readers are eagerly awaiting all the Star Trek fiction that is available.

Fan fiction had its beginning during the second season of the aired episodes and is still being produced at a phenomenal rate this very moment. Over the years the writers have gone through a series of phases in the content of the stories, beginning with the sequel stage. The majority of early fan fiction concerned itself with what happened to Zarabeth or the further adventures of Kevin Riley, characters the fans were enchanted with immediately. Then came Mary Sue, followed by "get Kirk" and "get Spock" stories wherein the development of the relationship was explored by a method called hurt/care/torture/comfort. Kirk is hurt, Spock cares, the pain is torturous, and Spock offers comfort. Or the other way around.

In the beginning there was Spock, and somewhere way out in left field there was Kirk. This was a concept even Shatner had to learn to live with. Some of the writers didn't quite know how to handle Spock, while others virtually ignored Kirk in order to develop the Vulcan. I am an adamant admirer of Captain Kirk, and this latter approach left me a little cold; I was glad to see the gorgeous captain take his rightful place in fan fiction. Then the scrutinization of Kirk/Spock began, and where it will end, only the fen* know.

In "Requiem for Methuselah," written by Jerome Bixby, there is an example of the rape of Captain Kirk as well as the existence of the Kirk/Spock relationship. Captain Kirk does not fall in love, instantly, with any woman. He may use a woman to get what he wants or needs, but to develop an emotional relationship requires some time. And the captain would never jeopardize his ship or his crew in any way, especially for personal reasons. We have already seen Kirk allow Edith Keeler to die in order to save his ship, his crew, and his world. However, the episode "Requiem for Methuselah" is overshadowed by the final scene in Kirk's quarters. McCoy and Spock are conversing while Kirk sleeps. McCoy says: "You'll never know the things that love can drive a man to—the ecstasies, the miseries, the broken rules, the desperate chances, the glorious failures, the glorious victories—all of these things you'll never know, simply because the word 'love' isn't written in your book." But Spock does know. And in one of the most moving scenes in aired Trek, Spock demonstrates he does know love by removing the more painful memories from Kirk's mind—a beautiful action which offsets one of the worst of the episodes.

Alone in the universe, Spock, at home nowhere except in Starfleet, and Kirk, bearing the loneliness of command, find the strength of love and friendship in each other.

One of the most valuable things to come from women's lib is "men's lib." A release from years of not being able to love, cry, express emotion, or assume the responsibility for changing the baby's diaper. Being a man, or a woman, has taken on new dimension wherein each is allowed to develop his or her interests and abilities to the fullest. And as has been said many times before, Trek was ahead of its time. The wide format allowed these two men to care about each other and to establish a love/friendship relationship. We didn't see Joe Friday and Frank Gannon hug one another or cry or even care about each other the way Starsky and Hutch are now able to express these feelings. In the past when two men cared for each other, and expressed it, they were eventually labeled gay.

* Fan term—plural of fan.

This has befallen Kirk/Spock, arrived at logically after years of writing, reading, and developing said characters, according to those who accept this premise. Unfortunately, it is out of character for both men, and as such comes across in the stories as bad writing.

After reading a sampling of zines, which were provided by the curator of *Memory Alpha,* the Federation Library and Bibliographic Center, containing stories, editorials, and viewpoints, there seems to be, in fanfic, a theory that after all the years of searching, touching, hurting, comforting, there is only one recourse open to the Kirk/Spock relationship, and that is the evolution of a homosexual relationship.

A relationship as complex and deep as Kirk/Spock does not climax with a sexual relationship. If such physical relationship is to be, it will be the beginning. When two beings meet and establish a rapport, sexuality allows a common bond of communication. Sex has a purpose above and beyond the perpetuation of the species, and that is to serve as a basis on which to begin a relationship, the common point where two people can begin to exchange ideas while enjoying the company and companionship of each other.

As time passes, these two people (and a meaningful, fulfilling sexual relationship seems to work best when limited to two people) learn other forms of communication, if they really care about each other. With a sexual relationship, in the beginning, no words are necessary; the primitive emotions and reactions are sufficient. But it does not last. There comes a time when communication must advance to the sharing of ideas. As this sharing becomes more pronounced, the necessity to touch seems to diminish, until a point is reached where a touching of hands brings more joy and pleasure than the uniting of bodies ever could.

At this point I always envision Sarek extending two fingers towards Amanda, and her response of placing two extended fingers against his. Touching briefly as a symbol of what they have shared in their relationship.

The Vulcans had added new dimension to the idea of two people being able to share, to communicate, to express feelings, in the form of the mind meld, wherein two minds are joined and thoughts are allowed to flow between the two. Kirk and Spock have experienced the mind meld on several occasions, so that the thoughts and feelings of one are able to become the thoughts and feelings of the other without the clumsiness of words. Once this advanced stage of communication has been reached, it would seem that returning to the first stage of communication, a sexual relationship, would be anticlimatic.

However, the broad format allows for several sets of circumstances in which Kirk and Spock are placed in a position where a homosexual relationship seems to be the only way out, usually because Spock's life is on the line. If Spock was pure Vulcan, a different set of standards would be used; but Spock is half human and that adds a new field of speculation.

For a scenario, the premise of *pon farr* seems to provide the most realistic setting. Spock is now in the advanced stages of *pon farr,* and because of his continued mind link with Kirk, the only person who can save Spock's life is Kirk. Needless to say, the *Enterprise* is parsecs from Vulcan. But Spock would never allow Kirk to know, and he would die.

If Kirk, being the industrious person that he is, discovers the problem at the last moment, he could force Spock to accept his help. Kirk, watching his friend near death, finds he has no choice: He either enters the realm of bisexuality or allows Spock to die.

In the sobering light of dawn, Kirk relives in his mind the events of the preceding night, and being the character that he is, he allows the seeds of guilt to begin to form and grow until they not only destroy the relationship, but the man himself.

Spock does indeed have strong feelings for Kirk, but he has also demonstrated a caring loyalty to at least one other human, Captain Christopher Pike. After serving for almost two years with Kirk, Spock risks everything he has, including his life, in order to give Pike the only chance at life he has.

Here is Spock, who supposedly has no feeling for anyone, stealing a starship and very knowingly accepting the death penalty for visiting Talos. The crimes he commits are the most serious in Starfleet, and Spock has no guarantee that anyone will intercede in his behalf. Pike will reach Talos and life while Spock will face court-martial and death.

There must have existed between Spock and Pike a strong relationship, but in my research for this article, through the many volumes of fan fiction, I could not find anything written concerning such a relationship. It seems very strange to me that over eleven years of a man's life have been omitted from fan fiction. Spock is not an ordinary fictional character. He is idolized, almost worshiped, by the fen, and yet, even though the entire history of Vulcan was constructed to provide Spock with a background, the eleven years, four months, and five days that Spock served under Pike have been neglected. Why? Does that relationship somehow invalidate the extent to which fan writers have carried the Kirk/Spock relationship?

There is another line of reasoning as to why the Kirk/Spock relationship has been developed to the physical. In the realm of fanfic it is believed that this relationship has evolved logically to a sexual relationship over the years while each gradually learned to touch and be touched, to hold and be held, to care and to love. I realize that the homosexual relationship did not just appear one day; it was reached after years of writing and reading. But I must wonder if it wasn't the result of the writers' having nothing left to write about. After all the hurting and torture and caring and comfort, what was left to write about?

Trek fiction has a problem unique unto itself in that the characters first appeared on the screen rather than in print, so that when one thinks of Kirk, one automatically envisions Shatner. Leonard Nimoy tried to deny that he was Spock and came to the logical conclusion that if he was not, then who was? Most fictional characters are created on paper to walk the pages of a novel long before being transferred to the screen. Not so with Trek. Roddenberry outlined the characters, Gene L. Coon directed the formation, but it was the actors who provided the form and substance, the personalities, the expressions, and the attitudes; all combined to make us, the viewers, really care about what was happening. Trek was special to each of these people who have had their lives shaped by the effect that Trek produced on us, the fen. We should remember their feelings as we express our own in fan fiction. Yes, we—the fans and the writers, and the artists, and all the rest—do have the right to freedom of expression, but only when that right does not infringe on the rights of other individuals.

Trek is a format for expressing rights, opinions, and ideals. Most every imaginable idea can be expressed through Trek, including homosexuality. But there is a right way. Kirk's actions in "The City on the Edge of Forever" and "Balance of Terror" showing his strengths and weaknesses. The wrong way can simply be illustrated with "The *Galileo* Seven." Fiction literature has long played an important role in the presentation of new ideas and concepts. When properly expressed, these ideas have started revolutions.

So, ladies—and gentlemen—man your typewriters (somehow, "woman your typewriters" just doesn't make it), and make Trek fiction the strong forceful tool it can be. Through the words we write here and now, Earth, 1978, we can very easily guide our nation, and even the world, from where we are to the point in time where Trek is—and maybe without their World War III. We can make all those things come true—the IDIC, the Prime Directive—but only if we are willing to work.

The ideal of Trek is truth and beauty, and when carried out in the finest form of fictional characterization, Kirk, Spock, McCoy, and the other members of the crew will join the realm of Antigone, Macbeth, and Tom Sawyer to live forever.

# 10.
# A SAMPLING OF
# TREK ROUNDTABLE

*We are most fortunate to enjoy that rarest of readerships: those who write letters. People who read a lot fall naturally into two groups: those who want desperately to write as well (and will do so at any opportunity), and those who are content to read only. Star Trek fans are those who want to write. Stories, poems, scripts—and letters. In any form imaginable, Trekkers want to get their feelings and opinions about Star Trek down on paper, and to share them with others. And we receive more than our fair share of these, as fans know that "Trek Roundtable" is probably the premiere forum in fandom for exchange of ideas. Enough. Let our readers speak for themselves. . . .*

### Betty Wynne, Kansas City, Kan.

First of all, I am going to nitpick a little with something that was written in Trek No. 7 concerning "The Trek Fan of the Month" in the Prime Directive section. I think it is just the wording of the following that bothered me, but it still gets me every time I read it, so I decided to comment on it:

"Let us see some examples of your writing, art, or any other skills or hobbies you may have. Include photos (if possible) of you, your ST collection, and any ST decorations or exhibits you may have assembled."

It seems to me that too many people think that you are not a real ST enthusiast unless you are surrounded by models, dolls, pictures, buttons, stills, and all the other trappings. I am not surrounded by these things, yet I (and I'm sure many others) are just as devoted to ST as those who do collect such items. I am not putting anyone down for collecting, but only stating that there are fans who do not go in for that.

The ST items that I have are just as dear to me as the

above-mentioned are to those that own them. I have invested my money in ST books, in ST magazines, and in tape recordings of the great guest talks and panel discussions at the cons I have been fortunate enough to attend. I have very few pictures, and those are of the stars, the fans, and the displays which I have taken myself at cons. (I must say that I do have three pictures that are my most prized possessions. They are pictures of the original *Enterprise* model that I took on a visit to the Air and Space Museum in Washington, D.C., this summer.) So let's hear it for fans who just enjoy watching ST and reading and listening to ST material as well as those who also collect it.

Now that I have aired my gripe, I think it only fair to tell you a little about myself. I have been a fan since day one, back in 1966; however, I was a closet ST fan until about two years ago. I finally told myself, "What are you doing? You love the show, why not say so?" And that is exactly what I did, and to my surprise, some of my best friends were also ST fans. Now we keep each other informed on the latest ST news.

I work for an airline and have been fortunate in that respect, for it enables me to go to other cities for the cons. I have attended the two cons here in Kansas City (they were both excellent), and I have also attended cons in both Los Angeles and Phoenix. I have been able to meet so many people who share my interest in ST and have acquired several pen pals as a result. I spend a lot of time reading and rereading all my ST books and magazines (and looking for new material all the time).

All I can say is that I thank my lucky stars that there are so many of us who realize what a great show ST was, is, and soon will be again. Thanks for listening and keep up the good work.

*When we wrote that invitation for candidates for our "Fan of the Month," we were asking for our readers to send us material on themselves which would be of interest to other readers—especially that which was quite unusual, such as the fact that one of our readers had discovered the original shuttlecraft, one had assembled a charming diorama using the Mego ST dolls, and yet another was a naturalized citizen who had found that the message of ST is truly universal.*

*As the perpetual victims of many askance looks when we reveal that we are the publishers of an ST magazine, we well know the image of the wild-eyed, costumed, grabbing-every-*

*thing-to-do-with-ST fan which many people have. And, to be frank, there are many fans who do collect everything even remotely concerned with ST—good, bad, or indifferent—without remotely fitting the above image.*

*However, we have to be responsive to all our readers, and they not only have a great range of preferences about ST, but they are of all ages and tastes. And as we are primarily a graphics-oriented magazine, we feel that publishing photos of collections, constructions, etc. serves the same purpose as the collections themselves: helping many of our readers to feel a little bit closer to the magic that is Star Trek.*

*We hope that this answers your questions (and those of others who have voiced similar ones). And we thank you very much for the beautiful photos of the Enterprise in the Air and Space Museum that you sent us. We were fortunate enough to tour this exciting and historical storehouse last summer also, but imagine how we felt when we discovered that our photos of the Enterprise model didn't come out! So we are doubly grateful for those you provided us with.*

### Leigh Rogers, Peoria, Ill.

I've enjoyed reading all of the letters in "Trek Roundtable." I collect every book, record, novelty, and paperback on Star Trek I see in our bookstores, and just recently bought Log 10 ("Slaver Weapon"), and "New Voyages 2," which are very interesting reading; also Fotonovel #4, "A Taste of Armageddon." Whoever thought of these fotonovels is an absolute genius! I can hardly wait to buy the ones for my favorite episodes, including "The Empath," "Balance of Terror," and "Obsession."

I like episodes which especially show Spock's gentleness, particularly to McCoy and the other crewmembers. As for Kirk, he's okay, but I like Spock's unaggressiveness better.

My favorite new superhero character is "The Incredible Hulk." It's wonderful to see a nice clean movie on television, instead of some of the trash that's on. *Hulk* was wholesome family entertainment, and I could watch it over and over again. I'm really looking forward to the Superman movie. I've got a feeling it could be a smash hit, just like *Star Wars*.

I'm puzzled about the Star Trek poster magazines. There haven't been any new issues released lately, and I also noticed that in Number 14 they didn't give a preview of next issue as usual. Would anyone know why new issues aren't available?

*Sorry we had to cut so much out of your letter, Leigh, but we can comment on your question. As far as we have been able to discover, the poster books have either been discontinued or suspended publication. Why this happened or if they will resume distribution we don't know. We suggest that interested readers write the publisher of the poster magazine and get the lowdown. Maybe if enough of you write, they will start appearing regularly again.*

*By the way, we enjoyed the* Hulk *program immensely also, and if enough readers think that it is a good idea, we could do a feature on the TV superheroes. Let us know.*

### John T. Gilmore, South St. Paul, Minn.

Am I to believe that racism is alive and well in the world of science fiction? I must assume so after reading your response to question number nine on your recent Fan Poll results. Mr. Spock is portrayed as an alien, and just look at his fan clubs. I have assumed until now that the phrase "United Planets," i.e. the Federation, meant all peoples, all nations, and all planets. I have believed over the past several years (since I have been reading s-f) that we (fans) are the elite! The best this world has to offer—the most open-minded of all!

I think M'Ress would be an ideal addition to the crew of the *Enterprise*. The script possibilities alone boggle the mind. After all, after Mr. Spock, M'Ress or another totally alien being is the next logical step.

Neil Armstrong was the first human being to set foot on the moon. Can you or I take that away from him? *No!* Nor would I want to.

This same line of reasoning applies to the crew of the *Enterprise*.

That any one or more of the crew would be slighted is ridiculous. Mr. Spock would undoubtedly enjoy having someone on board with whom he could play 3-D chess besides the ship's computer.

*Sorry, John, but we don't think that racism (either overt or unintentional) had much to do with the fans' veto of M'Ress and Arex. We think that the animated aliens were rejected because of backlash hostility toward the animated ST in general; and also by the antipathy of many fans to anything which is not the "original" Star Trek. This may be a form of chauvinism and closed-mindedness, but not racism.*

**Lynne Quinlan, Peoria, Ill.**

I just received my copy of *Trek* No. 9 yesterday, and enjoyed it very much. I especially liked the article on Dr. McCoy, and quite agree with you that he isn't given the credit due him. I really enjoy his so-called "arguments" with Spock, and feel he is a very essential character to Star Trek. I think that no one else could play this role as well as DeForrest Kelley.

It's a very good idea to have photorecaps only on particular episodes the fans enjoy. In the future, I'd like to see them on the following: "Balance of Terror," "Obsession," and "The Way to Eden." I know "Eden" isn't the most popular episode with most Star Trek fans. But I always liked this one, maybe because Spock was the only one who seemed to understand those hippies, and went out of his way to help them, too. Every time they rerun "Way to Eden," I always make a point of watching it. I particularly liked the scenes where Spock played his harp with them, and seemed to enjoy it too.

In future issues of *Trek,* I'd like to see more features on the great ST movies. . . .

*Think maybe you've got us confused with another ST'zine, Lynne. We haven't run photorecaps of episodes in some time. We feel that (even as much as fans seem to like them) they are pretty much "padded" space, and we prefer to use our available pages to delve into an episode or character rather than retread old ground which most fans know by heart already. Besides, the new series of fotonovels (which Leigh also mentioned in her letter) are doing this job so well now that anything we could do would pale by comparison.*

**Sherri Gilbert, Novi, Mich.**

I enjoy your magazine very much. It is one of the best that I've seen. The one thing I think is a little out of whack is the fact that the zine seems to have a lot of Kirk and Spock subjects. I'm not saying that they are bad characters, or that I don't like them, it's just that the other members of the famous crew don't seem to be getting equal time (or for that matter, hardly any time). In the recent poll that *Trek* issued, it stated that Kirk and Spock were equal with 43 percent of the total votes. But what about McCoy with 8 percent? There are some fans who might like McCoy (like myself), Scotty, Sulu, Uhura, Chekov, and Chapel. Maybe in your next issues you could include more articles and pictures on those unsung heroes and heroines. You wouldn't want to lose that 14 percent of your reading audience, would you? Thank you and keep your magazine rolling.

*We have to plead guilty to what seems to be an imbalance of Kirk and Spock articles in relation to the rest of the cast, but consider the ratio of Kirk/Spock to the other types of ST articles and features we run. We do not neglect the supporting cast, as witness the recent articles on McCoy and the interview with George Takei. The truth is simply that we receive more requests for Kirk/Spock features, and the majority of the submissions we receive are about one of the two. But we are making an effort to get around to each and every one of the supporting cast. An article on Uhura is in the works right now, and we have something very special in store for Scotty fans shortly. So stick around, and trust us. We're not going to forget anyone.*

## Chris Trepp

I just finished your great book *The Best of Trek*, and after reading Leslie Thompson's article "Star Trek Mysteries—Solved!" I'd like to send in a little mystery of my own. I'd like her answer to the mystery (if she has one!). While watching "The Man Trap" third time around, I noticed that Captain Kirk states in a log entry that a creature has beamed aboard the ship and can assume any form or shape it wants using the thoughts of others. (This isn't a quote, but that's generally what was said.) Now if they didn't know the creature had beamed aboard, then how could the captain put that fact in his log? Putting aside the theory that the log entries were thought up purely for summarizing the story for those who had missed the first half of the show, or that the log entry was made after the events happened (Kirk was speaking in the present tense), then what is your solution?

*Thank goodness this one's Leslie's! Take it away: "You hit the nail right on the head, Chris. The log entries were simply devices to bring the audience up to date with the action. But to us true believers, anything that happens in the ST universe really happened, right? So, how do we explain Kirk's seemingly psychic knowledge? Kirk (using testimony from crewmembers who had encountered the creature on the surface, and from his own eerie situation vis-à-vis McCoy and*

*Nancy) had tentatively come to the conclusion that a shape-changer was involved. And since there was no evidence that the creature was still on the surface, Kirk was using his usual caution where the safety of his ship was concerned, and risked looking like a bit of a fool in the log entry to ensure that a warning was given and action could be taken should he be killed or injured. There is an unspoken "maybe" in his statement, but Kirk, being the leader that he is, would rather be safe than sorry. And that is a solution which not only fits the known evidence, but is part and parcel of the character of Kirk as we know and love him." Satisfy you, Chris?*

**David G. Anderson, Bristol, Va.**

I am a Trekker of nearly seventeen years of my twenty-one. However, being from a rural community, I have not been able to attend conventions, but I did see Gene Roddenberry at East Tennessee State University and also Leonard Nimoy in 1977 when he visited Virginia Polytechnic Institute, where I study civil engineering. Thank you for *The Best of Trek*. I enjoyed it immensely. I did not previously know your magazine existed.

My present ST diet is the adapted stories by Blish, Alan Dean Foster's excellent ST Logs, all the fan paperbacks and novels, and my tenth or fifteenth viewing of reruns—depending on the whims of local stations. I believe your magazine will fill an important niche for me.

Being a "hard-core" SF reader, an amateur astronomer, and an engineering student (also the ST authority among my friends), I was particularly interested in "The Klingons: Their History and Empire," "The Romulans," "How the Time Warp Drive Works," and "Shortcuts Through Space in ST." The logical conclusions of the latter, however, are seriously contradicted by the galactic layout in the "Starfleet Technical Manual." Personally, I like Mark Golding's hypothesis. It has more possibilities.

I will close for now, until I lay my hands on a regular issue of *Trek*. I have much to ask and say about the *Enterprise*, the crew, the ST universe (from Klingon to Kzin), ST philosophy, and how that philosophy applies to science fiction, science fact, space colonization, and the society of Earth. Until then, a new but old friend. . . .

*Here's a good example of one of the things we keep on our readers about: Write an article! David mentions that he has much to say about almost every aspect of ST—so why not an article, Dave? And that goes for the rest of you readers, too. Write! We've been getting a very good response from purchasers of* The Best of Trek *who want to join in the fun, and most of these submissions have been very, very good. You'll start seeing some of them next issue. But why don't we get more submissions from the thousands of readers who have been reading* Trek *from the beginning?*

*We value everyone equally, but those of you who have become familiar names to us over the past couple of years hold a somewhat special place in our affections. And your letters and comments to us have often contained ideas that our staff is able to turn into an article. So please, if you have that idea, try to follow through with it, and see if it can become an article. Even if your writing talents are not up to Trek standards, the ideas and groundwork you present can serve as the basis for one of our staff to complete your work. Remember, writing talent is a gift and a skill—one which it is unfortunate that not all of us possess. But ideas can occur to everyone.*

*Love for ST, imagination, and the desire to share your feelings with your fellow fans takes no special talent or training, so why not get to work? Remember,* Trek *is directed solely at FANS, so why shouldn't fans do most of the writing?*

### Jeff Heine, Mound, Minn.

A wonderful book! *The Best of Trek* was one of the most pleasing reading experiences I got out of any ST book that I have ever read. I think that it's because this is the work of fans, not professional authors. I got the same feeling from reading the "New Voyages" volumes. I eagerly await *The Best of Trek #2*!

Among my favorite articles were the features on the Klingons and Romulans (don't ever lose Leslie Thompson—she's one person who can write!), and there were several other thought-provoking articles that I liked. One in particular that stirred me was "Star Trek Time Travels" by James Houston. His theories and comments were quite logical indeed, and I sort of question one of Walter Irwin's own views. In particular, "The Naked Time."

Now, when the *Enterprise* went back into time three days, it came out somewhere in the vicinity of Psi 2000. But when the *Enterprise* went back in time, what happened to the *Enterprise* of three days ago? Did it just simply vanish, removed from existence? That seems quite unusual. Because when *Enterprise* A goes back in time, *Enterprise* B cannot just cease to exist. If *Enterprise* B ceased to exist, then it could not go back into time three days later, thus disrupting the cycle.

It's all a complicated mess that I remember reading about in David Gerrold's "The Man Who Folded Himself." One of the premises called for the main character to go back into time, and see himself as an infant, actually be in the same room with the infant (or so my memory tells me). Now, had the character killed himself as a baby, the general theory is that he would cease to exist, thus removing himself. However, Gerrold stated that the character would remain, but he would have created another timeline where he never survived infancy. It's all a mess I hate to pursue. Now here, Walter Irwin's comment makes sense, for perhaps when *Enterprise* A went back in time, it created a new timeline where the *Enterprise* B never existed, but *Enterprise* A now existed. *Enterprise* A wouldn't necessarily have gone on to Psi 2000 again, but it would have to, since didn't Starfleet order it to go there? It could just hang around in the area and say that it had gone to the planet, telling of the adventure that it had experienced the first time.

To me, like Houston, the whole idea seems like a "golly gosh" type of ending thrown in to add a sense of all the marvelous things that can be done with that time period, and no one really thought about what was supposed to happen from then on.

Enough of that, I say! Miss Thompson's "Star Trek Mysteries" articles provided some very fitting answers to some of those inconsistencies. However, I do scratch my head about the idea of Spock "experimenting" with human emotions and such in "The Menagerie." It is very possible that it happened, and I could see Spock doing it. I think we all know the real reason was that at the time the pilot was filmed the Spock character probably wasn't worked out yet.

But some time ago when I was attempting to do a story on Spock's childhood after "Yesteryear," I had worked out a timeline of Spock's life that was quite accurate in that it fit—in age, *pon farr* cycles, etc.—all of those things that had to work out right in order to be consistent.

In my timeline, I blamed Spock's emotional "outbursts," if you will, on the fact that he was going through the *pon farr* cycle at that time. He managed to control it, but he did slip up by doing things that he had been suppressing so long—like smiling in satisfaction, crying out for the women's safety, etc. Leslie also said that these reactions looked forced. Could they have been in the act of being restrained, held back, with no success?

*Jeff had more to say, the most important of which was the fact that his letter in* The Best of Trek *incorrectly gave his home city as being located in New Mexico. Sorry. To make it up, Jeff, we are going to give you a chance to write an article for* Trek. *How about starting with that timeline of Spock's life that every reader out there is itching to get a look at? (Sneaky, aren't we?)*

*Walter is beginning to wish he had never written the addendum to Houston's time-travel article. Everyone has an opinion of time travel, it seems, and everyone wants to debate the issue—strongly. So, in our usual style of further fueling the flames of controversy, we have yet another time-travel article scheduled for the near future. This one is by Mark Golding, who wrote the popular "Time Warp Drive" and "Shortcuts" articles. And if you thought that Jim and Walter's comments caused a stir . . . hoo boy, wait until you read this one.*

*Although Leslie had some qualms about Jeff's explanation for Spock and had to be forcibly restrained from ripping out a short twenty or thirty pages on those qualms, she gives Jeff credit for coming up with yet another possible solution to that particular mystery. Along with, of course, her thanks for his kind words. And she promises that as long as there is a* Trek, *Leslie Thompson will keep writing for it. And that vow makes us just as happy as we are sure it does you readers!*

### Russell Bates, Andarko, Okla.

I do not follow fan publications or even have much of a perusing acquaintance with them. However, a friend directed me to pick up a copy of *The Best of Trek* so that I might read what was said about my animated Star Trek episode, "How Sharper Than a Serpent's Tooth." At first I was amused, then became somewhat thoughtful. The article that ostensibly "analyzed" the animated series went only a few cells deep and consisted mostly of opinion; unfortunately, analysis is not opinion, and most certainly opinion is not fact. As well, "The Animated Star Trek Index" consisted solely of the opinions of a handful and therefore cannot be granted any serious regard because it has but the barest iota of a statistic. If it had been the result of a survey of just your readership, the above would not be true.

Devotees of any media form or formula ordinarily operate in a vacuum, for they are self-appointed participants in that medium. My interpretation of the two articles in *The Best of Trek* is that they were written in ignorance, thus expanding ignorance into a sheer waste of competence. For your edification, I will attempt to provide facts which will demonstrate the levels to which that ignorance has reached.

"How Sharper Than a Serpent's Tooth" was written at the personal request of Dorothy Fontana; she alone approved it and accepted it. The eventual script so enthralled the studio that: (1) they allowed it to be nearly ninety seconds longer than the others and they went several thousand dollars over budget so that it might be done properly; (2) they even went so far as to render certain key scenes in motion-picture-quality full animation out of their pleasure with the script; (3) they were further pleasured with a deluge of favorable mail for that singular episode from parents, teachers, children, and other fans; (4) the episode was subsequently selected to be the American entry in Children's Programming at the 15th International Television Film Festival of Monte Carlo; finally, (5) when the animated Star Trek received a nomination from the Academy of Television Arts and Sciences, the studio submitted "Serpent's Tooth" and no other episodes as the credential for the judging committee. Solely on the basis of that episode, the animated Star Trek won a 1975 Emmy Award for Filmation Studies.

Those are the public facts. The private facts, which I would most happily have provided if I had been consulted, are these: (1) "Serpent's Tooth" bears plot similarity to "Who Mourns for Adonais" out of purpose on my part. Gene L. Coon (who wrote most of that latter episode, despite the credits) was my teacher and my friend. He had died just the year before I finally got to write for Star Trek and my episode consciously became a loving tribute to what he had done for me. (2) The mail from those who saw the show and understood it revealed that the cognizant TV audience (children included) saw beyond the mere *Enterprise*-meets-ancient God plotline and correctly divined the actual point. Since you and your writer seem to have missed it, I will spell it out though the episode did not and did not need to: Parents are gods to children and wish to make the children become what they, the parents, wish them to be. But there comes a time when the parents must let go, when the children must be allowed to go on their own, to succeed or fail by their own hands and minds. End of moral. Where is it, you say? When Kirk and the others finally confront Kukulkan as one-to-one.

KUKULKAN: But I regarded you as my children. I wanted to help you, teach you.

KIRK: But you did. Long ago, when it was needed most. Our people were children then, Kukulkan. But we've grown up now. (Not unkindly) We don't need you anymore.

Subtly, perhaps (and perhaps too subtle for network censors) the episode also addresses the fact that mankind will eventually outgrow its gods and become an adult race in both mind and culture. This was the essence of the best of Star Trek and it is also an essence which is totally lacking from The Best of Trek. Vacuum has no realities save for the one that it is empty. Realities lie not among the stars but on them and their bits of ground encircling. You are the people who look but do not see, taste but do not digest, whiff but do not seek the source, touch but do not respond.

What time is it?

At this retyping, it is exactly 11:45 p.m., Central Standard Time, August 16, 1978

And at 11:45 p.m. on this date, or any other, no unsubtle bit of mystical prose will change the simple fact that realities are indeed, realities.

In this case, Mr. Bates, the realities are these:

All of the points which you mention (except for two) were known to either Bill Norton or the editors (or both) at the time of the writing of this article. The exceptions are the fact that Dorothy Fontana requested and approved "Serpent's Tooth"—although it would be assumed that she would okay it in her position as story editor—and the fact that you wrote the episode as a tribute to Gene L. Coon.

However, to call the articles "ignorant" is folly. Regardless of your position, analysis is opinion, perhaps the purest sort of opinion. To not have intimate knowledge of your personal dealings with D. C. Fontana or Gene Coon is hardly working in a vacuum. How much do you know about Walter Irwin and G. B. Love?

*But back to "opinion." The fact that Filmation decided to give your episode more time and money (I'm sorry, but I am a lifelong animation fan, and I saw little of the "motion-picture-quality full animation" in the episode) is their opinion. The mail which you received was opinion. The decision to enter the episode in the festival was opinion. The decision of the judging committee to award the Emmy was opinion.*

*How then, basing your objections to the articles on the above-stated opinions, can you state that the conclusions of the articles are invalid just because they are—opinions? We won't have the temerity to stack up our opinions (or fan support of them) against Dorothy Fontana, or even the officials at Filmation, the festival, or the Academy.*

*However, they could be wrong, just as we could. And with that element of doubt entering into the picture, all opinions become equal in value.*

*Contrary to your belief, we did not miss the point of the episode. As if we could have. And we agree—growth, change, and development are perhaps the very essence of Star Trek. Our feelings on this are briefly stated in our introduction to* The Best of Trek, *which apparently you failed to read.*

*But we (and excluding Bill Norton here) saw "Serpent's Tooth" as a mere bow to the essence of ST. Setting up the "god" situation, and having your characters boldly state, "We don't need you anymore," is an easy way to show the development that Star Trek promises. It is much more difficult to portray this growth of understanding and freedom of man without a godlike antagonist. If this same message had been stated in much more subtle terminology, in a completely different format—through the actions and beliefs of the characters—perhaps we would have lauded your work, instead of giving it the little consideration we felt it deserved.*

**Paula Soloway, Morristown, N.J.**

I have dabbled in Star Trek since 1967, when it first occurred to me that it was the only portrayal of the future that didn't leave me fearing the world to come. It seemed a viable, real place to live.

In one of your articles a definition of different types of fans is given. I guess I've been all of them; Star Trek has reached me at all levels, all depths.

Things have really changed. On the network, Star Trek was

an embarrassing stepchild. Its fans, wierdos. When it was canceled, everything stopped and we all were numb. A world with no future? William Shatner saying, "Star Trek is dead," when I saw him at a summer stock performance talking to fans. Once ST reached syndication, I rushed to make tape recordings of all the episodes; by 1971 I had them all. Then slowly Star Trek began picking up momentum. Followers really seemed to emerge from the walls. Rebirth. Books, novels, etc. Lincoln Enterprises got a lot of business from me.

My interest remains at a guaranteed minimum which flares up at times. I still watch it, read it, listen to it, and dream. I avoid most of the third-season shows—they are hardly better than "Lost in Space" at its best, and painful it is to see things slipping before your eyes.

I hope whatever form this *Star Trek II* takes, it recaptures the high standards reached so many times in the first two seasons and puts us all back on that very familiar bridge amidst old friends.

### Debra Sara Greenblat, New York, N.Y.

I enjoyed *The Best of Trek* very much, so much that my check for a subscription is enclosed. However, I do have a couple of negative comments.

As a woman, I object to the part of your introduction where you say, "Star Trek is a very personal thing to each . . . fan. *His* hopes . . . are embodied in what *he* perceives ST to be. . . ." Don't you think in this day of increasing freedom to women, perhaps partially spearheaded by Star Trek, you could use "he/she" or "he and she"?

As a mathematics teacher, I object to " . . . but ST is still met by the average critic with as much love and understanding as integral calculus." You seem to be condoning the view that integral calc is worthy of such depreciation. It seems contradictory when compared to your later ". . . gain the necessary skills to change our technology and society."

Thanks again for an exciting experience.

*No slight intended in either case, Debra. To our way of thinking, the increasingly common use of asexual terminology in our language is not only awkard (such as amending useful and common words ending in "man" to "person") but, from the view of individual freedoms, self-defeating. The basic goal of human rights should be an ability to be recognized as part of the human race, regardless of sex, color, or the like. Adding on subgeneric suffixes to ordinary words only serves to point out differences, not disguise them. A congressman is still a congressman, while a woman is a congressperson. Aside from our desire to recognize all of our readers as equals (and a large percentage of them are women) we feel that the longstanding and technically correct usage of "he" is preferable to having our prose convoluted with patently artificial attempts to cover all bases.*

*In the case of calc, we plead guilty. Knowing that most of our readers had as little fun as we did with integral calculus in school, we associated it with a sharp pain in the nether regions. But we never had any intention of slighting its importance as a tool in helping to build our future. However, we feel that the analogy still stands. Most critics do not and most probably will not bother to understand or view Star Trek with any intelligence or affection.*

### Patricia Napolitano, Hillside, Ill.

I just finished reading my first issue of *Trek*. I enjoyed all the articles, but especially "Trek Roundtable." It's nice to be able to give a little feedback to a magazine. So here goes— my humble opinion on ST and S-F to share with other readers.

First, I'd like to say that the main reason I subscribed is to get some reliable info on the new ST movie. I've heard many contradicting rumors about ST returning, or not returning, as a series, a film, a special, with or without the original cast, etc.—but still no sign of a new ST show. I do not want details of the plot—I'd rather be surprised—but I would like to know if a new ST show is really in the works or not. I've written to TV execs asking for ST's return and would write again if it would do any good.

Assuming there will be an ST movie, here are my views on some subjects discussed in your last "Roundtable."

My objection to Arex and particularly M'Ress is not based on racism but on the credibility of the characters. Wouldn't a man-sized kitty like M'Ress roar, not purr; and be powerful and fast and move like a big cat instead of walking on hind legs and comfortably sitting on chairs, handling instruments, and wearing clothes designed for humanoids? The lady should be a tiger, not a cousin of the Pink Panther. I suppose that "in the flesh" she might look more convincing, but in cartoon form she made me wonder when Peter Rabbit or Mighty Mouse was going to turn up.

It has occurred to me that since she is not from Earth, she

might not behave like an Earth cat, but then why does she look like an Earth cat? I might accept an alien-looking felinoid, but not one that looks just like an oversize pussycat.

Also, while it adds atmosphere to dress up a scene with weird-looking aliens (like the cantina scene in *Star Wars*), if they were going to be a big part of the continuing story, they should develop some character. Spock is different not only in his physical makeup, but in his mental makeup as well. Arex and M'Ress didn't get much chance to show any character.

Of course I want to see more aliens, new ones never met before, and old "friends" like the Klingons. Personally, I'd like to see more Andorians. They were fascinating, so fragile-looking, yet with a self-confessed violent nature, and apparently they had a long and complex history behind them. Are there any more fans who want to learn more about the Andorians?

As to the time of the movie: I don't object to *Star Trek II* taking into account the years since the show has been canceled, but it certainly is not necessary. After all, the time depicted in the show was "dramatic" future time, not our present. Although the show appeared on our screens every Thursday, no one thought that Kirk and company saved the galaxy regularly once a week.

The show lasted an hour, but the events portrayed lasted several hours, or days, even months. References to past episodes and recurring characters gave a nice feeling of continuity and reality to the background or "world" created in ST; but, although some episodes obviously followed others, we were never told how long a time elapsed between shows.

Also, two interesting problems arise if *Star Trek II* takes place six years after the original: The *Enterprise*'s mission was only for five years. What happens after that? The only survivor of the *Enterprise*'s original mission seems to be Spock, who moved up to Number One's position of first officer. Surely after this mission, members of "the finest crew in the fleet" are due for some promotions and probably transfers. Possibly Spock would become captain of the *Enterprise* or some other ship. Kirk might be made an admiral or governor of a colony, etc. McCoy might be assigned to a mission to a new world or go into research on some colony, etc.

Also: I don't know what year of the mission it was that Spock went through his "amok time," but isn't it just about time for him to go through another?

I understand your magazine is not strictly ST and sometimes does articles on other S-F shows. I'd like to know if anyone else enjoyed, or even saw, that S-F comedy *Quark*. It has disappeared from my Chicagoland TV screen, and I assume it was canceled due to poor ratings. I admit I was disappointed in it at first, but something about the show kept me tuning in. It "grew on me," I guess. *Quark* definitely had its problems, but it also had some good, funny scenes. At least it *tried*—something that shows like *Lost in Space* and *UFO* seem unwilling to do. And after all, a show with a villain called Zorcon the Malevolent (not to mention his daughter Libido) cannot be all bad. I'd enjoy an article on *Quark*. I think that with more shakedown time, it might have developed a respectable following.

*We enjoyed* Quark *too, Patricia. We'd like very much to do an article on it, especially pointing up the parodies of ST contained in the shows. How would you readers like to see such an article?*

**Scott Hoyer, Olympia, Wash.**

Apparently the problem has not been solved. The debate as to what materials should be included in *Trek* continues unabated, and now that *Star Wars* has been dropped upon us, it would seem that it will get hotter instead of subsiding.

All right, let's analyze this in a logical manner. First off, *Trek* is a special magazine; its very name seems to indicate that this publication is, as it says on the cover, a magazine for Star Trek fans. Now, if you are going to be true to your cover, this automatically eliminates the running of articles of a non-Star Trek nature, mainly because Star Trek fans are interested in Star Trek, and if your magazine is going to be for Star Trek fans you must run what they are interested in. So you want to put a little diversity in, okay—what about *Star Wars*. But if that, why not *Voyage to the Bottom of the Sea* or *lost in space* (noncapitalization intended), and while you're at it, why not change your magazine to *Starlog II*?

You see, diversity is great but there is such a thing as going overboard, especially when it is diversity just for the sake of looking diverse. I think some of these letters to the "Roundtable" have been giving our dear editors a guilt complex.

What I find absolutely disgusting are those letters that claim we are betraying the Star Trek philosophy of IDIC because we voice disapproval of *Space 1999*. If you will look at the philosophy of IDIC, you will see that it advocates not just throwing together differences, but instead the combinations that those differences can make to produce meaning and beauty. And that's the crux of the matter—meaning and beauty. After seeing all the meaning and beauty produced by the combination of differences on Star Trek, I find it most unsatisfying to watch *1999* and, though looking, finding none of either. I do not wish to offend anyone, but *Space 1999* has a definite negative impact. When Star Trek came along it said, "Yes, man can succeed, we can have a wise and noble future, we can be masters of our destiny."

*Space 1999* says, "Oh, gee, we're lost in space again." Now *Space* had its good points—sets, SFX, costumes, competent actors—but it lacked what it needed most, what really counted: good stories, stories about something, stories with meaning.

So when we boo *1999* at conventions, it's not merely because it's not Star Trek; we boo it because a good set isn't worth a darn if it's misused, and more important, because it destroys all we dream about for the future of mankind.

Our editors still clamor for diversity, and the point is well taken. But think—do we really need to expand into the realm of fiction, when it would be much more valuable and probably just as exciting to expand into the realm of fact? One of the main reasons for Star Trek's popularity is the fact that many of the shows taught us something about real life. Star Trek covered just about every realm of human existence—from war to love, from religion to human rights, from the ideal man to lethargic nonproductivity, and if that's not diversity, what is? Star Trek was not Sunday morning with Billy Graham; it didn't say: If you do thus and such, mankind will achieve the stars.

Star Trek gave us a dream to work toward, but it is up to us to translate that dream to reality and figure out how to get there. *Trek* magazine is in the unique position to be able to carry on what Star Trek started. Let's get our brains together, and through the medium of this publication, let's try to figure out how to reach the stars, how to have a future such as Star Trek portrays. Let's try to find a way to end war, to instill people with the ideals of IDIC, to eliminate prejudice. It has been said that NASA could use a fandom like Star Trek's. Well, let's offer the services of that fandom. It has been said that support for the dream is support for the fact, and it's true, it's no good to just dream about it. We've got to work to get there, and this magazine might very well play a major role in getting us there. You want diversity? With a format like that you'll never run out of things to talk and write about.

*Star Wars*, as I have said before, might just add fuel to the debate fire. My hope is that you do not run articles about it ever again. *Star Wars* was just flashy mindless fun; I learned nothing about reality from it. I know, the cry goes up to quit trying to learn something from it, sit back and enjoy it. So I did, three times, and it was still mindless action. "But it was fun," some insist. Okay, it was fun. But every once in a while I'll be sitting around thinking about it, and I wonder—if killing bad guys and blowing up planets and death stars and assorted dogfights and ending human life is what we consider fun, then just what kind of people are we?

I think that the moral of this letter is: Reserve *Trek* for Star Trek. And if ever you feel the need for diversity, just remember the diversity of Star Trek; I'm sure you'll find something meaningful and beautiful and different. You need not go searching the sewers of the science-fiction world for something to write about in your magazine, in the name of diversity.

**Ken Janasz, Leavenworth, Kan.**

I must first commend Leslie Thompson on her fine article "A Brief Look at Kirk's Career." A most logical extrapolation of what little is already known about the good Captain. We were witness to the birth of a legend, learning more of just how special the man called Kirk really is. Once again Leslie has displayed talents that I'm sure Kirk would feel would qualify her for his crew.

And this is the sort of thing *Trek* should be primarily concerned with. *Trek* should always have one article dealing with an interpretation of the facts-without-fullness aspects of the Star Trek universe. You have done this in the past and should continue it in the future.

But filling in the gaps is only one direction this magazine should take. Keep the "Roundtable" and articles on the stars' lives and accomplishments outside of Star Trek. Then perhaps a couple more articles concerning ST. But, to paraphrase Kirk in "The Trouble With Tribbles": "Too much of anything isn't necessarily a good thing." *Trek* should take a new direction and delve into other aspects of science fiction.

Don't start mass-producing articles on anything, though. Choose one subject, such as the new science fiction shows on television as Leigh Rogers suggested, and examine them the way you've examined Star Trek. Continue each subject through two or three issues so that you can go in depth on the subject. And you need not print what every other magazine has printed; keep it on a personal level, what your thoughts and opinions are as well as those of your readers. Treat each subject as you have treated *Star Trek*, with respect. This kind of diversification will keep *Trek* at the top of the high-quality magazines.

*There you have it readers. The two sides of our dilemma. Half of our readers clamoring for nothing but Star Trek, others just as insistent that we feature more non-ST material. It is a question which has plagued us since the beginnings of* Trek, *and still we have no clear-cut mandate from our readership either way.*

*In answer to Scott, we do not feel that it is within our purview to offer "educational" articles. We always strive to keep as much of value in what we present as possible, but the resources needed to present factual and accurate articles on space, society, and our world are beyond both our means and our intent at this time.* Trek, *like Star Trek itself, is meant primarily for entertainment. If our readers learn a little something along the way, great, but only if they are enjoying themselves while doing so. We feel that the small part we play in helping to keep the dream of Star Trek alive is our greatest contribution to building a better tomorrow. If we tried to go any further, we would be cheating our readers in two ways.*

*Back to the question of non-ST material, however. As you have read at the beginning of the "Roundtable,"* Trek Special *is now to be a regular publication. And although we will continue to showcase ST in* Special, *it seems to us to be a better place for articles and features about other realms of s-f than* Trek. *So, in a way, our readers can have their cake and eat it too, as we will stick strictly to ST in* Trek, *and present the diversity many of you ask for in* Trek Special.

*Leslie thanks Ken for his kind words, but wonders just what a writer would do on a starship . . . and has an answer. Plus several other occupations you would not expect to find on the* Enterprise. *So you can expect an article very soon. . . .*

**Mary Jo Lawrence, Bartlett, Ill.**

We were extremely interested in your review of Marshak and Culbreath's *New Voyages 2* in "Trekviews." It was a sensitive and highly intelligent review. Your opinions, by the way, coincided *exactly* with ours. We even wrote the ladies to that effect. The "closed-shop" attitude, as you say, was disappointing, to say the least; but we were really more frustrated at the caliber and lack of imagination shown in the stories in *NV 2* (except for "Snakepit" and "Petard"). The stories in *New Voyages 1* were so much more interesting to us. What can compare to Spock's reaction to the irresistible "sprite" in 'The Enchanted Pool" or the depth of feeling expressed in "The Mind Sifter"?

In case someone hasn't read Joan Winston's book *The Making of the Trek Conventions*, it's a behind-the-scenes look at the organization and planning that went on during the New York (and some other) cons. While Miss Winston tries to tell us, as do Marshak and Culbreath, that the cons started out by a bunch of fans saying, "Hey, let's have a con!" to me the book said that if you don't call William Shatner "Bill" or DeForrest Kelley "De" or Gene Roddenberry, Jr., "Little Rod," you've missed the boat. Well, I'm sorry, but the closest I've come to any of them is tenth-row seats to see Shatner with the Chicago Philharmonic in June. He went onstage for about ten minutes to do a reading from Arthur C. Clarke. But that doesn't make me any less a loyal fan than Miss Winston. She just happens to be in a position to know people.

# 11.

# A NEW YEAR'S REVOLUTION

by Mary Jo Lawrence

*Discussing personal feelings and experiences is often a difficult thing to do, but Star Trek fans seem to have the ability to manage it a little more easily than the average person. This is not difficult to understand, as the philosophy of the IDIC welcomes the exchanging of individual views and experiences, and most Star Trek fans try to follow this example of sharing and finding joy in our diversities. Mary Jo Lawrence's story is a perfect example of this sharing between fans.*

This is the history of the transformation of a biased, Federation-snubbing science-fiction fan into a *Concordance*-carrying, story-writing, magazine-subscribing Trekker.

It all started with a pair of books—a friend's innocent-looking Christmas present. She had read one and liked it. Knowing that I've been a science-fiction fan for most of my life, she casually mentioned that she had a book I might be interested in. The title was *The Star Trek Reader* by James Blish.

To say that I accepted the loan of the book unenthusiastically would be an understatement. "Reluctantly" would be more like it. After all, I told myself haughtily, I'm used to reading the best: Asimov, Bradbury, Clarke, Heinlein . . . There's nothing worse than poor science fiction—"pulp." But Paula is my best friend (we've been like Lucy and Ethel since second grade) and, even though I didn't have much faith in her opinion of science fiction, I told her, "Sure, I'd like to read it."

That was in January 1978—twelve years and four months after Star Trek premiered on NBC television. It was also the beginning of my slide into the world of stardates and antimatter nacelles. In a few short months I became a confirmed Trekoholic with no desire to cure myself, and, after seven years of marriage, my husband had given up trying to find out what makes me tick and was trying to find out what makes me Trek!

I was eighteen when "The Man Trap" first aired on NBC—a ripe age to be swept up in the initial Trekmania— but somehow, although a few of my friends wouldn't miss an episode, I never saw one. I told myself that television always ruins science fiction and this would be no different, so I steadfastly refused to watch Star Trek. Eventually it faded into the recesses of my mind along with the withered corsages and sorority rushes that were all part of my college years. I was dimly aware that the local television station kept rerunning the series (and rerunning it, and rerunning it) but it simply held no fascination for me.

James Blish changed all that. By the time I'd read "Errand of Mercy" (the fourth story in the volume), I was hooked. Housework and children's baths all seemed very unimportant and far away as I eagerly devoured the seventeen remaining stories.

Soon I was on the phone to my friend demanding the next book, *The Star Trek Reader II*. She wasn't done with it yet and wouldn't give it up, but promised to bring it over when she finished. Impatiently aware that it could be a week before I got the book, I ran to my library and breathed a sigh of relief when I saw it sitting on the shelf, just waiting, I thought, for me to take it home. Ironically, that was the last time I ever saw it on the library shelf. Months later, after noticing its conspicuous absence, I questioned the librarian. She seemed surprised that I didn't know that the Blish books were rarely on the shelf. They are snapped up as fast as they are returned.

For a while, then, I was at a standstill. My friend and my library didn't have any more books. So I halfheartedly began to watch the television episodes, being careful to avoid the ones I haven't read yet. I had enjoyed Blish immensely, but I still couldn't shake the prejudice I felt about visual science fiction. I didn't want the series to ruin my enjoyment of the written word. Gradually it dawned on me that what I was watching was even more outstanding than what I was reading.

I was moving, episode by episode, into "Trekstacy"—stage 1. Every evening by 7:00 I had done the dishes and settled the children so I could sink down in front of the tube and, for an hour, lose myself in the adventures of my favorite starship crew. Soon I was scheduling meetings and parties "after 8:00," and woe betide the child who disturbed my viewing with anything less important than a gaping wound that required stitches.

My only concession in this area was my weekly astronomy class. It met between 7:00 and 8:00 every Tuesday evening. It killed me to give up an hour of Star Trek, but, as I'm equally interested in astronomy, I had to make a choice. Besides, my friend Paula was taking the course with me and she wouldn't be able to watch it either. You see, we have a friendly rivalry going on. She had been Trekking right along, on the basis of Blish, too. We felt lucky to have each other, since, we were certain, no one else was still interested in Star Trek. How much interest can a "dead" TV series command? (Little did we know.)

One day, Paula found a magazine called *Starlog*. It was a special Star Trek issue. She shelled out an unheard of $1.75 (Paula's a notorious nickel-nurser) and made me a present of it. I read all the articles with avid interest, but considered myself too aloof to subscribe to any of the "crazy" fan magazines I saw advertised.

The part of the magazine that really caught my eye was an advertisement for the Science Fiction Book Club. Volume III of Blish was one of the books offered for an introductory membership. I'd been wanting to join anyway, so I sent in my name and received, in turn, two copies of *The Star Trek Reader III*—one for me and one for Paula. She joined the club shortly thereafter, and we both ordered Volume IV, as a selection, a couple of months later. To complete my set, I also ordered volumes I and II.

Spurred on by the discovery, in March, of *Starlog*, I began haunting the local magazine racks. This was the beginning of my rollercoastering between peaks of sheer delight and depths of frustration and despair as I sailed into stage 2 of my Trekstacy. When I chanced to find something like a *Star Trek Poster Book* or the special Star Trek issue of *Science and Fantasy*, my spirits would soar and I'd walk on air until I could get home and dive into it. Then, weeks would go by and I wouldn't find anything. All the color would drain out of my life. My phone calls to Paula would be filled with remorse and self-reproach. Why hadn't I gotten interested in Star Trek back in college when it was a current rage? Surely there was a lot more available then. I was still painfully unaware of the wealth of books and magazines that are available. My conception of ongoing interest in Star Trek, like most of the uninformed, was that of the "Trekkie" and I was really put off by the image. I even heard about some guy calling himself a lieutenant in Starfleet who had established an "outpost" which I supposed was some sort of fan club. If this was Star Trek fandom I wanted no part of it! As much as I loved the show and as big a Kirkophile as I was becoming, I just couldn't picture myself as a thirty-year-old Trekkie! Maybe this could have been called "The Winter of My Discontent," which carried me into stage 3.

I was becoming resigned to my fate. While I continued to watch the episodes and wander aimlessly through the magazine section at the supermarket, I had abandoned all hope of finding Star Trek alive and well and living—anywhere!

Stage 4 was ushered in, again by Paula. She saw a book in a hobby shop near her mother's house. When I say "saw" I mean that she was unwilling to put out $6.95 for something called a *Star Trek Concordance*; but hoping to intrigue me into buying it, she told me all about it—stressing the fan artwork and the lexicon. Still put off by what I considered the Trekkie image, I told her something like, "Thanks, but no thanks."

A couple of days later, after a series of inner debates, I caved in. I decided that, if I'm a Trekkie, so be it! I called Paula and mentioned, as nonchalantly as I could, that if she happened to be in the vicinity of that hobby shop I guessed she could pick me up a copy of that *Concordance*. So it was that I was dragged, kicking and screaming, into actively pursuing my growing interest in Star Trek. And I pulled a curiously unprotesting Paula right along with me. It was the old Lucy and Ethel syndrome again. My first contact with Blish seemed ages ago. Actually, it had only been four months.

As I was making one of my by now routine tours of the local magazine racks, I spied something over by the paperback section. It was an anemic-looking little thing, put out by Bantam Books, with a picture of my beloved *Enterprise* on the cover. It was titled *Star Trek Book 12* by James Blish and J. A. Lawrence. I grabbed for it like a starving man clutching a Big Mac. The remaining adaptations (minus the Mudd stories) that weren't in my hardbound volumes! I was deliriously euphoric!

But the best part of the book was on the last page. There

was a list of *available books*! Every one of them was about Star Trek! At last! No more scrounging for pitiful out-of-date magazine articles! People were actually writing books about every aspect of Star Trek! Incredibly, they were even writing Star Trek novels and getting them published! After months of drought—rain!

I practically danced my way into stage 5. Realizing that I couldn't start spending dozens of dollars on paperback books (I was still rational enough to remember that my children need milk), I mobilized Paula and between us we started methodically raiding libraries. At first we hit the local ones and then the proximately local ones. By now we've plundered every library within twenty-five miles. Thank God for the interlibrary loan system!

What we couldn't find (and some of the things we did find) in libraries we continued to look for in bookstores. I was amazed to see Paula spending money like water, as long as it was for Star Trek. Slowly, inexorably, our own little libraries grew, and as our collections expanded so did our knowledge.

Pretty soon I felt that I hadn't missed so much back in the '60s after all. Books like Stephen Whitfield's *The Making of Star Trek* and David Gerrold's *The Trouble with Tribbles* and *The World of Star Trek* went a long way toward filling me in on the behind-the-scenes stuff that is so important to making you feel close to Gene Roddenberry's world of the future. I found myself using words like "Great Bird of the Galaxy" and "Organian Peace Treaty" and my speech was peppered with references to people and things like Larry Marvick and cordrazine. But best of all, I discovered the difference between "Trekkies" and "Trekkers". I decided that I definitely wanted to be a Trekker! I think the chapter titled "A Look at Star Trek Fandom" in *The Best of Trek* has an excellent description of the difference between the two types of fans.

"The Trek*er* is the backbone of Fandom—the more mature Fans. Trekkers run the various organizations, and are the workers, the editors, and officers—the doers and movers of Fandom. . . . [They] enjoy *Star Trek* for its dramatic impact, the interpersonal relationships and the ideas and ideals that compose it."

On the other hand: "The Trekk*ies* are the obnoxious little creatures that are forever underfoot at Cons and meetings: Running after the guests, demanding autographs and souvenirs in loud voices and drooling at the sight of one of the show's stars."

Well, I might salivate a drop or two "at the sight of one of the show's stars," but otherwise the description of the Trekker fits me to a tee and I was determined to become a "doer."

In May came the announcement of the Star Trek motion picture. My daily regimen began to include a quick combing through the newspapers for any further press releases, so how I missed it, I'll never know, but miss it I did. Paula to the rescue again! She called me one Monday and was all excited. "*He* is coming to Alpine Valley Music Theater." When I could get her calmed down enough to find out who *he* was, I found out that the Chicago Philharmonic Orchestra would be appearing in a concert that was to include selections from *Star Wars, Close Encounters,* and *2001,* and excerpts from science fiction to be read by (ta da) William Shatner!

It was obvious to us that we had to be at that concert. We'd read rave reviews about a similar performance he had given at the Hollywood Bowl with Zubin Mehta and the Los Angeles Philharmonic. However, it was equally obvious that Alpine Valley was in Wisconsin, two and a half hours' drive away! We began to speculate on how our husbands would react to us going all that way just to see William Shatner. They don't share our enthusiasm for Star Trek, and find it incomprehensible that we can spend so much time and energy on a television show. They feel that it's perfectly logical to spend fifteen hours every weekend watching football, however. The trials of a Trekker living with a non-Trekker could fill another whole article.

Paula's husband outright refused to go to the concert—so did mine, but I had an ace up my sleeve. It was scheduled for the same weekend as our wedding anniversary. So I wheedled him into it and when he finally, reluctantly agreed to take me, I innocently asked him if he'd mind if Paula came along too! Mumbling something like "It'll all come out in the divorce proceedings," he good-naturedly resigned himself to chauffering us to Wisconsin and back.

The concert was still six weeks off and the ad in the newspaper had been relatively small, so we were supremely confident that we'd be able to get some of the best seats in the house. We never thought that William Shatner would command much of an audience in a backwater little town in southern Wisconsin. Our first shock came the next day when we went to order our tickets. Already, the best seats available were in the tenth row, slightly to the left of the stage. At least they were aisle seats. Swallowing our disappointment, we went home with what we considered less than perfect seat designations; but when the night of the concert arrived we were thankful a dozen times over that our seats were as good as they were. We had underestimated the loyalty of the legion of Trekkers in the Chicago-Milwaukee area. Our second shock came when we filed into the theater. Alpine Valley is an open-air arena, and there were literally thousands of people spilling out of the seats and onto the grass all up and down the hillside.

Everyone sat politely through the musical portion of the concert. We tried not to get too restless as we waited for the star performer. Finally, after what seemed a millennium, the moment arrived. A hushed expectancy came over the audience, and then, as Shatner was introduced, the crowd exploded with a display of wild, reckless enthusiasm.

Our hero did a reading from Arthur Clarke's *Childhood's End* that seemed all too short, and exited to a standing ovation. Although Shatner did a superb job, Paula and I couldn't help but feel just a little bit cheated. The newspaper ad had specifically stated "readings" by William Shatner. He had done only one, for a total onstage time of fifteen minutes. We kept thinking that he'd come back on for an encore, but he didn't. All in all, though, even my skeptical husband had to admit on the way home that it had been a very enjoyable evening. The orchestra was excellent, he said, and even our "Captain Kirk" had done an adequate job! Adequate?! With that we ganged up on him and mercilessly spouted Trek trivia at him until he hollered "Spock!"

The concert was in the beginning of June and a long, sultry Chicago summer loomed before me, with little on the Star Trek horizon to look forward to. It was when June was stretching hopelessly into July that I read *Star Trek: The New Voyages*. Sondra Marshak and Myrna Culbreath became my new idols and I eagerly started making the rounds of the bookstores looking for their books.

By the time I got hold of *New Voyages 2*, I'd pretty much decided to take the editors at their bidding in the preface and submit a story for consideration in future volumes. Even if they thought my humble effort was terrible, at least it would be something to get me through the summer. I was now watching Star Trek three times a day on various channels (one of the advantages of living in a large metropolitan area) and reading voraciously. I was itching to put aside my passivity and use the knowledge I had been so painstakingly acquiring.

So, typewriter in hand, I plunged into stage 6, and, in what seemed like no time at all, my original (and two carbons) story was written and quickly (before I changed my mind) dispatched to Marshak and Culbreath in Baton Rouge. The reading public may never see it in print, but it's amazing how therapeutic it was just to write it! I'd had an idea clanging around in my head about how Kirk and Spock first met and was really anxious to marshal my thoughts and get it down in black and white. Meanwhile, I was writing letters. Letters to the Welcommittee, letters to fan magazines and letters to "Sondra and Myrna." My enthusiasm was running at an all-time high.

Stage 6 almost came to a screeching halt when I found Joan Winston's *The Making of the Trek Conventions*—a book that gives the reader an intimate behind-the-scenes look at Star Trek cons. The best thing I can say about Miss Winston's book is that it has lots of photographs and six great, hundred-question trivia quizzes. It's worth getting for those alone. But just when I was starting to feel secure in my abiding regard for Star Trek and Star Trek fandom, that book put me back about five stages! Miss Winston and her cronies were on the "inside Trek" and she obviously wanted us to know it. I began to feel like a little girl on the outside of a candy store with her nose pressed against the window.

My concern deepened as I found a dismal pattern emerging. Joan Winston, Jackie Lichtenberg, and Sondra Marshak (who collaborated on the popular *Star Trek Lives!*) were right in the center of an elitist group which expanded, as the narrative progressed, to include Myrna Culbreath (of course) and, to my growing consternation, such people as Shirley Maiewski and Connie Faddis. Now these are all very versatile and extremely talented people, but, as I checked back over the list of contributing authors in my volumes of *The New Voyages*, I found my suspicions completely confirmed. It was these, along with such obvious insiders as Nichelle Nichols and Jescoe von Puttkamer, Russell Bates (who wrote a script for the animateds) and Jennifer Guttridge (who was published in both volumes), who were getting their work into print. This was in direct conflict with what Marshak and Culbreath were purporting in their prefaces. It seemed that if you wanted to get anywhere in Star Trek fandom it wasn't *what* you knew, it was *who* you knew.

There are thousands of artistic Trekkers in the world, but only a handful of mutually supportive individuals are getting to share their talent and ideas with the rest of us. I was angry and hurt by what I felt was a betrayal of everything Star Trek fandom stood for. I could feel my enthusiasm ebb and my momentum come to a grinding halt.

I was right back where I started: If this was Star Trek fandom, I wanted no part of it. I continued to watch my episodes three times a day, but all the joy went out of my viewing. I even considered giving Paula all my accumulated Star Trek stuff.

Fortunately (for me—unfortunately for Paula's Star Trek collection), I'm a very resilient person and my love for the series and everything connected with it struggled to the surface. It wasn't long before Paula and I were hitting the bookstore trail again and I became very philosophical about the feelings that erupted as a result of Joan Winston's book. After all, I *am* a Johnny-come-lately and I'm probably destined to remain a little fish in a big pond; but what a "pond" it is! It's a midnight-blue sea that encompasses an entire galaxy of dreams and includes some of the brightest stars in the universe! I'm firmly convinced that I'm in great company, and I'm strangely comforted by the philosophy of IDIC. I feel that Star Trek fans are followers of a vision, and our strength lies in the combination of our diversity. I even have new respect for the "lieutenant" who established his "outpost." If this is Star Trek fandom, I want all parts of it!

My only regret, so far, is that I didn't become involved at least a couple of years sooner. As it is, I missed the big con that was held in Chicago in 1975, and there hasn't been one held here since. Besides, now that the motion picture is into production, it will be increasingly more difficult to get any of the *Enterprise* crew to attend a con. Also, in connection with this is the fact that I've never seen the famed "blooper reel." My brother saw it when Jimmy Doohan appeared at his college last year, and his descriptions of it merely serve to whet my appetite.

As to what the future holds . . . At every new plateau I was certain that I could go no further, and each time I was proved wrong. I've only been at this a year, but I'm certain that my faith in the concepts of IDIC will be justified and that Star Trek will continue to provide infinite source material to bolster an ever-changing fandom. Meanwhile Paula and I will continue to Lucy and Ethel our way through Trekdom overcoming occasional fits of despondency when things seem to stagnate.

Is there Trekstacy past stage 6? Maybe someone ought to write an article and tell *me*!

# 12.
# CAPTAIN KIRK'S DUTIES

by G. B. Love

*We've all seen Kirk save the universe a dozen times, but what does he do on a day-to-day basis? Surely he has to have some other job than ordering course changes and warp speeds. This question occured to G.B., and with typical attention to detail and a firm grounding in reality, he extrapolated a fairly accurate picture of what it means to be a starship captain.*

James T. Kirk is the Captain of the Starship *Enterprise.* This we well know, but how many of us know of or appreciate the extent of the duties and powers to which this position entitles him?

We can easily relate that Kirk is the commander of the *Enterprise*, he is assigned to seek out new life, new civilizations, etc., and that he has a complement of over 430 crewmembers. But as to specific duties . . . well, that is a little tougher.

As a starship commander, Kirk is required to perform the following (in the absence of any higher Federation or Starfleet authority):

He is military commander of any space sector in which he happens to be located. This means that Kirk is pretty much allowed the freedom to assemble ships in a fleet, mount or react to an attack, and declare his sector in a state of war. Lesser powers under this command are the ability to restrict travel and shipping, declare martial law, and take and hold prisoners.

Kirk is also automatically appointed military governor of any colonies, outposts, or expeditions in his space sector. In this capacity, he is the final arbiter of the disbursement of materials, persons, or facilities of these outposts. He is also authorized to settle any disputes over claims or territorial rights. If he feels the need is dire enough, Kirk may severely restrict the activities of these outposts, or even go so far as to completely shut them down.

Kirk is the supervisor of any interstellar commerce, trade, or shipping in his space sector. This gives him the leeway to either aid or restrict such trade according to the current conditions or requirements of the Federation.

He is the official representative of the Federation to any aligned or unaligned worlds or peoples in his sector. In this capacity, Kirk has the power to open negotiations, arrange for trade and cultural exchange, and make temporary treaties of peace or partnership. He is also responsible for the protection and stewardship of underdeveloped worlds and peoples according to the Prime Directive.

Kirk also serves as chief legal official of the Federation. In this guise, he is empowered to convene court-martials, trials, and boards of inquiry. He must see that local laws and customs adhere to Federation tenets, and that these laws are administered fairly and impartially. In some cases, he must act as a court of review or appeal. In other cases, he would have to serve as both judge and jury; in very rare and expedient cases, even as executioner.

All of these duties overlap to some extent, and there are many times in the experiences of a starship commander when even these explicit powers are not enough, and must be overstepped at the captain's discretion.

But what is a "higher Federation or Starfleet authority"? And in what circumstances can Kirk act on his own?

First, we must look at the hierarchy of Starfleet command, and see just where in that hierarchy a starship commander stands.

The United Federation of Planets is controlled by the Federation Council, which is made up of members from all planets in the Federation. The members are appointed by their respective planetary governments, but in extraordinary cases (such as that of the Vulcan T-'Pau) an invitation may be given to an individual from one of the member planets to serve on the council as an adviser. In this manner, the wisdom and experience of many beings are contributed to the council without their having to represent the interests of any particular planet.

Starfleet is the military and explorative arm of the Federation. A commander in chief of the United Starfleet forces sits on the council, and he is the head of the chiefs of staff who are responsible for the overall operations of Starfleet.

The chiefs of staff are all of admiral rank, and each is a representative of one of the following Starfleet sections: Infantry, the Fleet, Procurement, Security, Intelligence, Starbases, Science and Exploration, Colonies and Outposts, Diplomacy, and the Merchant Marine and private shipping. In the case of the far-seeking starships, these sections overlap in many areas, so line admirals are responsible for the actual operations of the ships themselves.

Fleet captains assist the line admirals in these duties, and each is responsible for a specific line of ships. Christopher Pike was promoted to captain in charge of starships before his debilitating accident. (On service records, fleet captain carries the rank of admiral. The title is only one of convenience, and most of the fleet captains still serve on starships—as opposed to a "desk jockey"—so they prefer the term "captain" as a mark of active service.)

The next-highest rank is commodore. Commodores serve either as commanders of starships or as heads of starbases. (Except for the admiral in charge of Diplomacy on the chiefs of staff, no diplomatic officer in Starfleet has a rank above commodore.) Currently, commodores who captain starships are in "training" to command the upcoming dreadnought starships, a position which many would rather have than an admiralcy.

Following them are the captains, with the starship commanders naturally taking precedence. They are supported by the commanders of destroyers, scouts, etc., according to rank and experience. The large conglomeration of commanders, lieutenants, ensigns, and yeomen make up the remainder of Starfleet personnel, along with the very large number of ordinary crewpersons.

On the civilian side, the large corps of diplomats, career civil servants, and Federation Council representatives serve in varying degrees of authority in all areas except starship and starbase operations.

In general, anyone who outranks Kirk, or who is the highest authority in a specific civilian field, is in charge in any given sector of space.

It is when none of these duly appointed entities are available that Kirk must take on his varied roles of commander, administrator, lawmaker, and diplomat. As the *Enterprise* covers almost unimaginable distances in space and often goes into unexplored regions, Kirk is quite often also called upon to exercise these duties. It is a mark of the highest confidence in a commander and his judgment when he is allowed to command a starship, for in the absence of higher authority, he is the Federation.

James T. Kirk has the hardest job in Starfleet, one which has destroyed many good and brave men. But it is a job that he believes in, loves, and does exceptionally well. Little wonder then that we can appreciate the kind of man he is when we realize the sheer weight of his duties and responsibilities, and still admire him for his humanity. That is why James Kirk has touched so many of us so deeply in so many ways.

# 13.
# A STAR TREK
# NEEDLEPOINT DESIGN

## by Beverley Wood

*Our readers' devotion to Star Trek takes many forms. We have had the pleasure of seeing sculpture, paintings, costume designs, dioramas (made with the Mego dolls), music, and much more. One of the most interesting of these, however, was the needlepoint design by Beverley Wood. We were so excited in our haste to get her excellent design into print that we inadvertently left her name off of the article! We're making sure it is on this time, Beverley, as we want all of our readers to know whom to thank when they are enjoying doing their own version of the needlepoint design.*

Star Trek fans have one thing in common (well, another thing, too): They are undeniably creative.

Science fiction attracts a creative audience (and highly intelligent, too—Isaac Asimov himself said so). And Star Trek is creative in the widest possible sense. Not only is the show itself a creative gem, it stimulates that quality in its viewers. Plots are subtly open-ended, so the audience can dream a little. Characters are cleverly understated, leaving shadowy corners that need investigating. Some of the most poignant scenes are only partly finished; cultures are hinted at, backgrounds left vague, remarks and expressions not always easily understood. Interpretation is left to the individual—and do we interpret!

All of which leads to the Star Trek Compulsive Creation Syndrome (a title invented by myself—and quite proud of it I am). The most usual symptom is a frantic urge to fit a pencil into the already clenched fingers and find (quick, please!) a piece of paper. Any paper will do—old bills (or new ones), napkins, torn envelopes, old rejection slips (or new ones), shirt sleeves, margins of newspapers.

But there are some of us whose hand fits a needle as well as (or possibly—sob—better than) a pencil. And those hands are not necessarily feminine either, needlecraft being a sport for all sexes.

My newest needlepoint project was fun to design and make, but displaying it in our living room is the most fun of all. Star Trek fans, of course, recognize the motto at once, but outsiders are interested and intrigued, too. Needlepointed on 10 mesh canvas it makes a stunning 18″ × 18″ pillowtop or picture. You can change the colors to suit yourself, but I found the stark black, blue, white, and grays appropriate.

You will need: 10 mesh mono needlepoint canvas, 22″ × 22″ or larger; blunt-pointed tapestry needle; and needlepoint or tapestry yarn in the following colors: black—85 yards, blue—55 yards, red—15 yards, white—125 yards, dark gray—15 yards, gray—190 yards.

Cut the canvas at least 22″ × 22″, leaving a 2″ margin on all sides. Bind the cut edges with masking tape to keep them from raveling and to keep the yarn from snagging on the thorny edges. You may work from the chart or copy the design directly onto the canvas with an indelible fine-tip felt pen. I find using the chart is the best way to work letters and borders.

Use lengths of yarn 30″ to 36″ long. To thread the needle (if sucking and twisting doesn't work), fold the end of the yarn around the needle and hold tightly. Slip the needle out and bring the eye over the fold. Voila!

When beginning a new length of yarn, don't knot the end; leave a little yarn on the wrong side and work the first few stitches over it. To end a piece of yarn, run the needle back through three or four stitches on the wrong side and trim off close to the work.

I work my piece entirely in Half Cross Stitch, but it can be done in Continental Stitch with the same effect. Or if you are an expert, other stitches can be combined for a textured look. Half Cross Stitch is faster than Continental and uses less yarn; Continental is stronger.

Whichever method you use, do *not* pull the yarn tightly or your work will gradually twist out of shape. No matter how carefully you work, it will not stay completely straight unless you use a stretcher frame to work on. Using a frame keeps the work nice and even, but it is rather a nuisance to use.

You really should sit at a table while stitching on a stretcher frame, as both hands are needed to push and pull the needle. Without a frame you can hold your work in one hand and stitch with the other while lounging in front of the TV (not during Star Trek, of course—you must lay your work reverently aside during that particular hour!).

If you work from the chart, start at the top or bottom and work in consecutive rows. Once the pattern is established, one color may be worked at a time, keeping to the chart. When you get to the lettering do all the letters first, then the background.

When the work is complete, dampen the back and pull it gently to straighten. Place the work face up on a clean board and fasten firmly around the edges with rustproof pushpins. Leave until thoroughly dry and frame, or sew to backing for a pillow. Then put your work of art in a prominent place and wait for rousing cheers!

(See photo insert for illustrations.)

# 14.
# A BRIEF LOOK
# AT KIRK'S CAREER

## by Leslie Thompson

*Who is James T. Kirk anyway? We know him as one of our best friends, of course, but we really know very little about him. In this article, Leslie Thompson uses her "speculative faction" to fill us in on some of the details and background of Jim Kirk. As usual with Leslie's articles, this one stirred up a storm of controversy when first published. Why? Well, read on. . . .*

The facts are known.

Name: James Tiberius Kirk. Service Record: Serial Number SC937-0176-CEC. Rank: Captain, Starship Command, USS *Enterprise* NCC-1701. Commendations: Palm Leaf of . . .

As we said, the facts are known. But what of James T. Kirk's early life? What factors shaped him into the man he is today, the starship captain, the explorer, the romantic, the passionate spokesman for all that is good in man?

We have never been given any hard information about Kirk's past, only inference and innuendo. In several episodes, we hear of people and places in Kirk's life—some important, some trivial. But a definitive personal history of Kirk has not been granted to us. Therefore, we must take the few given facts, and extrapolate one of our own.

Kirk was born in Greater Peoria, Illinois, thirty-four years before the first recorded voyage of the *Enterprise*. Shortly after this adventure ("Where No Man Has Gone Before"), Kirk celebrated his thirty-fifth birthday, which was marred by the loss of his closest friend, Commander Gary Mitchell.

When Kirk was still very young, his parents pulled up stakes and moved to Iowa. Rather, his mother did, as Kirk's father was serving in Starfleet as the captain of a destroyer (the *William Jennings Bryan*).

Young Kirk thrived in this new "country" environment, but he was still able to have the best of both rural and city life, as almost instantaneous civilian travel by transporter had become commonplace by this time.

In fact, the majority of Earth's population chose to live in the country, as getting to a job or school was as simple as walking into the next room; and over any distance on Earth . . . and even to the Moon!

So while little Jimmy Kirk lived and played in the rolling wheat fields of Iowa farmlands, he attended school every day in the Des Moines Complex, as did children from all around the state.

As his father was necessarily away most of the time, Kirk's major influences were his mother and his paternal grandfather, Peter Kirk. An older brother, George Samuel, was also quite important to the shaping of Kirk's early years, as he adored the older boy. It was a family joke that little Jimmy would follow "Sam" everywhere he went, often to the chagrin of George, who was developing an interest in girls just about the same time that Jimmy wanted to learn the finer points of zero-grav baseball.

From his mother, Kirk learned a great love of his fellow man and of all living things. She was a quiet and gentle woman who suffered her husband's long absences with a philosophical attitude. In Kirk, she instilled an admiration and love for the father he hardly knew by telling the boy of great deeds done and wonderful places his father had seen, and how he was sacrificing his home life to help keep Earth and the quickly expanding Federation safe from its enemies. So to Jimmy Kirk, his father was not an unknown cipher, but instead a giant, heroic figure. And the vision of space that his mother described would stay with Kirk for the rest of his life.

Old Pete Kirk would take Jimmy on his knee and tell him of the glorious history of the Kirk family. Even when quite young, Kirk found it hard to believe his grandfather's tales. The hardest to believe were his favorites: the ancestor who was raised by apelike subhumans in darkest Africa, the long-ago masked man who fought for justice in the old West, and the great bronzed figure who was the leading surgeon and scientist of his day. But until the day he died, old Pete Kirk swore the stories were true. James Kirk made a vow to himself to go to the census computers someday and check the stories out, but events swept him up, and the old man's tales soon faded into fond memories.

From them, however, Kirk gleaned an important message: A Kirk was expected to be brave, resourceful, and intelligent. A leader of men and a protector of the weak. Far above other men and better than the best.

This oblique message was probably the primary reason for Kirk's starting to drive himself at an early age. He had the native intelligence, reasoning, and intuition necessary for achieving just a little bit more than his fellow students, but he was no bookworm. Kirk excelled at both sandlot and school-sanctioned sports, and he was outgoing and popular with his classmates. Kirk was one of those rare youngsters who truly enjoyed school in all its phases, and he learned there to balance hard work and hard play.

When Kirk was fifteen, his father came to visit for a final time. Kirk was now old enough to realize that his father was not in actuality the giant hero of his mother's tales, but he was still somewhat awed by the huge and smiling man who strode back into his family's life every six months or so.

This was the longest visit in several years, and Richard Kirk was able to spend time with both of his sons, both together and separately. Sam Kirk was entering his third year in college at the time, and announced that he intended to become a biologist. Richard Kirk took this news stoically, as he realized that his elder son was no man of action, and his talents for organization and intuitive research would take him far in the scientific world. Seeing that his father approved, Sam also confessed that he was planning to marry a lovely young woman named Aurelan, and he wanted his father to be the best man.

Richard Kirk was immensely pleased, and when he turned to Jim and asked if he had considered what he wanted to do with his life, Jim spoke up: "I want to go into Starfleet. I want to be a starship captain!"

Once again, Richard Kirk was pleased. But he knew that his wife would be opposed; she already had enough to worry about. Too, it was a hard row to hoe. The boy had grit and brains, but it took much more than that to make it in Starfleet. Richard Kirk considered himself an intelligent and able man, yet he had never even come near the apex of his profession: commanding a starship. That was not for mere mortals. Starship captains were a breed apart.

So Richard Kirk gave his son a gentle smile and said, "There's time yet. You just might change your mind."

"I won't," answered Jim. Richard Kirk nodded slowly at his youngest son and then led both of his children back into their house.

Two days later he had left. Three weeks after that, he was dead.

Richard Kirk died a hero's death when he directed his ship to intentionally crash into a prototype Orion raider ship. Not only did this action prevent the destruction of a Federation outpost, it made the Orions think twice about challenging the Federation for supremacy in space and forced them into a policy of small-ship piracy and smuggling, ridding the Federation of a potentially dangerous enemy.

Kirk's mother never recovered from the news. Her years-long wall of reserve had been broken by Richard's death, and she became listless and uncaring. When she finally died of a broken heart a year later, Kirk considered it a blessing and comforted his grief with the knowledge that she was finally at peace.

To his surprise, Kirk discovered that his father's heroic death had qualified him to attend Starfleet Academy with the recommendation of his father's commander, Admiral Komack.

Although he would rather have earned the scholarship on his own, he was never one to look a gift horse in the mouth, and upon graduation from high school he entered Starfleet Academy.

It was hard, very much so. Not only did Kirk have to contend with the plethora of new and exciting knowledge presented almost every day, but in a curriculum designed to "wash out" cadets he was the butt of constant teasing and hazing because of the unorthodox way he had entered the Academy. Some of this grew to the point of brutality, and Kirk was ridden hard in particular by an upperclassman named Finnegan.

But it only made Kirk more determined to make it. He took the insults and jokes with grace, but being James T. Kirk, he remembered them all. Throughout the course of his academy days, he managed to repay them all in like fashion—all except Finnegan, who was always careful not to let the grim-faced Cadet Kirk catch him out of uniform.

During this difficult period, Kirk had an intense need for a hero, someone to emulate. He already had his father, but the memories were too painful, especially that of his mother, pin-ing away. This is perhaps where Kirk subconsciously developed his determination never to have a serious relationship with a woman.

But instead of one hero, Kirk found two. In Abraham Lincoln, Kirk saw a parallel with himself—a young man who started with very little managing to overcome adversity and rise to a high position. Too, Lincoln had to suffer the jeers of others, but still did not lose his humility and love for his fellow man. Kirk voraciously read everything he could get on Lincoln (particularly the Sandburg books) and vowed to himself that he would be at least half the man Abraham Lincoln was.

In Garth of Izar, Kirk found another hero, one who represented all that Kirk hoped to achieve as a Starfleet officer—a brilliant tactician, commander of a starship, fair and impartial in his dealings with both his crew and aliens. Kirk almost wore out his copy of Garth's textbook of starship battle tactics, and it was the greatest day of his life when Garth addressed the assembled cadets. If he wanted to be half the man Lincoln was, Kirk wanted to be twice the leader Garth was.

Eventually Kirk was graduated from Starfleet Academy—not at the top of his class; his marks in diplomacy and administration were a bit too low, as he considered these not necessary for a starship commander to know. Kirk didn't intend to be a desk jockey, he wanted to command a starship. And so he gave his greatest efforts to the disciplines he would need most to do so: tactics, math and electronics, space astronomy and exploration, and the physical needs—marksmanship, hand-to-hand combat, and helmsmanship.

However, Kirk still had to enter Command School, and before doing so, he had to serve time on a ship in deep space. He was consequently assigned to the scout ship *Jim Bridger*. However, midway through the voyage, Kirk contracted Vegan choriomeningitis and was remanded to a hospital on a nearby starbase.

Despondent over this setback, as the fast-moving world of Starfleet had no time for raw ensigns to recover from illnesses, Kirk utilized his recovery time to further his knowledge of starship operations and to make up some of the self-imposed deficiencies of his Academy education by constantly meeting and talking to the ever-changing parade of aliens and Federation envoys that visited the starbase. To his surprise, Kirk found that he had a natural ability to perceive and understand the problems and views of the aliens. This was not enough of a revelation to drive him into the diplomatic corps, but it did instill in him a respect for the myriad duties of a starship captain. It took more than an understanding of how a starship works and how best to blast an enemy out of existence to be another Garth. It was a lesson Kirk was not to forget.

Several days before Kirk was to return to the Academy for the long wait for reassignment to a ship, the starbase was the victim of a surprise attack by a Klingon battle cruiser. As Kirk was still on the inactive list and therefore had no specific battle station, he was able to place himself in a position where he could best see how the Klingons attacked the starbase. The outcome was a foregone conclusion, as the big guns of the starbase had the Klingon ship far outclassed, and Kirk assumed that the Klingon commander had gone berserk in the fashion that Klingons sometimes do.

Berserk or not, the Klingon was still a master tactician, and he managed to keep from being destroyed long enough to score a devastating hit on the life-support systems of the starbase. As the Klingon ship exploded, Kirk turned away only to hear the strident tones of a depressurization alarm. Without conscious thought, Kirk grabbed as many pressure suits as he could carry from a nearby storage locker and hurried down to the life-support bays.

Finding them sealed off by the automatic alarm systems, Kirk had a sudden inspiration. He hurried into the nearest transporter alcove, quickly estimated the range, and beamed the pressure suits in to the trapped crewmen. Several of them had already died from lack of oxygen and exposure, but Kirk's quick action managed to save the majority of the technicians.

Although Kirk couldn't see that he had done all that much, the starbase commander thought differently and recommended Kirk for his first award, the Prantares Ribbon of Commendation, Second Class. But more important to Kirk, his quick thinking allowed him to secure an immediate berth on a starship, the *Farragut*, commanded by the man who was soon to become his mentor, Captain Charles Garrovick.

Garrovick developed a soft spot for the young ensign when he discovered Kirk gazing longingly out of the starbase drydock at the majestic *Farragut*. He took Kirk under his wing, becoming almost a second father to him, and helped him to learn the essentials for starship service.

When the crew of the *Farragut* met with the cloud creature and Captain Garrovick died, Kirk blamed himself for not having fired sooner. His distress was especially hard when he learned that one of the last things Garrovick had done before being killed was to recommend that Kirk stand for command, and Kirk became more determined than ever to become a starship captain. He now had the added incentive of feeling that he must replace Garrovick, who was an especially fine commander, and therefore highly valuable to the Federation. He also vowed to someday destroy the cloud creature, a promise which he eventually kept with the help of Garrovick's son.

Back at the Academy for command training, Kirk become involved with Janice Lester, a fiery young cadet whose mercurial personality both attracted and repelled Kirk. Their affair continued throughout Kirk's training, but came to a bad end when Janice failed to meet the exacting Academy standards. Already high-strung, this unbalanced her even more, and she took the unrealistic view that she had been rejected because of her sex. She demanded that Kirk resign his commission in protest, and when he refused, she accused him of being "in on" the imagined conspiracy against her. Kirk wisely chose to stop seeing Janice, and after a while she drifted out of his life. He heard that she was training in astroarchaeology, but did not see her again until she used the ancient device of the Camusians to exchange minds with him in a vain attempt to usurp the powers of a starship captain.

Having graduated from Command School, Kirk was then assigned to the Starship *Exeter* as a helmsman. It was during this mission that he acted as orderly to his captain in the Axanar Peace Mission and was awarded another commendation for his services. Just before his tour of duty aboard the *Exeter* was over, Kirk was forced to report his old friend Ben Finney derelict in duty, causing a rift in their friendship.

Having compiled an excellent record, Kirk was then transferred to the destroyer *Chesty Puller* as first officer. It was during this voyage that Kirk was forced to take over the ship when his captain was injured and battle a Klingon cruiser. Choosing the better part of valor, Kirk ordered a retreat, but found his way blocked by yet another Klingon ship. This was a smaller but no less dangerous ship, and Kirk was forced to fight, as the large ship was jamming his communications.

Utilizing his ship's greater speed, he maneuvered the small Klingon ship into his sights, but held back on the order to fire. Thinking that the Federation ship was helpless, both Klingons moved in, and then Kirk ordered his men to fire while at the same time reversing engines at full warp.

This dangerous move had the effect that Kirk wanted. The smaller Klingon ship was hit by the phaser blast, while the battle cruiser's phasers hit only empty space. By the time that it could reverse course, Kirk's ship had gained just enough of a lead to call for help, and the Klingon, not wanting to face a starship in exchange for having eliminated a small destroyer, pulled away.

In reward for this action, Kirk was presented with the Medal of Honor, and the Karagite Order of Heroism. He also got something which was even more desirable to him: command of his own ship.

However, not right away. First he was to serve as one of the representatives to an exchange program that had been arranged with the Klingons. Luckily, Kirk did not have to travel to a Klingonese planet; he was assigned instead to serve as host and guide to a young Klingon officer, Kumara.

During the time that Kirk and Kumara were roommates at a Starfleet training facility (one carefully selected to reveal to the Klingons a minimum of Federation technology), they became good, if cautious, friends. They parted with a great amount of respect for each other, and each had the feeling that the other would one day be a foe to reckon with.

After completing this unusual assignment to his superiors' complete satisfaction, Kirk received his promised command: a brand-new ship, an experimental-model *Starstalker*, which was also its name. The object of the small, sleek ship was to act as a quick-moving and virtually untraceable weapon, much like the submarines of Earth's past. *Starstalker* was one of three models being tested by the Federation for this type of work.

Although conditions were rather primitive, the ship being strictly a shakedown model (with little provision made for comfort in any case), Kirk could not have been happier. He knew that it was an exceptional mark of confidence that he had been assigned the ship, and he was determined not to fail.

The early part of the cruise went well. The ship was virtually a flying phaser, with speed and firepower comparable to a full-sized starship, and Kirk forced his crew to the limit with every conceivable test the Federation could think of and a few that he invented on the spot. In this, he was ably assisted by a no-nonsense, hardheaded chief engineer named

Montgomery Scott, who had helped to design *Starstalker*. Kirk also had his best friend from his Academy days, Gary Mitchell, as first officer. Kirk had requested that Mitchell be assigned to *Starstalker*, using his prerogative as the first captain of a newly commissioned ship.

They ran into some trouble on Dimosous, where a group of hostile rodentlike natives attacked the crew, who had landed to check out a report that dilythium crystals had been discovered on the planet. Kirk was engaged in moving his men into a retreat when one of the natives aimed a poisoned dart at him. Mitchell threw himself in the way and took the dart that was intended for Kirk. When the crew reached the ship safely, Kirk ordered that the nearest route to a starbase hospital be taken, a route which brought the ship dangerously close to the Romulan Neutral Zone. The passage was uneventful, but Kirk received a severe reprimand for his action. His superiors were secretly pleased, however, as they themselves had taken similar risks for friends in the past. It was a mark against Kirk's service record, a mark for him in the eyes of his fellow officers.

After two years of experimentation, the *Starstalker* experiment was shelved and Kirk was assigned another ship. It was the usual procedure for one of his rank (which was at this time commander) to be assigned as second officer aboard a starship, or as captain of a scout. However, Kirk was immediately assigned as captain of a destroyer, which to his immense delight he discovered was the *Hua C'hing*, the first command of his hero, Captain Garth. Again, Kirk took Mitchell with him, along with another officer whom Kirk considered one of his planned "permanent staff," Engineer Scott. Aboard the *Hua C'hing*, he was to acquire another, who was at this time a raw ensign: Walter Sulu.

Kirk and company saw much action aboard the *Hua C'hing*. They participated in the opening of the Rigellian System (which had been pioneered a few years previously by Captain Christopher Pike aboard the *Enterprise*) and in several furious battles against the Kzinti, and in one exceptional raid they captured a Klingon warlord who had been in the Arualian System trying to undermine the Federation's influence. For their bravery in this raid, almost all of the crew received Awards of Valor, and Kirk was singled out for a Silver Palm with Cluster to go with his Medal of Honor.

Kirk served aboard the *Hua C'hing* for four years with similar success, and when Captain Pike was promoted to fleet

captain, he chose James Kirk as his successor to captain the
*Enterprise.* Starfleet Command readily concurred, and less
than ten years after he had graduated from Command
School, Jim Kirk had realized his ambition: command of a
starship.

Again taking along Mitchell, Scott, and Sulu, Kirk spent
the previous few days he had before assuming command in
gathering together the finest bridge crew he could find.
Among these was Lieutenant Uhura, whom Kirk had run
across at a starbase, chafing against the duties that kept her
from joining a regular crew. It seemed she had done her job
too well, and had been assigned as a communications instruc-
tor, a job she did competently but nevertheless despised.

Kirk also requested another fine officer, one highly recommended by his old friend Matt Decker: Lee Kelso, to be second navigator behind Mitchell. As backup helmsman, Kirk
chose Lieutenant Kevin Riley, a fiesty Irishman who had
been Sulu's roommate at the Academy.

Two of the men Kirk wanted had crossed his path in the
past, and he had ambivalent feelings about both. However, he
wanted his crew to be the very best possible, and so personal
feelings had to be put aside. He requested them both: Lieutenant Commander Finnegan as security officer, and Lieutenant Commander Ben Finney as records officer. He got
only Finney, as Finnegan was up for a captaincy, and learning this, Kirk didn't want to spoil his chances. But the lack of
a top-notch security officer would nag Kirk for several years,
and at times he dearly wished he had gotten the cocky but
competent Finnegan.

The post of science officer was already filled, as Pike's man
had requested to be reassigned to the *Enterprise.* Kirk was
leery about working with the Vulcan Spock, but was more
than happy to have him. Spock was generally acknowledged
to be the finest scientific mind Starfleet had, and Kirk knew
that he would prove invaluable in the months ahead. Just
how valuable even Kirk never suspected.

After a short shakedown cruise to check the modifications
and repairs to the *Enterprise* (Pike had been so active that
the ship hadn't had a thorough going-over in some time),
Kirk and crew proceeded on several important, if unexciting,
missions. Then, one fateful day, word came from Starfleet
that the *Enterprise* had been selected for an unusual mission:
to go where no man had gone before, through the barrier on
the edge of our galaxy.

This was the mission that resulted in the deaths of Mitchell and Kelso, and aided in the decision of Dr. Piper to retire from space. But it was also the baptism of fire for the new Captain of the *Enterprise* and his handpicked crew, and forged them together into a superbly efficient team.

With the promotion of Spock to first officer (in addition to his science-officer duties) and the assignment of Leonard McCoy as ship's surgeon, the complement of the *Enterprise* was complete.

James T. Kirk had achieved his youthful desire: He commanded a starship with the finest crew in the Federation. And the legend began to grow.

# 15.
# MORE TIME TRAVELS IN STAR TREK

by Mark A. Golding

*Jim Houston's article "Time Travels in Star Trek" (The Best of Trek #1) stirred up quite a bit of controversy and accounted for a large number of letters and comments. But Mark Golding, our resident expert in Star Trek technology, wasn't content with a few comments. Only a few days after Jim's article appeared in* Trek, *a bulky envelope arrived at our offices. In it was Mark's article. We were not only delighted that one of our favorite contributors had decided to have another look at ST time travel, but we were truly amazed that he could have written such a detailed study in such a short time. We think that you will feel the same way—especially when you remember that the series itself actually told us nothing about the inner workings of the various forms of time travel used, and Mark was forced to extrapolate known science from a scriptwriter's idea.*

Jim Houston, in his article "Time Travels in Star Trek" in the ninth issue of *Trek*, supposes that when the *Enterprise* traveled back in time in "Naked Time" that it would then go on to its adventure of Psi 2000 and be sent back in time, go to Psi 2000 and be sent back in time, over and over again until there were an infinite number of *Enterprises*. He supposed that such a process might possibly be short-circuited at some smaller number, perhaps seven thousand starships.

Actually when the *Enterprise* was sent back in time it appeared in a different place than it had been three days before being sent back in time—for the episode, which begins with the *Enterprise* just arrived at Psi 2000, just discovering the fate of the researchers it had come to evacuate, lasts for less than three days. Thus the starship must have been one or two days' travel distant from Psi 2000 at the moment when the *Enterprise* appeared from the future at a point which was only a few minutes travel from Psi 2000. This explains why the duplicate *Enterprise*s didn't detect one another, for the ship which had been thrown back in time left the solar system of Psi 2000 before the "original" *Enterprise* arrived.

It would be a very interesting situation. In "Arena," Kirk said that the *Enterprise* was the chief defense of the sector it was assigned to—one containing hundreds or thousands of solar systems; and in "Trouble with Tribbles," Korax said the same thing ("That sagging old rust bucket is designed like a garbage scow! Half the quadrant knows it—that's why they're learning to speak Klingonese!").

Since in "Tomorrow Is Yesterday" we are told that there are only twelve ships as powerful as the *Enterprise*, it seems to me that while the appearance of several thousand *Enterprise*s would be a pretty problem indeed for Starfleet Command, it would be a much worse problem for the Klingon and Romulan high commands!

Actually such a situation would not occur as a result of a simple trip three days in the past, as I have said. However, if desired it would be possible to multiply a starship by sending it back in time over and over again. Kirk can always escape from overwhelming numbers of enemy ships by multiplying the *Enterprise* through time travel. There would be certain limitations; the crew would grow too old after traveling back and forth through time for a few dozen years (ship's time).

Such a situation would not violate the laws of conservation of matter and energy. Time travel could not be possible unless time is one or more dimensions or directions as space is. In that case it would not be violating the conservation laws to move an object in the past to appear side by side with its earlier self, for the object would be simply moving from one location in space-time to another. To those observing the events from inside the flow of time it would appear as though an object had appeared side by side with itself and then one of the duplicates had later disappeared, but to an observer outside time and space it would seem as though an object had simply traveled in a loop before moving on.

If you were walking in a straight line, and then walked in a loop and continued on, a being which was aware of events inside a plane of space which intersected the loop you made, but which was not aware of the flow of time, would think that you had duplicated yourself, when actually you merely changed your location in space/time.

If the *Enterprise* was traveling backward in time, how could the crewmembers see the clocks going backward? Well, the starship as a whole was being flung back in time, but on board the flow of time was going forward, so that while going back in time three days, the crew aged and experienced the events of about five minutes.

But if the flow of time on the ship itself was going forward, why did the instruments show time going backward? Because the instruments in question were not atomic clocks or any other clocks which would show only the flow of time on board the ship, but clocks designed to show the rate of time flow outside the ship.

I have stated my opinion that the warp drive of the *Enterprise* works by speeding up time on board the ship, so that while the propulsion of the ship gives a speed of only say 0.0091248 percent of the speed of light, it would appear to outside observers to be travelling 512 times the speed of light. The elapsed time aboard the *Enterprise* for a journey would thus for the crew appear to be exactly as long as it would take to make the trip at 0.0091248 percent of the speed of light, even though to outside observers it would seem to take no longer than a ship traveling at 512 times the speed of light would take.

You may well ask how, since the time that a trip of one light-year would take would seem to be as long for the crew of the *Enterprise* as traveling one light-year at 0.0091248 of the speed of light (that would be 109.59144 years, which would seem to outside observers to be 17.121 hours), how they could live long enough to make even one star flight?

For one thing, I have postulated in some of my articles that there must be a series of space warps, which I call Gateways, leading between solar systems which make the distances traveled between two stars far less than the actual distances between the two stars. Thus the *Enterprise* could make a round trip of *about* 2,000 light-years in 1.7 hours in "Obsession" instead of the four years it would take, even at warp 8, if the starship had to travel the entire 2,000 light-years.

If the end points of the Gateways leading to and from a solar system are about 200,000,000 to 500,000,000 miles from the star, a starship traveling at warp 8 would seem to outside observers to appear out of one Gateway, cross the solar system in 0.06 to 0.16 minute depending on the exact distance and disappear through the Gateway on the other side. To the crew on board with time speeded up 56,000 times they would seem to enter the Gateway from one solar system, appear instantly in another, cross it in 56 to 145 hours, and then go through the Gateway on the far side and appear in another solar system.

In addition, it may be that inside the time warp which speeds up time on board the *Enterprise* there is another one which slows down time aboard the crew's quarters so that it appears to flow at the same rate as time outside the universe (or at any other desired rate; in "Menagerie" Spock said the trip from Starbase II to Talos IV was six days at maximum warp, yet the trip seemed to take only one day by ship's time).

Returning to the instruments of the *Enterprise*, it is not known if the *Enterprise* switches from one warp factor to another by increasing or decreasing the speed produced by its propulsion units while the intensity of the time warp remains the same, or by changing the intensity of the time warp while the speed produced by the propulsion units remains the same. If the latter case, which I prefer, is the actual case, the number of times that time is speeded up on a starship can vary, and thus it will be necessary to have ways of measuring the time flow in the outside universe to compare with the time flow aboard the ship.

It would be easy enough to measure the rate of time on board a starship by the use of atomic clocks, if an even more fantastically accurate means of telling time has not been developed by the time of Star Trek. The rate of time in the outside universe can be measured by astronomical instruments, for individual variable stars and stars of certain classes vary with specific periods, and then there are the rates of pulsars and the periodic variations of some quasars. Inside solar systems in which the orbits of the various bodies have been accurately determined, the positions of the bodies at any one moment will show the time in the outside universe.

Clearly, the "clock" that was showing on Sulu's instrument panel must have been a readout of the time in the universe outside the time warp of the *Enterprise* as determined by the computer system whose function it is to monitor the relative time rates of the *Enterprise* and the outside universe. No doubt the more important readout from that system, the ratio of time rates of the *Enterprise* and the outside universe, was displayed in a dial or counter which was just off-screen in the shot of the time dial. It is rather surprising that the computer was able to deduce that the *Enterprise* was traveling backward in time; it would appear that the computer was an extremely advanced model, and perhaps its programmers had anticipated the theoretical possibility of time travel.

Mr. Houston is wrong in stating that when in "Tomorrow Is Yesterday" Captain Christopher was transported back into his body of several days previously it would have resulted in a tremendous explosion as the mass of two human bodies was totally converted into energy. In order to convert a mass into energy all its particles must be placed into contact with the opposite antiparticles. Since the nuclei of atoms and even their electron shells occupy only an insignificant percentage of the total volume of an object, very few of the atoms of Christopher's bodies would find themselves in the same place. So even the much less violent release of energy which results from the breaking of the bonds holding together the particles which make up an atom would occur very rarely as the two bodies came to occupy the same space.

Since the molecules of the body also occupy a small volume out of the total space in the body, there would be only a small proportion of molecules materializing in spaces already occupied by molecules, and thus little breaking of the bonds which hold the atoms in each molecule together. However, all the spaces between molecules would be disrupted by the conflicting force fields between the molecules of the body that was being materialized in the same place where one already existed. Captain Christopher should have been reduced to liquids and gases.

But as we know, Captain Christopher was not "liquidated." And Mr. Houston's points about the *Enterprise*'s not vanishing from in front of Christopher's eyes merely because it was not traveling back in time is absolutely true, despite all the statements of the esteemed Mr. Irwin in his rebuttal. I'm afraid that Mr. Irwin, who states that an object can't be in two places at the same time (which is no more sensible than saying that it can't be in two different times at the same place), is still thinking in the world view devised by the great Greek philosophers 2,000 years ago, instead of the world view of modern science, in which time and space are equal, in which energy is just a form of matter and all solid "objects" are merely vacuums containing very thin concentrations of tiny particles which turn out to be nothing but volumes of space whose curvature is slightly different from that of the rest of space.

How do I explain what happened in "Tomorrow Is Yesterday"? Actually, I can't even begin to do so, because I have no evidence to go upon. That which we, the audience, see on our TV screen is logically and scientifically impossible, and Spock the supreme scientific adviser, Spock the most irrationally fanatical devotee of logic, not only does not protest at such illogic but actually thought up the plan, actually believed it might work!

But why go on about how Spock should have spotted the logical flaws in the plan and its apparent execution? It is enough of a wonder that all the other crewmembers didn't point out at once the logical flaws in his plan. I can't believe that there was even a single member of the *Enterprise* crew who didn't see the flaws in the plan—or wouldn't have if he had been allowed to think normally.

Clearly there was some outside influence at work, "clouding the minds" of the *Enterprise* crew to allow them to believe that their fantastic plan was working. What we saw on the TV screen during that sequence must have been the illusion created for the benefit of the *Enterprise* crewmen.

I do not know what happened to the air sergeant and to Captain Christopher after they were beamed down, or even if their being beamed down was also illusion. Since they were not beamed into their old bodies, reducing them to a liquid glop, what happened to them? Unless Spock's statement that Captain Christopher later became the father of a son who would head the first Saturn probe was merely another part of the imposed illusion, then we must accept as fact that what appeared to be a human body identical with that of Captain Christopher appeared on Earth and went through at least the outward semblance of fathering a son.

If it was in fact Captain Christopher, perhaps as Mr. Houston suggests he didn't know enough about the future to do it any damage. Perhaps his memories of his experience were erased—which in effect would be killing the Captain Christopher who lived aboard the *Enterprise*, though leaving alive the Captain Christopher, younger by a few days, who had not yet been taken aboard the starship. (These Captain Christophers I'm talking about are not different bodies but different periods of his memories stored in the same brain.) Perhaps his actions were controlled by some external source which prevented him from saying what he knew.

But we have no way of knowing if the body which appeared on Earth was in fact Captain Christopher nor even if such a body did in fact appear on Earth. If the captain and the sergeant were not, in fact, returned to Earth, what might have happened to them? Did they return to the future on the *Enterprise*, unseen by its crew, did they live for a million years in fabulous luxury on some distant planet to which they were taken, or did they die in hideous agony?

In "City on the Edge of Forever" and "Yesteryear" it is also impossible to say what actually happened. Did the time travelers change and then rechange the same time track, or did they switch the locations of their bodies and consciousnesses from one time track to another and then back to the first (or to a third)? Or perhaps all this happened on the same time track; the past was never changed, and the Guardian merely told them that the past had been changed in order to get them to go to the past so that they could fulfill their appointed roles in making history occur the way it had.

Indeed, it is quite possible that nobody has ever traveled in time through the Guardian of Forever. It might have the power to give those who visit it the illusion of traveling in time. *If* that was the case, would Spock have really died if in his illusion he thought he had failed to save his younger self, or would he have lived? Who can say?

It is a relief to turn from the unknowables to the simple answers to the problems in "All Our Yesterdays." It is said that the Atavachron prepares those who are sent back into past times so that they fit in physically and psychologically in the eras to which they are sent. If that is the case, why would the Inquisitor, who *had* been prepared by the Atavachron, still know that there were no such things as witches, when all the people of the "Charles II" era believed in them? Unless he was destined to be one of the reformers who abolished witchhunts, it would only cause him mental suffering to know that the "witches" were innocent and see them being executed for an impossible crime. Perhaps it would have been impossible to remove his modern knowledge without destroying so many memories as to destroy his identity, personality, and mind.

I do not see why the machine would have to prepare travelers physically before sending them back in time. Were the laws of nature different 1,000 years ago or 10,000? Was the gravitational constant or the cosmological constant different?

Was the universe and everything in it larger or smaller (it didn't look any different)?

Perhaps time travelers might be immunized against the various diseases to be found in the past, which were wiped out in the future and which they would have no natural immunity against. This would explain the concern of the Prosecutor for the unprepared Kirk. Whether the statement of Zarabeth that it would be fatal for her to return to her own era was true is not so easy to answer. I find it hard to believe that immunization for past diseases would be deadly for time travelers who returned to the future without having the immunization removed.

In Zarabeth's era, the Atavachron was not the long-known, familiar instrument which every Sarpied knew intimately, as it would be the means of saving his life, as it was in the time of Mr. Atoz and the Prosecutor; but rather a new invention, used as an instrument of terror by the evil dictator Zor Kahn. Do you suppose that Zor Kahn would have told the truth about the Atavachron to those of his victims he exiled into time if he could fool them into believing lies which made their situation seem even more hopeless? (Though by removing all hope of being returned such lies would make them less discontented with their exile in the past.) Perhaps Zarabeth had in fact made up the story herself in order to persuade Spock and McCoy to stay with her—but if she did, she certainly acted as though she believed it by refusing to go back to the future.

Incidentally, Spock told Zarabeth he had read about Zor Kahn. Perhaps he had had time to briefly scan a historical tape which mentioned the tyrant while in the library, or other ships had visited Beta Niobe before—though any such ships would seem not to have brought back any information about the Atavachron and the part it would play when the star was about to explode.

Spock's emotional behavior while 6,000 years in the past is easy to explain. In "Immunity Syndrome" we saw how Spock could detect the death of 400 Vulcans light-years away. Do you suppose that he is not constantly aware of the combined minds of all the millions or billions of Vulcans on Vulcan from even thousands of light-years away? In a sense all Vulcans share a sort of subconscious racial mind, even though their conscious minds have identities separate enough for T'Pring to scheme her schemes in defiance of the fate decreed for her by Vulcan custom.

Such a racial mass mind must have existed long before the Vulcans became logical. Thus it originally was emotional and illogical, and all Vulcans must have felt a constant pressure to behave emotionally—at least to follow those emotions considered proper by the combined minds of all the Vulcans.

This pressure may have been strong enough to make all Vulcans ready to die for their country or their cause, but not strong enough to make them all agree on which country and which cause. Thus there were wars more terrible even than those on Earth; indeed Vulcan violence may even have been a result of reaction against such a pressure to conform.

As we saw in "All Our Yesterdays," Spock's fierce determination to be rational was overcome by the power of all the combined illogical Vulcan minds of the time he found himself in, even though he must have been many light-years away from Vulcan. Imagine then what a struggle it must have been for Surak to completely change the psychology of the Vulcan people, especially without the use of force, as he seems to have done it. Clearly he was a great person indeed. "All Our Yesterdays" proves also that Surak's reforms took place long after the Ice Age on Sarpiedion 6,000 years ago.

Vulcan, it is believed, was colonized by the people of Arret, 600,000 years ago, and yet the reforms of Surak took place less than 6,000 years ago. Some time in that long expanse of time, Vulcans colonized many worlds. The Romulans are descended from one such warlike, emotional group. It would seem that their mass mind has split off from that of Vulcan as also the mass minds of the other Vulcan colony worlds, and the mass minds of any other colonies of Arret.

Still, it would seem that when Spock was aboard the Romulan ship in "The *Enterprise* Incident" the influence of the Romulan minds was enough for him to develop real emotions for the Romulan commander, which may give a hint to Nurse Chapel.

Now we get down to the nitty-gritty of time travel, the aspects of it which nobody seems to have paid much attention to. It is generally assumed that our universe came into existence 10 or 20 or 30 billion years ago. If that is the case, the first intelligent life, the first civilizations, must have appeared 5 or 10 or whatever billions of years after the creation of the universe.

Our planet is 5 billion years old, and life first appeared on it 3 or 4 billion years ago. The first life on land appeared a few hundred million years ago, the first tool-using pre-men existed several million years ago, while agriculture, the basis of civilization, is 10,000 or so years old. The use of metals is about half as old, the industrial revolution 200 years old. What will our civilization be like in the next 200 years, the next 5,000, the next 5 million, the next 5 billion?

Clearly civilizations develop at a fantastically rapid rate on the cosmic time scale, and one only 0.00001 percent older than ours as compared to the age of the Earth would have science and technology which would seem like magic to us—or to the crew of the *Enterprise*. And there may well be civilizations not merely hundreds of years older than ours but billions!

But such civilizations do not seem very obtrusive in the Star Trek universe. Our civilization may well be able to turn its citizens into energy beings, as the Organians did long ago, in just 300 or 400 years. There is no proof that any of the Star Trek civilizations must be more than a mere million years or so old. Perhaps the really ancient civilizations are so advanced we can't even detect their artifacts. Perhaps they have taken care to hide all evidence of their activity, to avoid changing history.

For even older than the civilizations which evolve naturally will be those which are founded by time travelers from the future who travel to the beginning of the universe to found civilizations which will be tens of billions of years old by the time of Star Trek. Try to imagine what one of those civilizations would be like!

Perhaps there are wars between rival time travelers to try to change history to make it more favorable for the civilizations of the future they represent. Perhaps our whole time line, our whole alternate universe, will be obliterated by the success of a rival time changer. Perhaps the past is unchangeable, and the time travelers watch countless tragedies they are helpless to prevent.

In "Paradise Syndrome," Spock said that there were several civilizations descended from Vulcan colonies known to the Federation, besides the Romulans. Some of them seem to use musical notes as their "alphabets." One of those worlds, whose natives must be still as emotional as the Romulans—in other words, of close to human personality—must have fairly close contact with Earth and is quite probably a Federation member. It is possible also that it may have a large human population, who have come from Earth since the discovery of space travel, or who were earlier brought in by the Preservers.

On this planet the fame of Mr. Spock, who may perhaps have played an important role in some important local event, is very great. For the first time, perhaps, the humans and the "Vulcanoids" of this planet are now aware of the possibility of successful breeding between humans and "Vulcanoid" beings, and with outstanding results.

Since the natives think and feel much more like humans than the Vulcans do, it should (perhaps) be easier for them to have successful marriages with humans, and such mixed marriages will become very common on that world, which perhaps has a long history of integration in other respects between the two races, in an attempt perhaps to promote interracial harmony.

So a large population of human-Vulcanoid hybrids will arise, who perhaps regard Spock as the being without whose example none of them would have been likely to have been born. Perhaps Kirk, McCoy, Scotty, and the rest of the *Enterprise* crew become heroes on this world too, because they are associated with Spock or because together they have saved the Federation (and thus all the people of the planet) from terrible dangers time and again. (That's assuming that all of the Star Trek episodes take place one after another on the same time line. I myself believe that it's likely that most of them take place in alternate universes from the other episodes.)

Time travel has been discovered by the Federation civilization in the time of the *Enterprise*, which in fact seems to be the ship which has made all the discoveries in that field. Accidents are of no use, but there are repeatable methods. Travelers can go back through the Guardian of Forever. In "Assignment: Earth," the *Enterprise* returned to 1968 Earth by means of the "Warp Speed Breakaway Factor," which could be either the method of time travel discovered in "Naked Time" or the one discovered in "Tomorrow Is Yesterday." Such a method may well become more common in years to come—which will mean that Federation starships will become more common in the years that were.

Sooner or later somebody is going to think of planting colonies at the beginning of the universe. Or perhaps the Klingons, or the Romulans, or the Tholians will conquer the Federation and the last remaining starships will flee into the past to escape. In any case, at least one starship whose crewmembers will mostly be human-Vulcanoid half-breeds from the planet I have talked about will travel far into the past.

Whether they will travel all the way back to the beginning of the universe to found their colony (as no doubt thousands and millions and billions of other expeditions from other civilizations have) or will be content with a much more recent time, I cannot say. But at some time and place they will found a great civilization. It will use musical notes for its alphabet, and will be of mixed human-Vulcanoid ancestry.

And they will think very highly of the heroes of the *Enterprise*, especially Spock, and consider both Earth and the Vulcanoid planet, and Vulcan before it, and Arret before Vulcan, as the sources of their civilization. They will have great knowledge of the history of what will then seem to them to be both the comparatively recent past of their ancestors and yet a remote future. But there will be many gaps in their knowledge of the history of the many worlds which make up the Federation and its enemies, gaps which they will want to fill.

So they will send ships forward in time to observe the blank periods of history. I do not know if they will have cloaking devices to hide them from the sensors of the Klingon and Romulan and Tholian and Federation and Orion and Gorn and Vedala spaceships of Star Trek's time, or if they will have to restrict their observations to less advanced times when they will be in no danger of being discovered.

Of all the species of intelligent life in the universe, no two are identical. Nowhere are there two planets with natives just like those on other worlds. With one exception.

On countless worlds there are human natives, supposed by some to have evolved independently through parallel evolution. Also there are several worlds whose natives resemble the Vulcans, but they are known to be descended from Vulcan colonies. Brooding on their ancestry, the members of that civilization are likely to deduce that all the humans scattered across space are likely to be descended from humans who came or were brought from some one world where they evolved.

The natives of the Amerind planet resembled some American Indian tribes. Even stranger, on planet Beta III, a man who lived 6,000 years ago had the French name of Landru, a name which wasn't evolved on Earth until just 1,000 years or so ago. His ancestors must have been brought back in time from a period of French history thousands of years in the future of the period in which they found themselves.

There are dozens of names from the various planets the *Enterprise* has visited which are similar to Earthly names out of only a few hundred known extraterrestrial names. Surely that can't be a coincidence; surely the ancestors of Mr. Hengist came to Rigel IV from Anglo-Saxon England; surely those of Melakon on Ekos came from some Celtic land where the memory of the mighty Maglocunnus the Island Dragon, King of Britain and King of Gwynned, Maelgyn Gwynned of later tradition, known also as Mailcun or Malachon, remained strong; surely the Zaons were descended either from pagan Semites or from Semitic or non-Semitic people who belonged to the Judeo-Christian-Islamic religious tradition.

Clearly some unknown society had taken Earthmen from the primitive societies of the past, who could not themselves have built spacecraft, and seeded them on distant worlds. If that had not occurred the history of countless planets would have been different—including, of course, the history of the world whence had come the founders of time-traveling civilization—as well as the history of contact and travel between the various worlds after the discovery of space travel. In short, none of the members of that civilization in the past would have been alive if not for that program of seeding humans on distant worlds, just as none of them would be alive if Mr. Spock had not shown the way for human-Vulcanoid marriages.

Investigating the process, a ship of this civilization watches as a starship gathers humans and takes them (or duplicates made of them) to other worlds. Making contact with the strange ship, they discover that it is waiting for them, that it is a ship from their own civilization a short time in the future. They themselves are the people who will and did seed humans on so many distant worlds, they themselves are the Preservers who used musical notes for their alphabet and placed the Indians on the Amerind planet and built the obelisk to protect them from asteroid collisions.

Many other things they may also do on their travels through space and time. The solar system of 40 Eridani, said to be that of Vulcan, contains a white dwarf star which must have exploded at least once as a nova or supernova. Such an event must have thinned the atmospheres of even the largest of planets in the system—and Vulcan is said to be a planet with a higher surface gravity than Earth and yet a thinner atmosphere. Could Vulcan be the solid core of what was once a gas giant, its thin atmosphere only the most insignificant remnant of the once tremendously dense atmosphere?

Who knows? But if that is the case, planets of similar nature will be found in only a small proportion of solar systems, those with the remains of exploded stars.

Since the Romulans and other cultures are descended from Vulcan colonists, and since the Vulcans are believed to be descended from colonists sent out from Arret 600,000 years ago, and since Vulcans and humans can survive if not flourish in one another's habitats, you'd expect that most of the worlds habitable for humans would have Vulcan colonists. Perhaps the Preservers wiped out the Vulcanoid colonies; perhaps the habitats of humans and Vulcans are too dissimilar for Vulcan colonists to survive for centuries or thousands of years on human planets.

Perhaps the Vulcans erroneously thought that they could only live on worlds of the same origin as Vulcan (the Preservers may have originated that belief), and so only colonized the few planets of that type, ignoring most habitable worlds.

It is possible that the Arretians, original ancestors of Vulcans, Romulans, and the Vulcanoids who married humans, and thus of the Preservers, were created by the Preservers, for we do not know if life could evolve naturally on a world such as it is possible that Arret was, a former gas giant stripped of almost all its atmosphere. It certainly seems strange that the Vulcans, products of independent evolution, and with a biochemistry which differs widely from that of humans in some respects, can mate successfully with humans.

Perhaps some of the Preservers were settled on Arret and carefully bred to bring out the Vulcan characteristics until they had produced a race like full-blooded Vulcans. Perhaps techniques of genetic engineering were used to create the first Arretians out of other forms of life. In any case, it can't be an accident that Vulcans can breed with humans, not when the Preservers would not have existed except for that amazing fact.

And what of the green Orion Slave Girls, the followers of Vaal (whose name is suspiciously like that of the Near Eastern god Baal), the black-and-white Cheronites, and other races who resemble humans but are like no type known on Earth? Couldn't they be descended from humans genetically modified by the Preservers who knew that history would be different if these variations on a familiar theme were not seeded on the planets they were recorded to occupy?

Come to think of it, who created the computer god Vaal and set it up as ruler of Gamma Trianguli VI? There are other civilizations which seem very unlikely to have evolved naturally, and it is possible that in those cases the Preservers created those cultures.

Strange it is to guess what role the Preservers have played in history. There are so many strange situations in Star Trek episodes which might, if no independent explanation could be found, be explained as due to the Preservers who wanted to make sure that recorded events would occur. A little thinking will show that the hypothesized origin of the Nomad/Tan Ru robot in "Changeling" is utterly fantastic, though I have come up with an explanation which doesn't require the Preservers.

Have the Preservers been content merely to watch and record the events of history with all their triumphs and tragedies? Did they cause many of those triumphs and tragedies, saving or killing many of the countless billions who have lived in the history of each planet? Did they try to make history better, even though it would have changed their past and made them nonexistent, only to find that the course of history cannot be changed?

Were the Preservers the people who maintained in the twentieth century (and probably many others) agents on Earth (and perhaps on other worlds) to help the natives survive the various problems they faced? Did they send Gary Seven to Earth, or was he sent by some other civilization?

The energy barrier which surrounds our galaxy might be natural, but if that was the case, you'd expect that the similar Andromeda Galaxy would also have such a force barrier. Yet in "By Any Other Name," the Kelvans mentioned running into the force barrier which surrounds this galaxy, speaking as though our galaxy was unique. Their ship was destroyed by the unexpeced encounter, but after seizing the *Enterprise* they soon discovered a way to penetrate the force barrier without any difficulty. *If* their own galaxy had had a force barrier around it they would have expected to find one around ours and would certainly have had enough time to devise a safe method of penetrating it in the 300 years it took them to reach our galaxy.

Could the Preservers have generated that force barrier as a

protection for this galaxy and for humans and Vulcans? If so, it is a very inadequate protection.

It has not kept out the Kelvans; nor the mind parasites ("Operation Annihilate"); nor the supposed "Doomsday Machine" which might well have actually been created to attack our galaxy; nor the giant, space-traveling, energy-absorbing ameba ("Immunity Syndrome"); nor Lazarus ("The Alternative Factor"); nor the vampire cloud ("Obsession"), which clearly must be a newcomer to this galaxy, for otherwise there'd be no life left; nor the planet-eating cosmic cloud ("One of Our Planets Is Missing"); nor the warmongering energy entity of "Day of the Dove"; nor the Kaladans and their deadly remains ("That Which Survives"); nor the humanoid makers from the Andromeda Galaxy and their too-helpful androids ("I, Mudd"); nor the two agents of the "Old Ones" ("Catspaw"). The last are the most sinister of all, for there seems to be a resemblance between them and some of the "Old Ones" in the Cthulhu Mythos.

I wonder how many dangers the energy barrier has kept out of our galaxy.

Notice too that all those extragalactic dangers appeared in the small fraction of our galaxy which is explored by the people to whom the ancestors of the Preservers belong. Have other terrible perils appeared in the other sections of the galaxy or are all these dangers directed only at the beings protected by the Preservers?

When you consider all the times that the crew of the *Enterprise* has just barely managed to save the galaxy from destruction, you wonder how it was possible for our primitive civilizations of 100,000 B.C. or 10,000 B.C. or 1000 B.C. or 1000 A.D. or 1978 A.D. to survive the attacks of the various terrible menaces which in their time there would have been no powerful space-traveling civilization to stop. Most of the civilizations which in the time of Star Trek are as advanced as Earth should also have been as primitive as ancient Earth at the time when Earthmen were living in caves. There are certainly many remains of ancient lost civilizations in the Star Trek universe. Perhaps they defeated the terrible dangers which threatened the galaxy in their times, finally succumbing to the pressure after buying time for younger civilizations to arise.

Perhaps whoever is responsible for sending those attacks against Earth's galaxy didn't start until the time of Star Trek. Or maybe the Preservers took up the task of protecting the infant civilizations that would one day form the Federation until they became powerful enough to defend themselves.

But when you come to think about it, hasn't the *Enterprise* beaten the odds too many times? In "Errand of Mercy," Spock calculated the odds against making it to Kor's office as 7,824.7 to 1, but they made it. Even the simple computers of the present operate thousands of times faster than human thought, yet the fantastically more advanced Nomad/Tan Ru, which should have calculated that suicide was the only way out within a split second, remained indecisive until Kirk had time to transport it far away from the *Enterprise*. And why didn't the robot compute that it was better to destroy both its imperfect self and the imperfect crew of the *Enterprise* than to merely destroy itself and let the humans go on polluting the universe with their noxious imperfections? Why didn't the androids of Mudd's Planet, with their knowledge of human deceit gained from a long experience of Harry Mudd, plus their knowledge that he had occasionally been known to tell the truth, at once see the obvious way out of the logical trap set for them?

I could go on and on. The *Enterprise* has always made it under the wire in its split-second countdowns with death. Its jerry-rigged emergency devices, often not only constructed but even invented during the current emergency, always perform with 100 percent efficiency and the theories behind them are always correct. The odds against the *Enterprise*'s surviving all of the dangers it has faced must be trillions to one, at a conservative estimate.

(Remember that the odds against the survival of Kirk and Spock through the entire first season must have been greater than the 7,824.7 to 1 they faced in just one episode. If the odds in the second and third seasons and the season of animated Star Trek were each exactly the same, the odds against their surviving all four seasons would be 7,824.7 × 7,824.7 × 7,824.7 × 7,824.7 to 1!)

Just as the Preservers were probably the beings who gave the crew of the *Enterprise* the illusion that they were solving their problems by transporting their two captives back to earth in "Tomorrow Is Yesterday," they probably played their secret parts in the course of many other adventures of the *Enterprise*, preserving Kirk, Spock, McCoy, etc. against all dangers and helping them to defeat the various menaces which threatened the Federation.

I suppose if this theory is thoroughly applied it may take

away some of the suspense of the various Star Trek episodes, knowing that the heroes of the *Enterprise* will always have their "guardian angels" hovering overhead, ready to save them from any peril they can't defeat themselves. But the theory is so reasonable that it should be adopted by writers of future episodes, taking care to describe its ramifications in a manner which will lessen the suspense in the least degree.

Did Zefrem Cochran independently invent the warp drive, or did the Preservers openly tell him about it, or use some subtle influence to make him imagine the theory of the warp drive? As I have elsewhere postulated, Cochrane's discovery seems to have included the time warp itself, a device for generating a drive that would propel a ship at a constant speed, and a device for locating the endpoints of Gateways—three great inventions from one man.

As I have reconstructed the history of that time, Cochrane must have discovered the existence of a society with a monopoly on interstellar travel, which mercilessly crushed any attempt of any other world to develop interstellar flight. If the Preservers had nothing to do with it, it was a lucky accident which enabled Cochrane to discover the existence of that monopoly without being himself discovered and destroyed by the agents of the monopoly.

Who created the system of space warps, which I call Gateways, linking the various solar systems of the galaxy? According to the evidence of the distribution of the worlds visited in Star Trek, some Gateways connect solar systems which are close to one another, while other Gateways connect solar systems hundreds or thousands or tens of thousands of light-years away. The system of Gateways doesn't seem to extend beyond our galaxy.

The stars within 1,000 light-years of Earth are only a tiny proportion of the total number of stars in the galaxy. And yet quite a large proportion of all the stars mentioned in Star Trek are within 1,000 light-years of Earth. Furthermore, of the twenty stars which at the present time appear brightest from Earth and thus are the best known to humans, a full thirteen have been mentioned as having been visited by Earthmen, and thus being easily accessible through the system of Gateways, though by the time of Star Trek perhaps no more than 0.001 percent of all the stars in the galaxy had been reached.

That is no coincidence. Whoever created the system of Gateways arranged it so that the stars best known to Earthmen of the twenty-second century would be among those it would be most easy for Earthmen to reach through the Gateways. I suggest that the Preservers would be likely candidates for the position of the powerful civilization strongly interested in the civilization of Earth which must have created the Gateways.

Did the Preservers arrange the marriage of Sarek and Amanda? Certainly no detailed explanation of how that seeming "odd couple" got together has been provided by the Star Trek episodes, though fans have attempted to do so. Certainly if any fraction of the importance of their offspring for the course of history had been explained to Sarek, his marriage with the human woman would seem "the logical thing to do."

This discussion by no means exhausts the possibilities of time travel. If time is like space, there should be at least three dimensions of time. Besides the familiar dimension in which the normal flow of time proceeds and along which time travelers pass to the past and to the future, there may be at least two more time dimensions at right angles to the first, dimensions along which one would travel to reach alternate universes.

Nor are the only episodes in which the subject of alternate universes would be important "Alternative Factor," "Mirror, Mirror," "The Counterclock Incident," "Is There in Truth no Beauty?," "The Tholian Web," and "Magicks of Megas'Tu." Instead, any discussion of alternate universes in *Star Trek* would have to mention every episode, and would overthrow all the current ideas about the chronology of *Star Trek* episodes.

But that will have to be a different article.

# 16.
# ANOTHER VIEW OF THE PSYCHOLOGY OF MR. SPOCK'S POPULARITY

## by Jack Lenburg

*Gloria-Ann Rovelstad's article "The Psychology of Mr. Spock's Popularity"* (The Best of Trek #1) *ranked second in the number of letters sent by readers. Many agreed with her comments; as many disagreed. But Jack Lenburg was not content with a simple letter commenting on Gloria-Ann's article. He wrote an article of his own. He left it untitled, but we didn't have any trouble giving it one. It is indeed, "another view."*

Gloria-Ann Rovelstad begins her article "The Psychology of Mr. Spock's Popularity" by writing: "We, as humans, watch to see him show emotion."

Whatever group of viewers she alleges to represent, perhaps the feminine contingent, she does not speak for me or any of my Star Trek-viewing friends.

Emotion abounds in the words and actions of Captain Kirk and Dr. McCoy in nearly every episode. Whether it evolves through the love of Captain Kirk for his ship and his women or through the vehement reactions of Dr. McCoy to the logic of Mr. Spock, it fulfills all quotas for man's foibles.

Almost every one of the many decisions arrived at by Captain Kirk is based on a combined consideration of the logical advice of First Officer Spock and Kirk's own emotional reaction to the situation.

Dr. McCoy's emotion is not merely confined to confrontations with Mr. Spock. Many times he is allowed to show his obvious affection and loyalty to the Captain. Also, we see that he is not immune to the charms of the opposite sex, as in the episode "Mantrap," when he nearly lets his love for Nancy Crater destroy the Captain.

Emotion is no stranger to Chief Engineer Scott, either.

153

Many times, while in command of the ship, he displays a fervor for the ship's safety which rivals Captain Kirk's. While intoxicated, Scotty becomes a virtual fountain of good cheer.

Additionally, the hate, lust, greed, avarice, and fear of each episode's villain or villainess only add to the total emotional impact of Star Trek.

One thing that Star Trek does not lack is a surplus of emotion! Added emotion from Mr. Spock is infinitesimal when compared with that of his co-stars.

On the other hand, the obvious friendship Spock displays for Kirk and McCoy is an integral part of his total portrayal. Many times Spock is willing to risk his own life and the safety of the *Enterprise* to save the Captain, even though it is "illogical."

Although Spock and McCoy often seem diametrically opposed, there is an underlying respect and friendship which is unmistakable. When McCoy becomes the helpless guinea pig of the Vians in "The Empath," Spock shows a genuine concern for the fate of the doctor. Spock knows that any time his life is in danger, Kirk or McCoy will willingly risk their own to save him. The first officer is more than willing to reciprocate.

This facet adds a dimension to the character that avoids predictability. Without periodic personal sacrifices on behalf of the Captain and the Dr. McCoy, Spock would be less endearing to the fans. Not even the most avid devotees of logic expect Spock to be a walking computer continually.

But the outstanding trait of Mr. Spock is his uniqueness, not his temporary outbursts of emotion. His unique appearance, unique philosophy, and unique way of relating to humans are what make him the ever-so-popular alien. His devilish countenance is a perfect mask for a man who has devoted his life to suppressing his emotions. While closeups allow Captain Kirk to display the entire spectrum of facial expressions, Mr. Spock is, for the most part, limited to the simple lifting of an eyebrow. And yet, with that lone unemotional gesture, Spock is able to project a whole panorama of hidden emotion to the viewer.

James Kirk portrays every emotion vividly and without restrictions. The subtle, deadpan appearance of Mr. Spock provides a unique alter ego for the Captain.

In many ways Spock is a superior being, with his computerlike mind and his emotionless devotion to duty. His Vulcan physique and endurance is an example to the rest of the crew which even Captain Kirk cannot match. Computing extremely intricate mathematical formulas and repairing advanced technical machinery are invaluable skills in which Spock was unequaled.

Another example of Spock superiority is the Vulcan Mind Meld. More than once this extraordinary ability saves Captain Kirk and the *Enterprise* from potentially disastrous situations. "Turnabout Intruder" provides a stirring example of the importance of Spock's nonhuman abilities. Only he could surmise, through the Vulcan Mind Meld, that the essence of James Kirk is imprisoned within the body of Janice Lester.

Spock's Mind Meld with the Horta in "The Devil in the Dark" ends a series of horrible deaths for pergium miners. No human could have accomplished this feat.

Captain Kirk, Dr. McCoy, and Chief Engineer Scott all owe their lives to the Vulcan Mind Meld in "The Last Gunfight." Without Spock's power to convince them that the bullets are illusions, all of them could have died.

The fact that an alien with such superior abilities has decided to align himself with a crewful of humans gives a feeling of superiority to the viewers.

Spock's confrontations with the parasites in "Operation Annihilate" provide the most impressive example of his extraordinary nature. What human with his entire nervous system entwined with stands of parasitic material could ignore the excruciating pain and return to duty? Only Spock's logical mind could overcome the effects on his invaded body through sheer willpower. Any man subject to emotional stress would have found this task impossible.

And when Dr. McCoy administers the "cure" for Spock's condition, what human could accept the resulting blindness so logically as Spock does? Again he proves his superiority through logic. Star Trek fans could only marvel at Spock's ability to cope with his environment.

Many times Spock's decision to "pursue the only logical course open" set an example for the rest of the crew to follow. In "Balance of Terror," when Kirk is undecided about what to do about the Romulan invasion, it is Spock's impeccable logic which convinces the Captain to attack the Romulan flagship.

Perhaps the greatest temptation Spock ever encounters is the female Romulan commander in "The *Enterprise* Incident." He is obviously attracted to her strength of will, her intelligence, and her kinship to his Vulcan ancestry. But these extraordinary qualities are no match for Spock's logical devotion to duty.

When Spock has carried out his mission and the Romulan commander asks, "Who are you that you could do this to me?" Spock's answer is simple but awe-inspiring: "First officer of the *Enterprise*." And then with a coolness that defied description he asks, "What is your present form of execution?"

His disregard for personal safety leaves fans with nothing but admiration for his strength of character.

In "All Our Yesterdays" when time regression threatens to metamorphose Spock into an illogical barbarian, only his logical mind allows him to retain his identity and overcome the baser desires which are trying to control him.

The science officer's relentless logic is the sole salvation for Captain Kirk in "Court Martial" when no one can disprove his supposed guilt for Records Officer Benjamin Finney's "death." Everyone, including Kirk himself, begins to doubt his innocence when the extract from the computer log seems to confirm his guilt. Logic alone allows Mr. Spock to perceive that the computer has been reprogrammed to falsify the log.

Spock's ability at deductive reasoning (which would rival even the great Sherlock Holmes) is evident in more than one episode. Given all the evidence, Mr. Spock is still the only person who can deduce the real identity of Mr. Flint and Rayna in "Requiem for Methuselah." Even when he reveals all of his findings to the Captain, Kirk is still mystified. But Spock realizes that Flint really is Johannes Brahms and Leonardo da Vinci and many others.

And, further, he surmises that Rayna is not human. Neither Captain Kirk nor Dr. McCoy even guess the answers until Mr. Spock tells them. Again, Mr. Spock's logical perception proves superior to the emotions of McCoy and the intuition of the Captain.

Many of Captain Kirk's decisions are directed by the unrelenting logic of Mr. Spock. In "The Lights of Zetar," Captain Kirk is unable to invent a defense against the life forms that are attacking the ship. Science Officer Spock has to advise the Captain that the only way to fight them is to "find an environment that is deadly to the life form." Spawned by logic, his advice is infallible.

One of the most popular of all episodes, "The City on the Edge of Forever," forces Captain Kirk to make one of the most difficult decisions of his entire career. It is again Mr.

Spock who unmasks the solution to their predicament: Edith Keeler has to die in order to set time right again.

Mr. Spock's brilliant repair work with the tricorder gives him the necessary information. Logic dictates the answer.

The time distortion is corrected thanks to Mr. Spock's deduction. Unfortunately, it is at the cost of Captain Kirk's figurative heart.

In "By Any Other Name," Captain Kirk is again at a loss for a solution to the Kelvan takeover. Not until Spock points out the peculiar reactions the Kelvans are displaying in their newly acquired human forms does Kirk realize the correct method of attack. It is Spock's logical evaluation of the situation which enables Captain Kirk to defeat another adversary.

Spock's logic serves as a delicate counterbalance to all the emotions displayed by Kirk and McCoy. This contrast of logic and emotions furnishes a perfect complement that never disappoints the viewers.

While the Captain's judgment is obviously clouded by his attraction to Rayna in "Requiem for Methuselah," Spock's levelheaded assistance keeps Kirk's perspective attuned to his duty. If not for Spock, the Captain's emotions might not be kept in check.

In "Court-Martial," while the captain wallows in frustration and Dr. McCoy approaches hysteria worrying about the fate of his friend James Kirk, Mr. Spock logically goes about the business of solving the mystery of the faulty computer log.

He provides the one cool head in a cast of players displaying almost every imaginable emotion. It offers a well-balanced contrast.

While Captain Kirk and Dr. McCoy exhibit fear, regret, despair, and anger over Spock's fate in "Operation Annihilate," the indomitable first officer accepts each catastrophe with the same selfless logic. His refusal to show emotion under such immense stress makes the performances of Kirk and McCoy that much more effective.

Infection and lesions on the body are the enemy which attack the *Enterprise* crew in "Miri." Captain Kirk is trying to handle the affections of a budding young lady diplomatically while slowly submitting to a shortened temper. Irritable and becoming increasingly frustrated, McCoy and Kirk are losing their ability to cope with the situation.

Spock, infected with the same virus, maintains his temperament and serves as a living stanchion who never falters in his pursuit of a solution to the problem.

All of the many emotions displayed by Dr. McCoy and Captain Kirk in Star Trek are tempered by the ever-present logic of Mr. Spock. The very presence of the *Enterprise*'s science officer gives hope to the viewer, no matter how hopeless a situation may appear.

Regardless of the pained or worried expressions on the faces of McCoy and Kirk, the viewer is secure in the knowledge that Mr. Spock will be unyielding in his quest for the solutions.

This interaction of emotions stemming from the Captain and McCoy, along with the calm resolve of the logical Mr. Spock, transmits a unique experience to the viewer unparalleled in television history. He can see and feel the pain, suffering, and apprehension of a particular event and at the same time be assured (almost subconsciously) that the perennial logic of Mr. Spock will somehow formulate or reveal a rationale for survival.

I admire and envy Mr. Spock for many reasons. His philosophy and way of life serve as an inspiration to many of us who are trying to survive in an illogical and frustrating society. The order and contentment which seem to surround his life-style invite mostly envy from the viewing audience.

Mr. Spock does not know frustration. He accepts each situation or problem as it materializes. After gathering all the information possible, he arrives at the logical solution, if there is one. Usually there is.

However, regardless of the predicament, Spock's logic has made him impervious to fear or hesitation. Undaunted, he always makes the decision or gives the advice which logic demands. Never does he regret or mull over a conclusion.

Humans make decisions daily and then wonder if it was the right choice. Not Mr. Spock! Very few people (if any) can claim the same supreme self-confidence which Mr. Spock displays.

The science officer's ability to discard emotional considerations when making a decision serves as an enviable example to every viewer.

In "Where No Man Has Gone Before," Captain Kirk hesitates to strand his mutated friend on a desolate planet. This emotional fixation could prove disastrous for the *Enterprise* were it not for Spock's logical advice when he reminds Kirk that this type of hesitation probably resulted in the destruction of the *Valiant*.

The *Enterprise* and the immortal nature of Star Trek could not have survived without the logic of Mr. Spock. His infrequent bouts with emotion only provide fans with proof that although he is superior, he is not perfect.

The quickness and accuracy of Mr. Spock's mind is also a wonder to behold. Calculating complicated mathematical formulas in his mind that the captain cannot even comprehend on paper is a common occurrence for the *Enterprise*'s first officer. His understanding of scientific phenomena and computer technology is unmatched in Starfleet. Every man or woman who watches Star Trek wishes he or she could master the intricacies of his chosen field half as well as Mr. Spock does.

Spock's intellectual explanations of space phenomena and physical laws elevate television vocabulary to a new height. He is one of the few characters on TV who does not insult the intelligence of the viewer.

New technological terms flow from his dialogue in every episode. Those who understand, or wanted to understand, listen a little more intently every time Mr. Spock speaks. We do not listen to hear a statement of emotion, but to accept the weekly challenge of fathoming the explanations and conclusions of the science officer of the *Enterprise*.

And when the challenge is occasionally too much we go one step further and learn a new fact.

Very few other series or characters can make that claim. Mr. Spock offers more than entertainment to the viewer. He offers an intelligent vocabulary for intelligent viewers.

Mr. Spock does not make a success out of Star Trek by himself any more than Captain Kirk does. He fills a character void in the total puzzle of Star Trek.

As a starbound "Errol Flynn," the Captain portrays a charismatic swashbuckler type that has long been missing from the screen. He sweeps the ladies off their feet, vanquishes all foes in single combat, and instills undying loyalty in his crew. All this is done in as dramatic and flamboyant a manner as possible.

Spock also titillates the ladies, distinguishes himself in every physical conflict, and commands lasting respect from his shipmates. But as an anti-Kirk character he accomplishes these feats in a subtle, casually unemotional manner.

By himself, Captain Kirk is a good character. With Mr.

Spock's aid, he is a great Captain, believable and immortal in the hearts of his fans.

I watch Mr. Spock because he portrays an approach to life which I feel is superior. My adoration for him stems from his Vulcan supremacy, not his human weaknesses. If I ever feel sympathy for him after one of his romantic entanglements it is because he has been forced to relinquish his logical characteristics for an emotional personality. Logic is his strength, emotion his weakness. I prefer a strong Mr. Spock.

After my quick conversion to a Star Trek fanatic, I did not make application for admission to the Air Force Academy or NASA. I did not grow pointed ears and my blood is still red.

But when my temper flares or the weight of the world rests itself on my shoulders, I sometimes stop and think, "Would Mr. Spock allow himself to be upset by this situation?" And sometimes I can choose logic over anger or despair.

I do not pretend to be as smart or logical as the famous Vulcan, but within my own limitations I do try to emulate his philosophy for coping with reality.

The logical Mr. Spock inspires followers and exemplifies a way of life that many of us find superior. The minority of Star Trek fans who watch only to be entertained watch to see Mr. Spock show emotions. The rest of the intelligent audience watch not only to be entertained but also to have their minds stimulated and their knowledge enhanced. They watch to see Mr. Spock exhibit a logical way of life.

# 17.
# KIRK AND HORNBLOWER

## by G. B. Love

*Gene Roddenberry called his vision of the* Enterprise *captain "A space-age Captain Horatio Hornblower." But it takes more than a glib phrase aimed at studio executives to create a character, and in creating his captain, Roddenberry took himself at his word, and did indeed go to Horatio Hornblower for his inspiration. In the following article, G. B. discusses why Hornblower was such an excellent choice for the Kirk role model, and further looks at the similarities and differences between the characters.*

When Gene Roddenberry first began to develop the story line for his proposed science fiction television series Star Trek, he knew from his television writing experience that a strong leading character was essential to the success of a show. He envisioned his protagonists to be adventurers and explorers in deep space, serving in a vessel which would be away from its home port for long periods of time. In other words, a ship of the line, much the same as the old sailing vessels and warships of the British Empire that explored and colonized much of the known world.

The analogy was perfect. The spaceship of Star Trek would be a far-ranging, virtually autonomous arm of Earth's (later the United Federation of Planets') space forces, finding new worlds and new adventures each week.

As the parallel between his proposed space vessel and the old sailing ships grew in Roddenberry's mind, he also realized that his ship would require that one factor which helped to make the ships of the British Empire so successful: a strong, determined, and superbly well-trained captain in charge.

The rare breed of men who were captains of England's ships had to have not only an excellent working knowledge of seamanship, but also a smattering of diplomacy, battle tactics, trading, and stewardship. Often thousands of miles away from home port, a captain of a British ship of the line was very much on his own. He represented not only the naval and military aspects of his government, but also acted as its official ambassador as well. Communications could take months, even as long as a year, to reach his superiors, so he often had to make life-and-death decisions on his own—decisions which could very well affect not only his current mission, but conceivably the safety and security of his homeland.

They were amazing and fascinating men. Roddenberry that he had to capture much of these qualities in his space-faring captain for the show to have a good chance for success. But exactly what qualities should his captain have? How should he react to a given situation, an attack, a crisis of galactic proportions? Roddenberry needed a model for his captain, a place from which to start to build the exceptional character that a man-in-a-million of the future would surely have to possess.

Luckily for Roddenberry, such a model did exist. In fact, he was one of Gene's favorite fictional characters, and perhaps the germination for Star Trek was originally a subconscious desire to translate his adventures to the science of the far future.

He was Captain Horatio Hornblower. And by extension, Captain James T. Kirk.

The exploits of Horatio Hornblower were first presented in the novel *Beat to Quarters* in 1937. Hornblower's creator was a shy, unassuming man named Cecil Scott Forester. Forester was born in Cairo, Egypt, in 1899, the son of a British army officer (not a naval officer as one would expect). He was educated in London, where he studied medicine until joining the British army as an infantryman in World War I. After a short term of service, he decided to give up medicine and tried his hand at poetry. He was not very successful, however, and soon turned to writing biographies and fiction.

It was with fiction that Forester found his greatest success, writing such best-selling novels as *The African Queen* and *The General*. After the success of his first Hornblower novel (the fifth in the series chronologically), he concentrated his efforts mainly on the immensely popular adventures of the dashing sea captain.

At the time of his death in 1966, Forester had completed eleven Hornblower books, all of them best sellers. It took him many months to write one of the Hornblower sagas, because he thoroughly researched and authenticated all the action, time periods, and settings of each book. One can see the immense amount of planning and detail that went into the Hornblower books, as the complete set makes up a perfectly logical and consistent chronological story of Hornblower's life and career; yet they were written out of sequence.

The Hornblower saga is as readable and as exciting today as in the past, and if you are not acquainted with it, you are missing some of the greatest adventures ever written.

It was inevitable that Gene Roddenberry would find parallels between Hornblower and the captain he envisioned. There was the added incentive that the Hornblower character had proved to be both popular and enduring with readers over many years, so a Star Trek captain with many of the same qualities would have an excellent chance of catching on with the viewing public.

But how much of Horatio Hornblower really went into James Kirk? We must remember that Roddenberry never intended that Kirk be a carbon copy of Hornblower, only that Forester's hero serve as a guide. The captain of the *Enterprise* would have to be a man of his time and his technology, and that made for a great difference between the basic characters from the very start.

Through the eleven books in the Hornblower saga, we see how he went from a young and inexperienced midshipman to admiral of the fleet. His character was thus enabled to mature with each new experience, and the reader is able to see the events which shape a youth into the sort of man who could command one of her majesty's warships.

But Kirk was to arrive on the television screens of the nation full-grown. The imperatives of getting on with the story did not allow for idle talk about his past experiences; and to attempt to follow a Starfleet officer from midshipman days through his captaincy was not the intention of Star Trek (although such a story would make for a fascinating TV miniseries!).

So the viewer had to know immediately that the captain of the *Enterprise* was an exceptional person. In order to effect this instant identification, all of the best qualities of Hornblower had to be in Captain Kirk—and even more so.

Then the qualities which one may find in Hornblower will not give a completely representative picture of Kirk. Hornblower was created to be much more of a realistic historical character than the "classical" hero type, and this may be verified by the large amount of tedium which is an integral part of Hornblower. That is, tedium in the sense of the day-to-day routine of shipboard life, of the necessary exposition required to follow the slow progression of events in Hornblower's world. And it is not boring, by any means.

But the adventures of Captain Kirk cannot be told in as leisurely fashion as in a novel. Television requires that the story and action begin immediately. There is little time for the exposition, the tedium, that makes for a well-rounded character.

Even over the course of three seasons, and the continuing efforts of both Roddenberry and Bill Shatner, little was added to the basic structure of Kirk. The overblown, almost super-hero qualities of the character dominated. Kirk didn't just feel emotions, he agonized over them. Kirk didn't just love, he fell head over heels. Kirk didn't just command a starship, he was the first commander, a living legend.

Not much can be done with a living legend, no matter how hard subsequent scripts try to humanize him. He is still *Kirk, the Captain of the Enterprise.*

In Hornblower, we see the gradual development of the admirable qualities that were literally flung at us with Kirk. We like Kirk, and want to emulate him, but until a mental process of "building" a past for Kirk takes place, we cannot appreciate him as a character—or as a person.

For example, in one of the early Hornblower sagas, the young and inexperienced Hornblower slides barehanded down a rope. We feel his pain and embarassment, and we know just as well as he does that he will never make that particular mistake again.

But upon hearing about a similar mistake on the part of a young Ensign Kirk, we would only be amused, as we have not been allowed to experience it with him. Further, such an elementary mistake doesn't fit into our perceptions of the eminently able Kirk. Why? Because we have not followed him through his learning process, and since we have therefore never seen Kirk make such a stupid mistake (and seldom a mistake of any kind), we cannot accept it as part of him.

This is not necessarily bad. Kirk is, after all, a hero. And heroes aren't supposed to make mistakes—not lasting ones, anyway. What we were presented with by Gene Roddenberry was a man of exceptional qualities, in the prime of his life and career. Such a man serves as a springboard to the series, both as protagonist and antagonist, and occasionally as a chorus.

Kirk does not lack any of the essential things that make up an adventure hero. We have the stated prerequisites: bravery, loyalty, intelligence, skill, youth, and virility. And what we are not overtly given, we may infer: compassion, humor, cunning, self-sacrifice. And even a certain amount of flaws: vanity, arrogance, chauvinism.

These things we impart to Kirk not only through actions written into a script, but by the mental building processes by which we define our own personal requirements for a hero— specifically, for the captain of the *Enterprise*.

When Roddenberry used Hornblower as his basic model for Kirk, he realized that unless the viewer was able to pick up on these unstated things that make up a likable, admirable, and popular character, that character would fail. By making him an overblown hero, Roddenberry gave us a head start on the building process, and it was up to us to make Kirk more than just a superman in space.

Thus it is due to the fans of Star Trek that Captain Kirk is a real and valuable person. Through our dreams and imagination, we have made a man out of a simplistic prototype; we have created a true hero. And a friend.

Thanks to this, today Kirk can stand proudly next to Hornblower as one of the most-loved and exciting characters in fiction. C. S. Forester created Hornblower's saga. We have created James T. Kirk's. And don't you think that Gene Roddenberry and Bill Shatner kind of planned it that way?

# 18.
# THE RISE OF
# THE FEDERATION
## Part I:
## The Eugenics Wars

### by Jim Houston

*Wow, did this article ever pull in the letters! Jim Houston turned his attention back to Star Trek after a long absence, and he did it with a vengeance, prompting one writer to comment that "Houston thinks he can rewrite history"! As to what could elicit such a charge, you can judge for yourself. (One comment: This is Part I of a multi-part article, which other writing considerations have kept Jim from completing. However, he promises it soon, and we promise it to you in The Best of Trek #3!)*

**1969**
Men land on the Moon.

**1980**
First space shuttle flights.

**1982**
Construction begins on Starlab, the first permanently manned space station. Though inhabited mainly by Americans, the space station also utilizes many foreign scientists on its civilian staff.

**1983—February**
Dr. Adam Charon begins his genetic-control experiments. Using thousands of subjects from all over the world (including his own wife and son), Charon attempts to improve the human race artificially by editing out "bad" influences in genetic structures, and adding in "improvements" which will maximize the potential mental and physical development of

the subject fetuses. The children resulting from these experiments will eventually grow up to be almost perfect examples of human developments.

### 1983—August
The United States, Russia, England, France, Germany, Japan, and Australia begin construction of a permanent base on the Moon. The purpose of the base is twofold: first, to prove that different nations can indeed cooperate on a large-scale space project (thus helping to relieve political tensions); and second, to demonstrate the practical value of space exploration by mining heavy metals from beneath the lunar surface.

### 1984
Starlab completed, full operations begin. Agricultural experiments are added to Moon Base One.

### 1985
Moon Base One completed, and full operations begin. A crew is selected for the first manned flight to Mars. Though the crew is composed of American astronauts, the ship itself will be built in the lower gravity of Moon Base by members of all participating nations.

### 1986—March
The success of Starlab prompts its backers to begin plans for an even larger space station which will house over 10,000 permanent inhabitants and be man's first true colony in space. To further emphasize the practicality and importance of space exploration, plans call for the station to be manufactured primarily from materials mined from the Moon, and if possible, from Mars. The station is to be built in sections, and as each section is completed, it will become immediately operational, thus allowing the station, in effect, to build itself. If successful, this ambitious project will represent man's greatest space achievement. It will not only include scientific and industrial sections (making such items as frictionless ball bearings, which can be produced only in weightless conditions), but will also grow its own food and provide reliable solar energy via microwave to a power-hungry Earth.

### 1986—July
The first manned Martian mission is launched from orbit around the moon.

**1987**

The first manned Martian expedition lands on Mars. Unlike the first lunar flights, all of the Martian crew will visit the surface. The main mission ship, the *Willy Ley* (named after a pioneer rocket experimenter), will remain in orbit while its three shuttle crafts, the *Isaac Asimov*, the *Ray Bradbury*, and the *John Carter* (evidence that the Martian mission crew remember earlier "visitors" to Mars), ferry the astronauts and their experimental devices to and from the surface. This will allow the crew to explore much of the Martian surface—more, in fact, than the total surface of the Moon explored by all of the Apollo missions combined. At the end of their three-month stay, the astronauts will board a recently arrived ship (the *John F. Kennedy*), which has been launched unmanned from Moon orbit for this purpose. The *Willy Ley* will remain in Mars orbit, along with the three shuttles and permanent experimental and information devices on Mars' surface, to serve as a base for future missions. Thus, following journeys to Mars needn't be encumbered by a large ship and can be launched for much less money.

**1988**

The *John F. Kennedy* lands at Moon Base One. The data brought back by the Martian expedition prompts the decision of scientists to attempt to build a permanent colony on Mars.

**1989**

Construction is started on the giant spaceship *Martian Genesis*, planned to carry over 1,000 people, all specially trained volunteers who will begin the task of making the Martian surface habitable for man. Instead of remaining in orbit around Mars, the *Martian Genesis* is designed to land on the surface, serving as a temporary home for the colonists until permanent facilities can be constructed. The *Genesis* will then serve as a power source for the colony with its nuclear generators.

**1990**

The *Martian Genesis* lands on Mars, and the colony is successfully launched. The colonists begin the difficult task of building a permanent home on the Martian surface.

**1991 to 2000**

Mankind enters what appears to be a golden age. Due to the technology developed in the colonization of the Moon and Mars, the standard of living goes up radically the world over.

The Martian colony flourishes and grows to over 10,000 in population. Further colonies are established in the asteroid belt, and on the moons of Jupiter and Saturn. An automated station is landed on the surface of Jupiter to "mine" the rare chemicals from the atmosphere. The Martian colony, augmented by new arrivals from Earth, splits into three more locations. Three more Starlab-type space stations are established, one of which is devoted solely to farming. With no seasons, droughts, diseases, etc. to affect growth yields, the farm satellite produces three times the foodstuffs an equal area of land on Earth does. World famine is greatly reduced, and the promise of more farm satellites gives humanity freedom from the fear of hunger. Solar power, in the form of microwaving from space, now supplies more than 75 percent of Earth's power needs. Thus, two of the largest problems facing the people of Earth seem to be solved, and public support for exploration and utilization of space has never been higher. The future of man is assured. Or so it seems. . . .

## 2000

Alex Charon, the son of Adam Charon and one of the first of the "superbabies" bred through his father's experiments, graduates from Harvard at the age of sixteen. He stands 6'2" and weighs 200 pounds. He was first in his class and played quarterback on the first nationally rated Harvard team in many years. Thoroughly convinced of his superiority over the rest of mankind, he decides the quickest way to obtain power is by entering politics. Thanks to the extent of his father's experiments, he has over 10,000 superbaby contemporaries, with more being born every day. Many people consider him to be a monster.

## 2006

Man now has a foothold on most of the inhabitable planets in the solar system. His unmanned ships have explored the inner-and outermost planets, as well as the deepest reaches of the seas. Advances in weather-control techniques and the influx of foodstuffs from the space stations have ended Earth's food problems. The standard of living throughout the world has never been higher. Power and raw materials are abundant and luxuries once considered beyond the reach of most of Earth's population are now commonplace. Major wars, which a few short years ago seemed unavoidable, are now unthinkable. With his immediate needs satisfied, man turns his attention and major efforts to reaching the stars. Without faster-than-light travel, interstellar expeditions must be considered a one-way trip. At first, five missions are considered. Three are of the generation-ship variety. Two hundred volunteers are chosen for each large ship. The ships contain their own ecosystem, producing food, water, and power indefinitely. Launched from one of the colony worlds, the ships will eventually build up speeds near the speed of light. The actual trips will take thousands of years in normal time, but due to the time-dilation effects of near-light speeds, it will appear much shorter to the passengers. Even so, it will be the descendants of the original passengers who arrive at the destination.

The remaining two interstellar ships are to be sleeper ships, in which the passengers are placed in a state of suspended animation to be awakened upon arrival at the destination programmed into these computer-guided ships. These ships are much cheaper to build, as they do not need to have the built-in ecosystems of the generation ships, but the element of risk is much greater.

## 2010
The five interstellar ships are launched from orbit around the outer planets. Alex Charon is defeated in his bid to be elected to an assembly seat in New York State, his planned first step in his political career. All over the world the maturing supermen are finding their efforts to enter the human world frustrated by fear and distrust, and by the disapproval of most organized religions.

## 2012
Fear that the supermen plan to replace normal humans reaches a stage of witchhunting when Gerald Vance, a crackpot evangelist, publishes his *Children of Satan: How the Supermen Plan to Conquer the World*. The book is the ravings of a deranged fanatic, full of half-truths, scientific inaccuracies, and out-and-out lies. Vance details the plans of the "superman conspiracy" to take over the governments of the world by subterfuge, and "eventually establish concentration camps where all of the normal human males will be used as slave labor and worked to death, and all of the women will be genetically 'reprogrammed' to produce only supermen children." The innate human need for an antagonist left vacant by the elimination of war found a handy target in the form of the supermen, and the fact that several of the supermen had already endeavored to enter politics and business led to a

ready acceptance for Vance's bigotry. The book leaps to the top of the best-seller lists, and waves of hysteria follow in its wake.

## 2015

Alex Charon loses his class-action suit to have *Children of Satan* suppressed. The publicity resulting from the trial only serves to bolster the book's popularity and lend credence to the rumor that Charon's people would end freedom of speech.

## 2017

Charon tries again for elective office. By now, resentment against the supermen is so high that Charon is driven from every platform where he tries to speak. Twice he narrowly escapes lynching. Disgusted with America, he gathers around him an elite band of superman scientists and administrators and leaves the country. He offers their services to any underdeveloped nation that will allow them to live in peace. Still suffering the effects of overpopulation, India gratefully takes them up on their offer. But Charon seeks more than a home for his people. He intends to eventually take control.

## 2018

In Germany, things are going somewhat better for the supermen. The leader of the superman faction is a man named Rupert Hentzau, the hereditary Baron of Ruritania. Hentzau proposes the return of the aristocracy to power as rulers of the nation. The most amazing thing about Hentzau is that he finds a receptive audience in his German countrymen. Especially attractive to them is his insistence that East Germany, which is still under Russian influence, be reunited with West Germany. Skillfully using world opinion against the Russian and East German rulers, Hentzau later in the year manages to convince the United Nations to authorize the unification of the two German nations.

## 2019

Germany becomes a whole nation again, and a celebrating German people declare Hentzau to be Rupert I, Emperor of all the German Peoples. Other Europeans view the title as a sign that Rupert will not be satisfied with the German nation alone.

## 2024

After seven years of maneuvering, Alex Charon takes over direct control of India. His plan is to now aid supermen in other nations to gain power in their own lands. Since the powerful and socially secure Western powers are not about to hand themselves over to superman rule, Charon turns his attention instead to the Third World.

**2032**

Alex Charon's plans are succeeding beyond his wildest dreams. By now, ten nations are controlled by supermen: India, the Empire of East Africa, the Republic of Central Africa, the United Nations of North Africa, United Indochina, Manchuria, the Republic of the Congo, Burma, Pakistan, and the Empire of the German Peoples. Of all these, only the German Empire does not owe its allegiance to Alex Charon.

This is a flaw Charon plans to correct. He succeeds in concluding an alliance with the volatile Rupert. Though he controls almost one-third of the world's population, Charon knows it is the poorest third. The only nation on Earth that Charon can even look to for help, and that has technology and wealth enough to battle the Western nations when the time comes, is Germany. So Charon enters into talks with Rupert for an alliance of their powers.

During their discussions, Charon discovers that Rupert's desires for power rival his own. Although they do not trust each other, they have no choice. Charon needs Rupert's technology and wealth, Rupert needs Charon's almost inexhaustible supply of people. The alliance, which on the surface appears to be no more than an exchange of information and raw materials, is in fact a plan for dividing up the world. They form tacit agreements: Charon would retain control of Africa, Asia, and sections of South America; Rupert would gain dominion over his hated enemies, the other Europeans and Russians, plus most of North America.

Back in India, Charon faces a threat to his power when a native superman, Ram Singh Kahn, begins to build a power base for himself. Using the resentment that has grown against Charon because of his practice of rounding up the sacred cattle that roam freely through India and selling them to foreign markets, he quickly becomes the favorite of the people. He also receives the support of many of Charon's generals, who resent having to follow a non-Indian and a white man. Though small at first, Kahn's power continues to grow as Charon increasingly turns his attention to world conquest.

**2033**

Rupert faces his first serious test. When the Council of Spacefaring Nations (the international body that controls space travel) meets, other European nations show their distrust of Rupert by introducing a resolution to have Germany expelled from the organization for "certain warlike intentions." To be exiled would deny Germany access to the advanced resources of space technology, and more important to Rupert, would ban Germany from launching and operating its own satellites. In a vicious behind-the-scenes fight, Rupert manages to keep his nation in the Council, but his bitterness against his neighbors is now beyond the point of reconciliation.

Later that year, in a now brazen show of disdain, Rupert launches a series of "observation" satellites, and although to an extent they are for observation, their primary purpose is much more chilling. The satellites contain ground-controlled laser cannons, positioned in orbit so that they can be targeted anywhere on the globe in a matter of minutes. They can also defend themselves against missile attack. Weapons such as these have been banned since the twentieth century, and consequently, no other nation has an effective defense against them. They are to be Rupert's major weapon in his coming bid for world domination.

## 2034

Rupert now has dozens of laser cannons in orbit. Beginning to fear his intentions, the other European nations demand inspection of the satellites. A team is dispatched by the Council, but they are blasted out of the sky by one of the lasers. Now that the true nature of the satellites is known, the nations of the world demand that Rupert dismantle them. His response is to open fire on nuclear-missile silos in England and France.

Russia is his next target. Even as the Supreme Soviet is in the process of declaring war upon him, Rupert's lasers are in the process of destroying their weaponry. Able to pinpoint targets at will, Rupert quickly brings Europe to its knees. He then turns the lasers on the United States.

But for once, someone acts without bureaucratic haggling. The United States launches its small complement of missiles at both Germany and the satellites. A desperate but futile effort, as over three decades of peace have led the superpowers to destroy most of their defensive weaponry. Only four of the satellites are destroyed.

## 2035

The West's last-ditch effort to stop Rupert is launched. The spacefleet based on the Moon attempts to destroy the satellites, but is destroyed by the laser defense system. Fearing further attacks from the moon, Rupert turns his lasers to Moon Base One. It is this action which proves his undoing. Now that the war has come to their doorstep, the satellite colonies decide to intervene. Converting their powerful communication and power lasers into destructive weapons, they are able to take Rupert's technicians by surprise and eliminate his satellites. In a rage, Rupert orders his missiles fired at the colonies, and they too are easily destroyed. Although the brunt of Rupert's threat is now gone, he still controls most of Europe, and a formidable array of sophisticated weaponry. Even with the sword of imminent destruction removed from their heads, the Western Allies still face a long hard fight to free Europe. A year of fighting has given Kahn control of the western half of India. Most of Charon's old allies have now sided with him. But Charon still has a foothold in eastern India, and as this is the section that contains most of the heavy industry, he controls the nuclear missiles and the technology to use them. A stalemate is thus reached, and the East girds itself for long and bitter war.

**2036**

The Western Allies invade Europe. They are aided by underground groups which have sprung up under Rupert's despotic rule, but get no further help from the space colonies. After the threat of the laser satellites was removed, the colonies ignored all attempts at contact. They appear to want no more to do with the problems and wars of Earth.

The war in the East is still going in Kahn's favor. All of Asia and Africa (except for Charon's East India stronghold) is under his control. But his hold on these lands are shaky. He is running out of food and materials. His repeated attempts to overrun Charon have failed. His followers are beginning to mutter of revolt. And he always must fear a victory by Rupert, which would naturally lead to an attack upon Kahn's forces and lands. Deciding that he must have an impregnable base from which to retrench his forces, Kahn decides upon Australia. Able to attack it with the whole of his forces, Kahn takes control of Australia in a matter of days. He then turns his attention to administration, and an unspoken truce is formed between him and Charon.

**2037**

The easy victory that Rupert once seemed to have is now an empty dream. By the summer, his forces have been driven back to the German borders. Even though he has brought them to ruin, the German people are still loyal to Rupert, so an invasion of Germany would mean at least another long, hard year of fighting against a still rabid citizenry. The Allies decide to sue for peace instead. The terms of the treaty would require Germany to destroy all of its military machinery and to aid in the restoration of Europe. It also requires that Rupert abdicate the throne, and that the new emperor not be one of the supermen. In return, the Allies will allow Germany to remain an independent state, something they would not allow if an invasion was required. Though he is a despot, Rupert still loves his people, and realizing that the war is lost, accepts the treaty as the best thing for them. To assure the continuance of his power, Rupert appoints a distant relative, Joseph Slegberg, Baron Rustaheim, to be emperor. In January of 2038, he becomes Emperor Franz Joseph I.

The war in the East has gone badly for Kahn. One of his allies, K'huarba Insebe, Emperor of East Africa, attacks Kahn's unprotected rear in an attempt to widen his power. Kahn realizes that this is but the first of such revolts by his allies. Instead of attempting to defend a crumbling empire, Kahn takes the cream of his supermen and retreats to his Australian stronghold.

## 2038

K'huarba, giddy by what he feels is a major victory over Kahn, assembles the dregs of his armies and attacks Charon. He is easily defeated, but the effort, coupled with famine, leads to the fall of Charon's empire as well. His armies desert, and driven almost mad by the failure of his dreams, Charon singles out Kahn for blame. His last act before committing suicide is to launch his remaining missiles at Australia.

The devastation caused by this attack allows a strike force of Western Allies to move on Kahn's fortress and take him and his main body of supermen followers captive. He refuses to renounce his ambitions, so he and his people are placed aboard a sleeper ship and launched into space.

The long struggle with the supermen is over. The results: an Earth in ruins. Widespread starvation and disease. The loss of an incalculable amount of knowledge and resources. And over one-third of the Earth's population destroyed. Surveying the carnage, no one would suspect that man's finest hour was at hand.

# 19.
# SPECULATIONS ON SPOCK'S PAST

by Pamela Rose

*What was Spock like as a child? Why did he clash with his father and enter Starfleet? Why did he hold such a deep and abiding love for Christopher Pike? Exactly what happened in Spock's life during the many years preceding the time we first encounter him on Star Trek?*

*All of these questions (and hundreds more) have been the subject of literally thousands of articles and stories by Star Trek fans. And, as you may well imagine, almost each and every one of them has a different answer to those questions. But we feel that Pamela Rose has come about as close as anyone ever will to the "real" story. See if you agree.*

On a diplomatic mission to Earth, Ambassador Sarek of Vulcan met a Earthwoman named Amanda Grayson.

Amanda was a teacher, very intelligent and compassionate. And she was a very beautiful woman—a fact not lost on Sarek, although he considered it of secondary importance. She rapidly fell in love with the handsome, stoic Vulcan, but it took somewhat longer for Sarek to feel the same way.

However, the chemistry between them could not be ignored. Eventually Sarek proposed marriage, in a very calm and logical manner, of course, and Amanda had no difficulty in deciding to accept.

Although Sarek was in his sixties (relatively young by Vulcan years), he had never married. It seemed that his sperm was not compatible with a Vulcan female; therefore, it was considered illogical for him to be bonded when no issue could be expected of the union. This may have been the reason he permitted himself to fall in love with a human female. But, then again, Amanda was undoubtedly an unusual woman. Perhaps Sarek was not as coldblooded as he led us to believe. That he loved Amanda was undeniable.

It was later discovered that Sarek was indeed fertile when mated with an Earthwoman. It was a difficult pregnancy, as Amanda's blood type was far removed from the child's, but not impossible. Vulcan obstetrics were extremely advanced and proved quite capable of handling the many problems involved.

Sarek was concerned with the dangers this pregnancy presented to his wife, but he could not help but feel pleased. On Vulcan everything revolved around custom, family, and inheritance. With this child, the line would continue. In a very logical reaction, he made plans for its future.

The child was born and, with the exception of some disturbing human elements in his blood, appeared completely Vulcan. He was named Spock.

As young Spock grew, he began to realize that he was different in some way. When he felt the urge to laugh out loud or cry, he sensed that it was wrong. He wasn't sure what he was doing wrong, but when he caught Sarek's disapproving gaze, he would wither. As time went on, he learned quickly to keep it inside; he smothered his feelings, until they became easier to hide.

At the age of seven, he was properly bonded to a lovely little girl named T'Pring. He wasn't unduly impressed as, at the time, he wasn't quite certain what it meant.

He was a very intelligent child. Perhaps even more so than was ordinary in Vulcans. Part of the reason for this could have been his hybrid makeup. It has been remarked that crossbreeding often results in greater intelligence and stamina than pure strains. His curiosity was insatiable. He wanted to know everything all at once.

On the whole, he was an exceptional child. Sarek was well pleased with his son except for one thing which he deemed a fault in Spock's personality. Spock was a dreamer.

Sarek had found Spock staring at the stars, eyes wide, the emotions within him easy to read. He occasionally strayed from the path of logic to seek answers without facts to base them on. He questioned constantly, always wanting to know why, instead of concentrating on the facts themselves as was proper for a child of his years. Much of this Sarek attributed to the Earth literature Amanda gave to Spock, which he devoured eagerly. However, Sarek felt it was only a matter of time before Spock would be able to control these unfortunate human tendencies.

Sarek was correct. It did not take Spock long to adjust to his environment (or perhaps conform is a better word). He was a Vulcan, and Vulcans behaved in a logical manner. They had no room for dreaming or emotionalism. The other Vulcan children made it quite clear that it was not acceptable behavior. They did not taunt him as human children would have done. There were no fights or namecalling. They were much more subtle. They simply turned from him, not including him in their activities. He was half human; therefore he must be inferior.

Spoke stubbornly set out to prove that he was as much a Vulcan as any of them. In the process he made himself more stiff and controlled than even his father. He resolutely put aside the human literature and poetry his mother had given him and concentrated on science instead. Art, even Vulcan art, was closer to emotions than was safe. Only his music was kept—and that in private.

Other than his pet *sehlat*, Spock was friendless. He refused to get close to anyone—perhaps because he feared rejection, perhaps because he felt his human half might slip out.

He entered the Vulcan Academy of Science at an unusually young age and quickly rose to the top of the class. He earned the equivalent of a doctorate in mathematics, computer science, and biophysics.

When it neared the time for him to be offered a permanent position in the Academy, as his father had been (and his father before him), Spock's mother stepped in. She wanted Spock to spend time on Earth to learn some of his human history and culture. Sarek wasn't enthusiastic about the suggestion, feeling that anything could be learned more factually on Vulcan, but he couldn't, in logic, refuse such a desire on Amanda's part.

Spock had very little to say in the matter, of course. On Vulcan one does not question the wisdom of his elders until he comes of age, and Spock was not quite twenty. He was far from eager to return to Earth, however. He had been there once before at the age of ten, when he had gone with his mother to visit his aunt and cousins. He felt humans were, on the whole, quite uneducated and prejudiced.

He did not find them much changed in the ten years he had been away.

However, he did meet a most unusual human. His name

was Christopher Pike, and he was slated to take command of the Starship *Enterprise* when Captain April was promoted.

Pike contacted Spock to talk to him about becoming science officer on the *Enterprise* when he took command. Spock was puzzled, as he was not even entered in Starfleet Academy. Chris Pike was aware of this, but the Vulcan had been highly recommended to him by one of Spock's professors, who thought he was definitely Starfleet material. Pike knew Spock's intelligence and academic record. He felt certain that with little more than a year of cadet training, Spock would be eligible.

Spock understood what he was driving at. There were not many Vulcans in Starfleet, especially in anything other than research. The whole purpose of Starfleet went against the Vulcan philosophy of nonviolence—although it was publicly supported by the Vulcan government as a necessary evil.

However, Vulcans were greatly in demand for their logic and intelligence. Pike knew this, and he also knew that he wanted one as his science officer. Specifically, he wanted Spock. The *Enterprise* was scheduled to go into deep space. He needed someone who could be logical and unemotional in a dangerous situation.

Spock could not help but be intrigued by the possibility of scientific investigation in totally unknown areas. The freedom of space also attracted him. But he considered it illogical to give up a position at the Vulcan Academy for an uncertain career in Starfleet.

His life had been carefully plotted, almost from the moment of his birth. His career, and even his choice of wife had been arranged in careful Vulcan style. Very little was left to whim or chance. Although the human in him might feel stifled from time to time, the Vulcan in him saw the logic in careful planning.

When he returned to Vulcan, however, he found that his position at the Academy was not as certain as he had thought. There was some controversy about adding a human element. They felt they could not logically overlook any aspect of Spock's psychological makeup. Since he was half human, could there not be a possibility of emotions coloring his work? It was extremely subtle prejudice.

The decision was not really in question. They could hardly refuse to admit someone of Spock's very apparent qualifications.

But somehow Spock could not help feeling that the fact

that Sarek was his father had a great deal to do with their decision. Sarek was very influential on Vulcan—he was not a man even the Academy could afford to offend. Sarek, of course, felt differently. He thought Spock should stay and force them to see his worth.

But Spock was weary of trying to prove he was totally Vulcan. He wasn't that certain of it anyway. He knew there was much of his mother in him, and that he *did* sometimes have trouble controlling it. It was a hard decision, as his home was very important to Spock, but he decided to leave Vulcan and join Starfleet. Perhaps there he could discover what he really was—Vulcan or human. Or maybe he'd be able to reach a compromise between the two.

Sarek strongly disapproved of Starfleet, and Spock's decision to join the service kept them at odds for eighteen years. This hurt Spock deeply, for he loved and respected his father, but he had learned to control these feelings just as he controlled his pain at parting from Vulcan. A part of him always remained a little homesick.

Starfleet Academy presented no problem for Spock. The discipline there was nothing like what was normal on Vulcan. It was not long until he was assigned, at Captain Pike's request, to the Starship *Enterprise*.

Pike became something of a father figure to Spock. A father who could show compassion—something Spock had lacked. He was patient with Spock's futile attempts at being human, and understanding about his failures. He encouraged, lectured, scolded, and praised. In short, he gave Spock the things Sarek had been unable to give. Spock loved him. He was loyal to Pike to the extent that, in later years, Spock was to risk his career, and even the death penalty, to save Pike from a death-in-life by taking him back to Talos IV.

When Pike was promoted, Spock was uncertain how to deal with the situation. His best choice was to remain on the *Enterprise* as science officer. Here he had a secure place. He felt at home.

He was also a little uncertain of how he felt toward the new captain, James T. Kirk. Pike had personally chosen Kirk as his successor. It was an unusual move, but one which Starfleet surprisingly honored. Kirk was said to be a man of unusual bravery and command potential. But Spock could not give his loyalty easily; it would have to be earned.

The new officers that came with Captain Kirk were quite satisfactory, however. Especially the chief engineer, Montgomery Scott. Spock could not be less than impressed with this man's genius at mechanics and engineering. Sulu and Uhura were also extremely efficient.

Unfortunately, Spock could find little to admire about the new first officer, Gary Mitchell. He was loud, brash, and conceited. He was also not above telling Vulcan jokes within Spock's hearing, forcing Spock to grit his teeth in irritation.

Although Mitchell was very proficient at his job as navigator and first officer, Spock could not understand Kirk's fondness for him. They were apparently extremely close friends. Spock could not comprehend how a man of Kirk's obvious intelligence did not see the shortcomings in Mitchell's character.

Then they were assigned to the mission at the edge of the galaxy. It had happened very quickly. The barrier/forcefield. The unfortunate change in Mitchell. Kirk's decision to strand his mutated first officer on Delta Vega. Mitchell's death.

Spock saw the pain in Kirk's eyes. The terrible responsibility of command decision when it involved a close friend.

Spock spoke those words of regret at Mitchell's death and never regretted them. Kirk's pain had seemed to lessen in the sharing.

They became closer after Mitchell's death. Spock was promoted to first officer, and Kirk seemed to need someone to confide in.

Of course, Kirk also had Dr. Leonard McCoy, the man who had taken Dr. Piper's place as chief surgeon. Kirk and this man he called "Bones" seemed to understand each other very well.

Spock wasn't quite able to form an opinion about McCoy. He was a difficult man to pin down to a category. He could be cynical and sarcastic, but he was also sentimental and emotional. And he was undoubtedly an extremely adept surgeon. Part of Spock liked him, another part was leery of him. He sometimes cut too close to the bone. He saw too much, and yet sometimes not enough.

Still, Kirk turned to Spock more and more.

Danger shared. Knowledge gained. Quiet games of chess.

They became friends.

And (to borrow a phrase) the rest is history.

# 20.
# BILL SHATNER:
# AN ACTING CRITIQUE

### by Mark Schooney

*When we asked longtime television fan and historian Mark Schooney to do an in-depth article on William Shatner's career, he answered with a snort. "Give me the entire issue, and I'll start on it." Having only three pages scheduled for the article in our Special Kirk Issue (Trek No. 10), we were forced to agree to Mark's suggestion that he concentrate only on Bill's acting style—and that only in brief. But we were more than happy with the result. And who knows? Maybe one of these days we'll have a Special Shatner's Career Issue!*

There are many actors who appear on television and in movies with great regularity, yet their names are usually unknown to the average viewer. These persons work often because they have those qualities which make directors and producers very happy: They are extremely talented and competent; they are "quick studies" and always ready to perform when the camera starts; they show a decided lack of temperament and ego, taking direction well while still contributing to the quality of the production; and they are agreeable personalities who instantly establish a comfortable rapport with the audience.

Such actors are extremely valuable to films and TV; they are even more rare. That is why you see them so often, and are usually pleased to do so. Not only do they help to guarantee that your viewing time will not be wasted, they are like old friends.

Such an actor is William Shatner.

In the past twenty-odd years, William Shatner has appeared in almost one hundred television shows and movies, in dozens of theatrical productions, as a regular in three TV series (and the pilots for several others), and in many commercials, public-service announcements, and guest shots on game and talk shows.

Shatner is the complete actor, able to command a starship just as well as he can essay the works of William Shakespeare, or make a sincere pitch for margarine as smoothly as he portrays Alexander the Great. It is this versatility which has made Shatner one of the most popular and busiest actors in Hollywood, and a familiar face to viewers everywhere.

As the basic facts of Bill Shatner's career are already well known to most *Trek* readers, we will not go into them in any great detail here. The basic facts are that Shatner was born in Canada, where he was educated at McGill University and was active in campus theatrical productions. At the same time, he acted with a stock company and performed on numerous radio shows. After graduation, he joined the National Repertory Theatre in Ottawa, which led to a stint with the Stratford, Ontario, Shakespeare Festival.

From there he went to New York, appearing first on the stage and later in many live television productions. When the majority of television work moved to Hollywood, Shatner decided to give up most of his stage work and followed the jobs (and the money) West. He has worked steadily ever since.

This is, of course, an oversimplification of Shatner's career. Many specifics are left out, such as his struggle to learn his craft and his agony over the decision to give up the personal satisfaction of the stage for the more regular employment of films and TV.

However, we must look at Bill Shatner's career from a very special viewpoint: the affection and respect we have for him as Captain James T. Kirk. It is sad to say that many Star Trek fans either have little interest in Bill's other work or, upon seeing it, are disappointed because it is not just another variation of Kirk.

Although Shatner is able to handle any type of role, he does have a very distinctive and somewhat unusual acting style. As one gets the opportunity to review some of his earlier work, this style can be seen developing. The sweeping arm movments, the studied hesitations of speech, the swagger, the slight upturning smile, the subtle eye movements—all are part of the learning process which Shatner has refined over the years.

These are all elements of Shatner himself, and he has wisely amplified them to good effect. Many fans do not realize that William Shatner already had perfected his acting style and presence long before becoming Captain Kirk; the mannerisms are his, they are not written in the scripts. Which leads to the complaints of other fans: that Shatner is always playing Kirk.

So damned if he does and damned if he doesn't. Shatner is in the unenviable position of being accused of doing the wrong thing in any part he plays.

But although William Shatner played Kirk in seventy-nine episodes of Star Trek, we must remember that his other work numbers more than twice that many appearances. And a majority of it was done before Star Trek.

So when you hear someone complain that Bill Shatner is riding the coattails of his success on Star Trek, simply remind him of the fact that Shatner has been acting on TV, in movies, and on the stage for over twenty-five years; and at the heart of any role he plays is William Shatner, not Captain Kirk.

Although television is the surest way to "overnight success," it didn't happen that way with Bill Shatner. He paid his dues, and the quality of his work (both before, during, and after Star Trek) proves it.

No, Bill has not yet achieved his aim to be "an Olivier-type star." He is, however, an excellent actor, and respected by both his fans and his peers. That is quite an achievement for any actor to aspire to; and who knows, Bill may yet be another Olivier. After all, he gets better every day!

One of the most complete filmographies of William Shatner can be found in *Enterprise Incidents* No. 4, along with comments on many of his acting jobs. We highly recommend it for the fan wishing to see the varied types of roles that William Shatner has played over the years.

# 21.
# JIM'S LITTLE
# BLACK BOOK

by Walter Irwin

*If there's anything you can say about Captain James T. Kirk, it is that he certainly does like the ladies! This facet of Kirk's character has been the subject of many stories and articles (and a few female fans' fantasies!), but we think that Walter's is one of the few which takes the time to examine not only the many women in Kirk's life, but the underlying psychological basis for his actions. You may or may not agree with all that he says, but we do guarantee it will set you to thinking.*

As outlined by Gene Roddenberry, the character of Captain James T. Kirk was based on the mythos of the old-style Earth sea captains—daring, slightly imperious, hell-raisers and women chasers, and possessing enough autonomy to virtually rule whatever part of the world their ships traveled to. Over the course of the series, these attributes were toned down considerably (causing Kirk to become a milder and more bland character as the series progressed); and of them all, only the womanizing was not given short shrift. After all, doesn't a professional sailor (or spacer) have a girl in every port?

However, due to the type of series Star Trek was, Kirk actually had far less to do with the ladies than we would generally assume. Many episodes were focused on other characters, who became the object of the "love interest" rather than Kirk. Others had no featured female guest star; others still had no guest stars at all. So during the three-year run of Star Trek, Kirk's dalliances (and occasional conquests) pale beside those of other television heroes, say for instance the typical private eye.

It is inherent, however, in the stated character of James

185

Kirk that he appreciates the female of the species to a degree which causes some other *Enterprise* crew members to seem virtual monks. But we can see that most women do not really mean much to Kirk. He has an unfortunate tendency to use them—both for purposes of seduction and conquest and to further the aims of his assigned missions. When he does meet a woman who stirs a deep reaction in him, he is torn between his almost maniacal devotion to duty and his desire to build a lasting relationship. Only once is he forced to the ultimate choice, and duty wins out.

Kirk has, for a short while, an on-board love interest—or "titillation" interest—in Yeoman Janice Rand. He is very obviously taken with her youth and beauty, as he often shows by being, in turn, brusque, embarrassed, and charming in her presence. In "The Corbomite Maneuver," he even goes so far as to rail against "the idiot who assigned me a female yeoman."

It is unlikely that Kirk ever has any real feelings for Janice. True, her obvious physical charms attract him mightily, but he is too often cast by circumstances in the role of protector and father figure to allow himself even a minor slip. And, to be honest, Janice Rand is a bit too feather-brained for the demanding Kirk, who (as we shall see) is always attracted to strong-willed and fiercely independent woman—incidentally, two of the strongest factors in Kirk's own psychological makeup.

But Janice is severely infatuated with the Captain, and it shows. It is obvious to everyone in the crew (especially Kirk), and it is a fair assumption that Janice takes a good amount of ribbing about it from her crewmates, both male and female. This ribbing must become pretty rough after the events of "The Enemy Within," when the "evil" Kirk attempts to rape her. But this would not be what prompted Janice's decision to leave the *Enterprise*. That decision is made after "Miri."

The solicitous care which Kirk shows toward her in that adventure must convince Janice that he really cares for her, and she would be bitterly disappointed when she finds that nothing has changed when they are back aboard the *Enterprise*. Realizing that Kirk is married to his ship, and that she has no chance of winning his love, she requests a transfer.

The only problem that arises here is that a rookie yeoman would hardly be able to have an immediate transfer granted just for the asking, especially during the middle of her first tour of duty. So it is obvious that Kirk, understanding the situation, pulls some strings for her. One theory holds that this happens during an emotional scene between them, when Janice desperately confesses her love; but that doesn't fit the characters of either. If Janice had the will to confront Kirk, she would be more the type of woman he preferred; and Kirk is the kind of commander who confronts problems, not transfers them out. It's more likely that Kirk, having to approve all requests for transfer, realizes immediately why Janice wants to leave and arranges matters without Janice knowing anything about it.

Kirk's first outside-the-ship involvement we are told about is with one of "Mudd's Women," Eve McHuron. It is pretty much one-sided, with the romantic Eve seeming to fall for "a captain" as much as she does for Kirk himself. Kirk returns her affection in a mild way, but his aim is to find out exactly what it is that Mudd is hiding. This is the first instance we see of his penchant for using women to gain results in the line of duty, and with the frequency that it occurs later, one can assume that Kirk also has a tendency to use women for personal "results" as well.

The unbelievable transformation she undergoes notwithstanding, however, Eve is a realistic woman, and she is obviously quite prepared for Kirk's rejection. After all, marrying the lithium-rich Ben Childress is a much better deal than a temporary dalliance with Kirk, no matter how enjoyable.

One can only feel sorry for Andrea, the beautiful android in "What Are Little Girls Made Of?" She has humanlike emotions which she doesn't understand and can't quite control; and along comes Kirk, utilizing her childlike naiveté to the utmost—once again in the line of duty. She meets a sad and somewhat noble end, and deserves better during the brief time her awakened emotions have enabled her to enjoy truly being alive.

"Miri" is another female who falls for Kirk in the first flush of burgeoning emotions, but hers are in the natural course of things, and could more accurately be classified under the heading of a schoolgirl crush rather than passion.

Kirk fails to realize his effect on the girl, and it almost leads to his landing party's deaths when he no longer has time to flatter her with offhand charm. To Miri, this is outright rejection, and so she turns against Kirk and crew. However, to Kirk's credit, he later realizes his mistakes and treats Miri with a little more sensitivity and tact. It would be interesting to see Miri return in a new Star Trek series, now that she is an adult. What would her reaction to Kirk be then?

Kirk falls deeply in love with Dr. Helen Noel in "Dagger of the Mind," but it is an artificial love processed into him by Dr. Adams' neural neutralizer. Beyond an innocent flirtation at a Christmas party aboard ship, there is nothing between Kirk and Helen, which is probably the deciding factor in Kirk's being able to throw off the effects of the brainwashing device. To Helen's credit, she handles the situation very well. It seems a little strange that Kirk does not develop more than a mild interest in her, as she is the type of willful woman that he prefers. Apparently, the necessary spark just isn't there.

Once again Kirk uses his charm and position to involve himself with a woman to gain information in "The Conscience of the King." His stalking of Lenore Karidian is a little more coldblooded than usual, however; perhaps because of the hatred Kirk holds for Kodos the Executioner, whom he believes her father to be. Kirk's legendary ability to "read" women takes a licking in this episode, as he never suspects that it is Lenore who is doing the killing.

"Shore Leave" offers us our first look into Kirk's past with the inclusion of Finnegan, his old Academy tormentor, and Ruth, his long-lost love. What we learn about Kirk and Ruth's past is mostly between the lines, but we are told that they were in love during his Academy days. Obviously, it was early on during his education (around his graduation he was involved with Janice Lester), and most likely the pressures on the new cadet pulled them apart. She was important to him at the time, probably his first serious love; but he does not grieve for her. Ruth's appearance on the Shore Leave planet was prompted more by Finnegan's appearance and Kirk's musings on Academy days than by any deep-seated urge on Kirk's part to regain her love. Ruth's reappearance is a chance for him to relive earlier days, without the pressures and anxieties which plagued him in real life.

Areel Shaw appears from out of Kirk's past to act as the prosecutor in his "Court-Martial," but we are told very little about what took place between them years before. Their manner toward each other is friendly enough, so we can assume that they parted as friends. She is merely one of Kirk's old girlfriends (and there must be plenty of those!), and played no important role in his life or development as a person.

Kirk is mildly intrigued by the cool beauty of Mea 3 in "A Taste of Armageddon," but is more interested in stopping the computer war of Eminiar and Vendikar and saving his ship.

No sparks are noticeable between them, and it is unlikely that anything serious would develop even if more pressing matters weren't present.

Edith Keeler. The one and only true love of Kirk's life, and the woman he is literally ready to sacrifice a universe for. Rather than discuss the love they share (so much has already been written about it), time would be better spent in examining exactly why Kirk falls so deeply in love with Edith.

Many fans have voiced the hypothesis that Kirk's great love for Edith Keeler is based solely on circumstance; that the time, place, and the desperateness of the situation lead him into feelings which he would not otherwise allow to develop. Part of this theory is based on the belief that Kirk does not truly love Edith until he discovers that she is doomed to die in order for the universe to go on. In other words, it is more of Kirk's callousness toward women: Either Edith will die, in which case Kirk can freely feel love, knowing that her necessary death will prevent a permanent arrangement; or events will not be reversible, in which case Kirk will be set up with a lover to help him get over the fact of being stranded in the twentieth century.

Not very nice thoughts, but such an occurence could have happened in the light of James Kirk's previous track record of using women for his own purposes. We, of course, know the Captain a little better than that, and so are able to reject the theory immediately. But we are then left with the question of why Kirk falls in love with Edith.

Surely this is no minor infatuation. Kirk feels (and goes on feeling) Edith's loss too deeply. And if it is just another fling, why should Kirk even hesitate to let Edith die when confronted with the alternative? It has to be more than mere physical attraction.

The answer lies in the one thing which first attracts Kirk to Edith: her mind. Her personality. Her character. Her beliefs. In toto, her *soul*.

To understand this, we must review those things which are strongest in Kirk's own character: strength, determination, bravery, compassion, intelligence, and, above all, independence. Edith matches Kirk in all of these. That is why he is attracted to her, and that is why he—however unwillingly—falls in love with her.

As an immensely strong and dynamic individual, Kirk is constantly on the lookout for any woman who can bring the same intensity to living and a relationship that he contributes.

Throughout the run of the series, we have seen again and again how he is almost irresistibly drawn to such women—good or bad—and how he eventually rejects them. Invariably, they fail to meet his demanding unconscious standards—and the *Enterprise*, as ever, wins again.

However, Edith is a different story. Her boundless compassion and love for her fellow man is probably much stronger than Kirk's. Her independence and determination to achieve her views is dauntless; and her bravery is without question—she is ready to take on the worst our civilization has to offer. She is a totally alive and functioning human being.

Kirk cannot help but respond. Edith is a female version of himself. And after having finally found the "perfect woman," he is understandably loath to let her go. But he does.

This brings up perhaps the most important aspect of the Kirk-Keeler relationship—one which is the source of much controversy, even extending to Harlan Ellison, who wrote the original script.

It is easy to say that Kirk prevents Bones from saving Edith because of his position, the need to preserve what is to be, one life against millions, etc. And they are good and valid arguments. Kirk is that sort of person—he must be in order to be the Captain, the hero, we admire.

But consider that one tiny split second when Kirk has to actually and finally make up his mind. What thoughts go racing through his brain? We are not privy to know, but one can reasonably assume that he is thinking: "What would Edith want me to do?" The answer is obvious. And so she dies.

We mourn for Edith, and more so for Kirk. It is obvious that he will spend the rest of his life searching for another woman like her—if one exists—and it is very likely that he will never marry because of it. And if there are any of you out there who do not consider James Kirk to be one of the classic tragic heroes . . . well, *you* take a hand in destroying the only woman you have ever loved, and do so hundreds of years before you were even born!

The next woman that Kirk is involved with appears quite a bit later, and even though we can assume that Kirk, being Kirk, does not carry his grief for Edith outwardly too long, it is evident that he has little to do with even casual flirtations for a good while.

But in "Mirror, Mirror," Kirk is back to his old tricks—namely, quite cheerfully making love to an "enemy" for the sake of completing his mission. His not-quite-successful disguise as the evil Kirk of the mirror dimension requires him to dally with Lieutenant Marlena Moreau, "The Captain's Woman"; and if the time spent does not prove necessary to their own dimension, it does help in keeping Kirk away from the scrutiny of Spock-2 and other more observant minions of the Empire. And once the problem is solved, she does help in the final escape attempt, proving that (like Spock-2) she has not been totally corrupted by her environment.

This is doubtless due more to circumstances than to any "magical powers" of Kirk's lovemaking, but he does help her to see that better people and a better world can exist. And however unintentionally Kirk shares this with her, it is more than he often gave to other women he used in the past.

(An amusing afternote to this adventure is Kirk's discovery that a Marlena also exists in our universe. We are not allowed to know how that relationship turns out, but we can assume that things probably proceed as Kirk obviously intends when he approaches "his" Lieutenant Moreau.)

(Another afternote: Does the villainous Kirk-2 also have an encounter with the Edith Keeler of his universe? If so, it is likely that upon discovery of the necessity for her to die, Kirk-2 casually pulls out his phaser and blasts her out of existence—after raping her, of course.)

In "Catspaw," Kirk once again uses a woman for his own ends, but in this case, his job is made much easier by the fact that the exotic Sylvia is in reality an alien in human form, and the new emotions which she is experiencing make her quite a willing target. The only thing of note about the relationship is the ease with which Kirk seems to fall into the role of a cad. It has become almost automatic for him by this time; but whether this is due to the fact that he does it so often, or whether feelings for Edith have left him embittered, it is difficult to say. It does not bode well, however, for any future relationships—real or "in the line of duty." Kirk is beginning to play the part too well.

Another of Kirk's old flames returns in "The Deadly Years," but this time Kirk is in no condition to rekindle the fires. He and several others of the crew have been affected by abnormal and rapid aging. We do see, however, a major aspect of Kirk's attitudes toward women in this episode. Part of Kirk's appeal for women lies in his power as a starship commander and his animal-like virility. And it is obvious that he considers both to be even more necessary than women do. Therein lies one of Kirk's major strengths and flaws: his vanity (yet another requirement for the "classical hero").

And when age removes his power and potency from him, he perceives Janet Wallace's feelings toward him—whatever they might be—as pity. Since Kirk must always be the strong one, this is a situation which he cannot abide. So he breaks off any kind of contact with Janet. Because of this action, we are not allowed to see what kind of relationship they had in the past, or would have in the present. Beyond a few references to "back then," it is not discussed. But it is a safe bet that Janet was just another girlfriend, and in no way important to Kirk as a person.

In "The Gamesters of Triskelion," Kirk does use the beautiful and innocent Shahna to a certain extent, but it must be realized that he is forced into contact with her and does not seem to enjoy the "gigolo" part in this instance. He also obviously is attracted to her naiveté (enough so as to regret leaving her), showing us a side of Kirk we have never seen. Perhaps this is an indication of a subconscious rejection of the hopelessness of ever finding another Edith. This time Kirk intends to leave Shahna with a vision of another world, and we can assume that it is a way of saying "I'm sorry."

Kirk is supposed to fall in love with Nona, the "witch woman" in "A Private Little War," because of the potion she uses to save his life. But beyond a slight haziness and some verbal innuendoes, it doesn't seem to work too well. Too bad, as this would have allowed Kirk to be on the receiving end for a change, and would have helped to curb his tendency to use women a bit. But once the action starts, Kirk doesn't even spare Nona a second glance.

Kirk goes through a beautiful and ages-old love affair in "Return to Tomorrow," but it is by proxy. His body is used as the receptacle for the alien Sargon, while Sargon's wife, Thalassa, resides in the lovely body of Dr. Ann Mulhall. It is regretful that Kirk will probably never find another woman with whom he can be as loving as Sargon was with Thalassa, as the tenderness which his face and actions express through Sargon is quite touching. And it is doubly a shame that Kirk and Ann do not continue to follow the romance up on their own, as it would be interesting to see how Kirk reacts to a woman of his own age and experience.

Once again Kirk performs in the name of duty in "By Any Other Name," but this time his purpose is a little different. He romances the human-formed Kelvan, Kelinda, to take advantage of her newfound human emotions; but his main objective is to make her consort, Rojan, jealous, and thus force him to realize that his kind cannot survive in human form. And to be fair, Kirk does not seem to relish the job. Perhaps he is on the verge of having enough.

Perhaps this growing revulsion on Kirk's part for using women is responsible for his short-lived and halfhearted attempt to romance Kara, the woman who stole "Spock's Brain." Or maybe (like most viewers) he feels that the whole situation is too ridiculous to get worked up about.

The relationship that is sometimes referred to as "Kirk's other great love" takes place in "The Paradise Syndrome," but it can be logically argued that in this instance Kirk is very much "not himself."

However, his love for and marriage to the Indian maiden Miramanee can be viewed as an eloquent desire for a simpler life, with a simpler woman. As with Shahna, Kirk is immediately attracted to Miramanee because of her innocence; and having lost his memory, he immediately and fully responds to that attraction. His love for her may not be as strong and as compelling as his love for Edith Keeler, but it is a much more basic, purer love. For without his memory of his duties and obligations, Kirk is able to respond on a totally emotional level, unencumbered by the necessary give-and-take of a "civilized" relationship.

Miramanee would have little attraction for a normal Kirk, whereas Edith has much. Kirk loves Edith with his head, Miramanee with his heart. And who can say which is greater?

There is a return of sorts of Kirk's attraction for the self-sufficient type of woman when he meets Miranda Jones in "Is There in Truth No Beauty?" But one can also see that Kirk could unconsciously realize that Miranda was blind, and therefore be interested in her because of the diverse mix of strength and helplessness she represented. It is a moot point, as he never goes beyond more than a casually stated admiration for Miranda, and no indication is given by either of them that anything further can develop.

Kirk is forced to give Lieutenant Uhura a reluctant kiss by "Plato's Stepchildren," and it is obvious that each of them is too angry and embarrassed by the situation to get any sort of pleasure out of it. But a question arises. Out of 125-odd women on the starship, why is Uhura selected for Kirk? A valid question, and one which will be discussed later.

In "Wink of an Eye," Kirk is as much used by the

Scalosian, Deela, to help perpetuate her race as she is used by him to get information to Spock and McCoy. Again, Kirk really has little choice about being involved with Deela, and even though he obviously enjoys his tryst with her, he enters into it rather reluctantly. The only important item about the affair is that it is the only instance in which we are given overt evidence that Kirk has had sexual relations with one of the women featured in an episode.

"Elaan of Troyius" also affects Kirk with a love potion (administered through her tears), and although it proves more effective than Nona's, it is still not strong enough to overcome his devotion to the *Enterprise* and duty. Beyond a few heady moments for Kirk, nothing important comes of this brief interlude—luckily for Kirk, as life with the spoiled and selfish Elaan would certainly not be too pleasant.

Kirk tries his old trick of romancing the enemy once too often in "Whom Gods Destroy," and almost ends up with a knife in his back. The sadly insane Marta wields the weapon because of her compulsion to kill all of her lovers (Kirk doesn't even get close!); but mad though she is, she deserves a better end.

Kirk once again is used by the people of the planet Gideon when he is forced into contact with the beautiful Odona in "The Mark of Gideon." Although she falls in love with Kirk (probably caused more by her exultation of sheer room than anything else), Kirk is only mildly attracted to her. He does try to use her as a means to get back to his ship, but in the end, her welfare becomes his primary concern. Again, we can see that Jim is attracted by the relative innocence of Odona, but when she begins to mature as a person and accept responsibility, he more than gladly gives her up. By this time, Kirk is very much avoiding the independent women. Quite a reversal.

If Kirk falls in love with Edith Keeler because he is fascinated by the reflection of his own qualities that he sees in her, it is little wonder then that he becomes so completely enamored of Reena Kapec in "Requiem for Methuselah."

Because she is an android, and one without emotions, Reena is quite able to assimilate and reflect all that Kirk has been feeding her as input since the moment she met him. And Kirk responds.

But one gets the feeling that the situation is a bit too pat, that Kirk falls a little bit *too* much in love, a little bit too fast. Perhaps Flint is forcing Kirk's emotions in some way, or warping Kirk's perceptions enough so that he will react abnormally. This seems likely, as following his recent patterns, Kirk would respond to Reena the Innocent, but would back off quickly as he perceived her intellectual qualities.

An added bit of evidence to the theory that love for Reena is "implanted" in Kirk in some way is that Spock is required to use the Mind Meld to rid Kirk of her memory, something he does not have to do even when Kirk loses Edith and Miramanee.

The tables are completely turned on Kirk in "Turnabout Intruder" as he is forced to exchange identities with an ex-love, Janice Lester. Beyond Janice's hatred, there are no feelings left between them at this point, but it is apparent that they shared a stormy and passionate relationship in the past. Janice is psychotic, and from what we glean of their earlier affairs, she was not too stable even then. When rejected from Starfleet Academy, Janice refused to realize her own problems and shifted the blame to Kirk. However much Kirk was in love with her at the time (if at all), he was too determined to get on with his career to take the time to pacify Janice—or, as she probably insisted, to resign from the Academy. He was left with regrets, she with hatred.

It is a bit of a shame that we are not given more insight into Kirk's reactions upon finding himself in the body of a woman. It would be quite interesting to note the reactions of a man who has used woman so often (and so well) to suddenly find himself one. And one of his rejected lovers, at that!

This is the weakest aspect of the "Turnabout" script, in that beyond an initial horror and amazement upon awakening, Kirk seems to take the entire experience just a little bit too calmly. As it was put in the play *Goodbye Charlie*, it is terrible "to be a gourmet all your life and suddenly wake up a lamb chop!"

In summing up, we can see Kirk's major failing in his relations with the female sex. He can relate to and understand them as people; but not as women. And with only two known exceptions, he is unable to form complete and lasting relationships with women. Again, it stems from Kirk's basic psychological makeup—and more important, his conception of himself as a loner, married to his ship and his duty. One could accurately say that although Kirk loves women, he actually doesn't like them very much. And that is the main reason why James T. Kirk will most likely end his days as a bachelor.

Except maybe for . . .

We promised you more on Uhura, and why she is selected to pair with Kirk in "Plato's Stepchildren." It seems evident that along with their psychokinetic powers, the Platonians have a limited amount of telepathy. After all, they cause Kirk and Spock to recite a nursery rhyme that they could only have found in Kirk's subconscious; and they know that Spock can be affected by experiencing strong emotions when no mention has been made of the fact. So it is reasonable to assume that the Platonians are able to tap into the subconscious minds of those they control with psychokinesis.

When women are required for the "orgy," the Platonians simply dip into Kirk's and Spock's thoughts and beam up the two women who are uppermost in their subconscious minds. Christine Chapel is a natural for Spock, as the problem of her love for him is never far from his thoughts, and he has stated that if he were capable of feelings, he could care for her. But why Uhura for Kirk? Could it be that he has unstated and unshown feelings for her? Even love?

It is possible. There is much circumstantial evidence to support the fact: Whenever there is any sort of disturbance on the bridge, Kirk's first thoughts (after the safety of the ship) are of Uhura. It has not been blatant in any of the episodes, but there is a feeling that Uhura can get away with a little more than anyone else on the bridge crew, both in word and action. Plus many other things: Kirk's tendency to touch Uhura in a comforting manner, the quick glance he gives her every time he enters the bridge, and other, subtler things.

But we still return to why Uhura is drawn from Kirk's mind. Do the Platonians know what even Kirk does not realize, that he loves Uhura?

The answer is unknown, as of yet. You may have your own opinions, according to the way you perceive the characters, and according to your likes and dislikes of Kirk and/or Uhura. But it would make for a damned interesting story, wouldn't it?

Again, it is highly unlikely, for a number of reasons, that James T. Kirk will become seriously involved with (or married to) any woman in the foreseeable future. Or perhaps not at all.

But you can be sure of one thing: When Star Trek returns, we will see our gallant Captain involved with just as many beautiful and exciting and exotic women as ever. And frankly, we wouldn't want it any other way!

# ABOUT THE AUTHOR

Although largely unknown to readers not involved in Star Trek fandom before the publication of *The Best of Trek #1*, WALTER IRWIN and G. B. LOVE have been actively editing and publishing magazines for many years. Before they teamed up to create TREK® in 1975, Irwin worked in newspapers, advertising, and free-lance writing, while Love published *The Rocket's Blast—Comiccollector* from 1960 to 1974, as well as hundreds of other magazines, books, and collectables. Both together and separately, they are currently planning several new books and magazines, as well as continuing to publish TREK.